SUBMODERN

ALSO BY MARK WALLACE:

Notes from the Center on Public Policy (Altered Scale Press, 2014)

The End of America, Book One (Dusie Kollectiv, 2012)

The Quarry and The Lot (BlazeVox, 2011)

Felonies of Illusion (Edge Books, 2008)

Walking Dreams: Selected Early Tales (BlazeVox, 2007)

Temporary Worker Rides A Subway (Green Integer, 2004)

Haze: Essays, Poems, Prose (Edge Books, 2004)

Dead Carnival (Avec Books, 2004)

Oh Boy (Slack Buddha Press, 2004)

The Monstrous Failure of Contemplation with Aquifer by Kaia Sand
    (self-publish or perish, 2001)

My Christmas Poem (Poetry New York, 1998)

Nothing Happened and Besides I Wasn't There (Edge Books, 1997)

Sonnets of a Penny-A-Liner (Buck Downs Books, 1996)

In Case of Damage To Life, Limb, or This Elevator
    (Standing Stones, 1996)

The Haunted Baronet (Primitive Publications, 1996)

The Lawless Man (Upper Limit Music, 1996)

Every Day Is Most Of My Time (Texture Press, 1994)

Complications From Standing In A Circle (Leave Books, 1993)

You Bring Your Whole Life To The Material (Leave Books, 1992)

By These Tokens (Triangle Press, 1990)

CRAB

SUBMODERN

CRAB

a novel

MARK WALLACE

ACKNOWLEDGMENTS

An earlier version of chapter one appeared in the online anthology *DC Poetry*. Thanks to the editors.

Many thanks to Suzanne Stein, whose deft suggestions have made this book much better than it would have been without her.

Crab is a work of fiction. Any possible resemblance to anyone can be only a weird coincidence.

Copyright © 2017 by Mark Wallace

Printed in the United States of America
Designed by James Meetze
First Edition

ISBN: 978-1-943899-03-6

Published by
SUBMODERN BOOKS

The riddle of the Carnival crab was known to all, crab-Johnny, crab-Charlotte, as the mutual devouring principle within a chained civilization, North, South, East, West… The intricacy of all these relationships, their fullness, their abbreviated texture, their half-eclipsed initial capacity in the riddle of the crab at death's door was not entirely lost upon Sir Thomas.

Wilson Harris, *Carnival*

Old age is like a crab, we don't all age in the same way. It gradually stretches out its claws inside us. At times it starts from the back, others from the legs, others from the head. In my case, it began from the dreams: I started to dream almost every night about people from my past.

Osman Lins, "Retable of Saint Joana Carolina"

ONE

The Crab lurched forward, steel joint against steel screw. From behind the glass wall, the operator, hovering over the control panel, couldn't hear the Crab cross the table, although after many months of long work hours it almost seemed he could make out its high-pitched metallic whine. It wasn't efficient—what could that mean now?—though still able at times to work. If he was careful.

Occasionally disjointed, prone to seizures that threatened to send it tumbling to its back, legs flailing, the Crab reached, without faltering, the far side of the table and crawled up the body of the patient in the chair. The patient's cheeks and chin were tightly vised, not enough to hurt, but more than enough to hold him still when combined with the straps across his arms and legs. Should he be unlucky and wake from his drug-induced unconsciousness, he wouldn't be able to change his mind. His eyelids were open, held back by a pair of small steel claws. Fluid dropped into the pupils, so far with proper regularity, from the small pumps poised above them.

The Crab straddled the patient's face. The operator, behind the glass, turned towards the monitor to coordinate the rest of the work. The monitor kept flickering. The operator wondered whether, soon, anything would function at all, whether there would be time to get even a few people into the intended state before things ceased, although time would continue, of course, like an unseen wave across a vast motionless ocean. He shook his head, trying to throw away the thought. The monitor, again. It worked well enough. The flickers lasted only a second, the moments of clarity perhaps ten.

The operator felt himself flickering also. He had been at this too long, not just today. There weren't enough people who could operate the Crab. There weren't enough people to do anything. So he worked long after he was too tired, after it seemed he would never feel rested again. He had been doing fourteen, sixteen hour shifts for weeks. The world smelled like disinfectant.

At his command, the Crab released the pincer in its belly. It punctured, swiftly, lightly, the strapped patient's eye. The patient jerked. Not a perfect incision, but close. The tube, functioning properly for now, rolled out of the Crab's belly. The tiny, white viscous egg appeared at the tube's tip. The tube, pressing down against the punctured surface of the eye, pushed the egg through. The tube pulled back into the belly, out of which came the laser. With a brief flash, the laser sealed the eye. The patient remained motionless. It was unlikely he felt pain. "Dream," said the operator, as if it was an order. There was some chance it would work. Some small chance for some of them.

The Crab clambered down from the man's face, landed on the table again. After a moment it lurched across the table's slick surface. One of its forelegs slipped; the leg landed not even on the first small joint but all the way up on the second, near the body. The Crab crumpled forward. Before the operator could stop it, its legs pushed until it flipped over entirely, kicking at the air a moment before the operator shut off the mechanism. "Damn," he said, thudding his hand hard against the control panel. He would have to wait at least an hour before it was safe to go in and pick up the Crab in a carefully gloved hand. Each delay only made things worse. Delays were also inevitable, given the materials he had to work with. It hadn't always been like this, although it was hard now to think of other times, and no use. One simply pushed on through, lurching like the Crab, and handled delays as efficiently as possible. Since the goal was to leave the world behind, to never see again what was left of the city of Mytros, to find another world somewhere else in a burgeoning and unimaginable dream, one could hardly expect much from the world one was abandoning. And the Crab had laid the egg successfully. "The egg and the eye," the operator said, pressing his elbows in at his sides in a sudden desire to warm himself. "The egg and the eye."

*

"Sooner or later," Marinda said to the man and woman with her at the table, "I expect to be blamed. Get me another drink, would you?"

Pushing his chubby hands against the table, the man stood. A wave of flesh rippled underneath his polo shirt, rising towards his chest then settling back. Marinda stared at his gut, unashamedly fascinated. "That's funny," she said. "You need to start exercising, Jerry. I've heard Manhattan has these things called gyms."

"Go to hell." Jerry's eyes scrunched under puffy cheeks, then brightened as he looked towards the bar, where people lined up several deep in spring clothes of the Manhattan moment. Moody ceiling lamps added to the silvery sheen of the walls and gave everyone's appearance a metallic coating. "Hey, lots of chicks at the bar now. I hadn't noticed. Want gin?"

Marinda put her hand in her jacket pocket, fiddled a moment. "If you can buy it for me. I forgot to bring money."

"Again?" Jerry said.

"Yes. And bring back a chick for both of us."

"You have no faith in me."

"I have nothing but faith in you," Marinda said. "It's easier than expectations."

"And the winner of the bitchiest comment of the evening is…" Jerry mockingly drew a star in the air with his finger.

"You brought me here because you wanted me to be a bitch."

Jerry's eyes glittered. "Marry me."

"And be more alone than I am already? You're melting me, really. Go."

"You'll see." He walked away.

The third person at the table, Geena, had been watching their exchange silently. A short woman, her blond hair was piled high on her head, in contrast to Marinda's, which was clipped, stylishly tousled, and black. Geena was a bit plump, although less so than Jerry. She looked energetic in her sparkly dress, another contrast to Marinda's slender emaciation in tightly cut blue jeans and a black shirt. Even when Marinda *had* slept, she never looked like it. Her eyes seemed hollowed out. The sharp asymmetrical lines around her mouth highlighted her air of withdrawn charisma. "You're pretty hard on him," Geena said. Her eyes were genuinely shocked.

"He needs me to be mean sometimes," Marinda said. "It helps him relax. Have you noticed that when people hate themselves, having someone around who can express that hostility is a relief? I wish having people be mean helped me. If it did, I'd be calm right now. As it is I'm a wreck."

"Heard from Steve?"

"No. He still doesn't know where I am, and with luck he won't find out. My parents hear from him though. He writes letters, calls my mother late at night to say she was a bad parent and ruined my life. He thinks it has something to do with my father's church. He says if I wasn't so repressed, I'd still be with him."

"He says that to your parents?" Geena's head turned to the side, like she didn't understand.

"My mother anyway. My father won't talk to him."

"Why does your mother talk to him?"

"I don't know." Marinda smiled wearily. "Maybe she thinks she can help him, or that she can do something to keep him away from me. I've got the restraining order but how good is that? Right now, he has no idea I'm in New York. I just hope my mother doesn't let that slip."

"Think she might?"

"Honestly, no. But Steve's devious. He doesn't know he's devious, but he is. As far as he's concerned, he's a good honest guy I've mistreated, because I hate men, or because of my father, or because of any other reason he can invent. I've read the books. As far as he's concerned, it's all my fault and I just don't see it, but if he shouts at me and insults me and throws things long enough, I'll change my mind. To think I was actually in love with such a textbook case. Maybe that's the best I'm ever going to do. Sometimes I wonder."

"Stop it," Geena said.

"No, no, mark my words," Marinda said. "I'm going to be blamed. I'm too obvious a target."

"I hope Jerry comes back soon," Geena said. "Do you see him? He's so funny." She giggled, a girlish flirtatious giggle. Marinda looked sharply in her direction. Could Geena possibly…?

"I wonder sometimes whether Jerry's gay," Marinda said.

"What?" Geena said. "He isn't."

"I'm not sure," Marinda said. "I know he always talks aggressively about women. He almost never follows through, especially lately. I'm not sure he's serious."

"Jerry's never claimed to be gay."

"True," Marinda said. "And he's had girlfriends before, a few weeks here or there. Maybe he won't admit it, even to himself. He doesn't understand himself and doesn't want to. And that's true even if he's 100 percent straight."

"I think he's cute," Geena said. "I love the way he goes after what he wants."

Marinda started to laugh, then checked herself. "Not that I hold it against him. Not knowing himself, I mean. Nobody knows themselves anymore, that's the thing. No one even thinks they should know themselves. It doesn't help anyone get ahead. That's one of the basic lessons."

"We were just at his place," Geena said. "It's a guy's apartment. He has posters of baseball players."

"Ambiguous, isn't it?" Marinda said.

Then Jerry was there, smiling, drinks in hand. When he tried to be charming, it was clear that he could be good-looking in a boyish way if he took better care of himself. He had soft, dirty blond hair cut neatly and a mischievous grin that turned too easily into a pout.

"One for the Queen of Death." He placed a glass in front of Marinda with an exaggeratedly polite swoop of his arm. Geena giggled again.

Jerry sat. "Couple of real babes at the bar." His voice boomed confidence. "If I wasn't with you ladies, I might have had to take them with me."

"Jerry picks up women in bars all the time." Marinda winked falsehood at Geena. "I'm desperate and jealous."

"With good reason," Jerry said.

"Oh Jerry," Marinda said. "You know ultimately you're mine, despite all your bravado." She turned to Geena again. "It's wonderful to have male servants, you know. Much better than emotional give and take is emotional take and take."

"Maybe you'd like to take things further," Jerry said. "Or maybe Geena would and you could watch."

Geena shifted uncomfortably in her chair. The eager glow of her presence dimmed.

"You needn't worry, Geena." Marinda put her hand on the other woman's arm. "He's all talk. He wouldn't dare follow through."

"Try me," Jerry said.

"Or maybe instead we could talk about something other than your manhood?"

Jerry shot her an icy glance that said this time he was close to being genuinely offended.

"Tell us about your new job," Marinda said to Geena. She wasn't changing the subject because there had barely been one. "It wouldn't hurt Jerry to hear about what it's like to work. He hasn't done it in almost forever."

"I could work if I wanted," Jerry said, his face back in its standard pout. "I want the right job, not just any job. And I'll have it too. I've got plans."

"The great advantage of having money," Marinda said, "is it gives you free time to drive yourself crazy. I've invented whole new ways to go out of my mind." She took a drink. Her eyes surveyed the room as if searching for someone, then gave up. "What have you been doing lately, Geena? Jerry and I don't need to spend all evening boring ourselves to death with our own problems."

*

Steve so often felt abandoned in his dreams that it was almost comforting, if a feeling could be comforting and devastating at the same time.

The long burnt field in front of him vanished. He found himself going against his will through the blue glass doors of an anonymous building. He knew he worked there because he felt no connection to it. He belonged to places like this, places that ripped him away from himself until he became no more than the rip.

He pushed the elevator button repeatedly. The elevator didn't come. Nothing and no one ever came. He took the stairs.

He walked several flights with excruciating slowness, hand grabbing the metal rail like he wanted to break it. He came through a door, walked down a hallway, and found himself in his parent's dining room.

"Steve, help your mother." His father's voice pushed him into a chair. "Your mother needs help."

"My mother's dead," Steve said.

"She makes excellent roast beef," his father said. "And these potatoes are just right. Stop sitting there whining like a girl and get to it."

His mother pressed herself close to him. A dark-colored flower print dress, a reddish fleshy leg. Steve tried to bury his head in the dress. The flower opened and drew him inside.

"Nothing like a big leg of mutton on a solid bone," his father said. "You should have been a girl."

Steve pushed further into the flower. Sexual arousal hit him like a slap. He rolled into a ball.

"Can you get these reports out by the end of the day?" His boss leaned over his computer monitor, rings on his fingers flashing. "It's crucial."

The anonymous blue building spread out around him. It had wings. The office could fly. The building was nothing more than the dreamscape of another world. That world had forgotten how to dream and was sending people through artificial dreams into another dreamed world that was somehow this one. In so doing, it altered everything. The dreams of one world and the waking facts of another intermingled in such a way that the dreams didn't know which world they belonged to.

"This isn't my dream," Steve protested.

"But it's excellent roast beef," his father said. "And it's an excellent mother."

"Do you love your mother?" said his mother.

"He loves her too much," his father said. "You want to fuck your mother, don't you, boy? Or maybe you're not a boy. Maybe you're a girl."

"Get that done in the next hour and drinks are on me," his boss said. "Go down on it right away."

"I don't understand," Steve said. What if being awake was no more than a filter to keep out other possibilities? Like he put on clothes so people couldn't see what he was thinking? "Where's Marinda?" he asked no one. "Why are they keeping me from Marinda?"

Cynthia stood there. She worked in a cubicle on the other side of the office and came to talk to him all the time. She was pretty, with big startled eyes and shoulder-length curly brown hair. She wasn't skinny to the point of non-existence like so many women these days—like Marinda was trying to be and couldn't—but had a good build and solid female energy that carried him away from what he didn't want to know. She was hard-working and friendly. "What's he got you doing?" she asked. "Can I help?"

"You could help me finish this beef," his father said.

Pain cracked through Steve's head. He shouted, reached his hand up to the pain. Dirty pale blue light floated through the cracks in the blinds. His head throbbed. The smell of sweaty sheets surrounded him. He was awake. He had turned himself all the way around and had hit his head on the wall against the side of the bed.

"It hurts," Steve said into the blue light. "Those fucking bastards. I'm going to make *them* eat it."

*

Sarah sat near the back of the room, behind people's heads, where the words would be less overwhelming. They were still there, lighting up a sleeve, a hand, a wall or a door: "Foolish in Brown," "Confused," "Emergency Exit." At times like this, more intense than most, her surroundings often blurred with words. Tonight the words stuck especially to people's foreheads. Maybe she shouldn't have had so much coffee.

The balding man at the front of the lecture hall, in rolled up sleeves and skinny tie, droned on. "Having developed the proper tools, one might proceed to access the brain. Several main hypotheses are currently in place regarding how best to tap into the dream state's energy…" and blah blah blah. Sarah sighed. She had hoped to learn at least something she needed to know, had even put on a professional pantsuit of a kind she rarely wore, in order to seem like someone in the field, in case after the lecture she wanted a detailed discussion with "Highly Regarded Dream Scientist Dr. Pennington," according to the flier. The flier's heading, "Accessing the Dream State," had popped out at her from a local paper's upcoming events list after weeks of research at the New York Public Library, searching national and international news sources, and scanning discussion boards and university websites. She could barely listen to Pennington's pedantic rendering of the details. His forehead several times tossed out the word "Misinformed" in gaudy lettering. Once it even read "Don't Get It," the words taking off from his forehead and fluttering around the crowd, landing on one person and then another, settling finally in the third row on a woman in her early thirties who was watching the lecture intently, the word "Worship" winking on and off beside her in an aggressive red that clashed with her outfit.

It was too much. Sarah stood. She was far enough towards the back that she could leave without disrupting anything, although one man looked at her with the words "Annoyed because I can be" popping off the furrows above his glasses. In the hall she avoided the scrawled fury of the message board. She pushed through the "Door Caution Door" into the night air and could breathe again. For a moment there were no words, just sky and, at the far side of the campus park, the city lights.

She didn't know where to go. Home was no good. She didn't want to write. The total lack of words to see there, except for the covers of her books, would feel in her heightened state like absence, not relief. She didn't want to spiral into emptiness, a strong possibility right now.

The messages of the last month had been unlike any she had ever seen. They had occurred several dozen times now, far too many to be some new personal oddity that she hadn't learned to understand. She couldn't identify where they came from. They didn't belong in the city. "Dream," they insisted, even raged. Sometimes they appeared in the air or on the pavement, where there was no reason for words and no words should be.

Of course, the origin of any word, wherever it appeared, wasn't easy to determine. Sometimes words emanated from people's bodies. Sometimes they leapt out from the signs that covered so many of the city's human-built surfaces. Sometimes they bounced around or were volleyed back and forth. The distinction between a word emanating from a person and a word imposed on that person could be unclear.

The word "Dream," as it had been appearing lately, was not an imposition in the way she had understood impositions before. Ordinary impositions were human creations that got loose in people's frenzied desire to cover everything with language and tried to burrow into anyone they could. But the word, the command, "Dream," not only didn't belong in the city, it didn't seem to belong in the world at all. She didn't know how that could be true, but it was. The word was from elsewhere and had broken loose. As a command, it wasn't working. Yet. It happened randomly, popping in and out of focus, sometimes burning with fury yet still landing wrong. Commanding the side of a wall to "Dream" didn't make the wall dream, however insistent the command.

Sarah was back on the city streets now, away from the college. It was a lively spring night in New York. People were going to or coming from plays or movies or restaurants or bars or just taking walks for the pleasure of walking. She felt comfortably anonymous. Despite her abilities, no one looking at her would have seen anything other than an ordinary attractive professional woman in her late thirties, with short brown hair and thoughtful eyes, though the professionalism contrasted with what was, at the moment, a bewildered expression. She looked like one more person overwhelmed by too much motion. She was glad no one could tell *how* overwhelmed.

Several boys brushed her as they hurried past, dropping the words "suburbs" and "lost" at her feet as their eyes studied her. Soon after, she passed a tense couple, the woman nervously eyeing the man, who wouldn't return her stare. As he went by, he gave off the word "CHEATING" in big green capital letters. At least he had money for the coming divorce. Sarah's mind still felt active, but thankfully, here on the street, more restrained than before. There were occasions when words from the evening streets bludgeoned her and she would have to go home, close her blinds and shut off the lights until the words went away. Tonight, despite the intensity around her, her energy was focused, even after the disappointment of the lecture. She felt she was getting closer to what she needed to know.

A few minutes later, there it was, in the distance, poised above a streetlight yet having nothing to do with the streetlight. "Dream." It had no color. There was no doubt, as there hadn't been: it was lost. She decided to follow it, maybe had already known that she would. "You don't want to be revealed but I can reveal you anyway," she said to it before it winked into nothing.

Once she reached the streetlight, the question was which way to turn. There was no clear path to follow. She went down a smaller side street, darker, where words held themselves back, a relief, since she could feel herself becoming overloaded. So here she was, walking the back streets of the city, looking wherever her own instincts led her for… well, for what?

There it was again. "Dream." It moved this time, crashed into a wall, bounced off and shattered. It was directed, she was sure. It was meant to go from elsewhere to here and to find something once it arrived. Having arrived, it didn't know what to do.

Sarah walked a few more blocks. The city became rougher. No more crowds. There were still occasional rowhouses, now broken up by mechanics' garages and small fenced-in lots littered with junk. They smelled of purposes she didn't try to understand. Two men leaning against a fence on an opposite corner eyed her a moment. She got no words from them and hurried on. The city night was still a purplish glow that gave her enough light to see, even in patches where no street lamps shown. But there was real darkness here, places where people could hide. Maybe I should go home, she said to herself. Numbers giving the addresses of the buildings were small comfort—1472, 1474, 1474 ½. For the most part, there were no words anywhere.

Then there was a man in front of her, a block away, sitting awkwardly on some porch steps. "Drunk," his forehead flashed quickly, then again. The word flickered oddly, as if something had interfered with it. She was close to him now. The man groaned, then whimpered. His head pitched forward into his hands. "Sick" roared off him and splashed onto the pavement.

Just beyond him, a small alley turned off the street. Sarah caught a blip out of the corner of her eye, knew what it was. Would she really go down there? She had done more questionable things. But going down the alley was pretty questionable.

There were a few cars parked in the alley, which ran between the small yards, garages, and storage sheds behind two rows of houses. A cat dashed past her feet and under a fence. Amazing how few words animals gave off, although an occasional dog could be plastered with them. Why was she walking here? What did she expect to find? The alley opened out onto another street. I'm wasting my time, she told herself.

A few blocks down the street, she came to a subway stop. Home wasn't far, though she'd have to transfer lines. Down in the subway, words were everywhere: on the token booth, posters on the wall, signs. A few people moved through the stop, giving off bits of low key language. After the intensity of the past hour, her energy was becoming muted. When she got on the first train, then the second, people were mainly quiet, staring ahead tiredly or looking at the floor.

If the words didn't know what they were doing, how could she? One could sift through the confusion of other people's words and find the sense that the people themselves didn't know how to make. That involved seeing the context of their words from a position they couldn't. But her ability to do that depended on having some sense of the context. How to understand the context of something that didn't belong anywhere yet still was here? Maybe she had it wrong. She couldn't rule out the idea that what was happening was just her own aberration. Oh yes I can, she thought. Those words are coming from somewhere. It wasn't like her to question her ability. Her self doubt only emphasized how odd the situation was.

She exited the subway at her stop. It was late now, but people were still on the street. That was one of the things about the city, that there was rarely a time when the streets were empty. Her head hurt. She'd been focusing hard for too long.

Then, once more, there it was. A quick red flash, "Dream," in the air above her, attached to nothing. Her head twitched painfully. Had the word come close to landing on her? Words needed attachments.

If this word was attached to nothing, it would try to change that. They're missing their target, she thought. Will they keep missing or will they eventually catch me or somebody else? What happens then?

Once in her building, she felt unable to look at the names on the mailboxes and hurried up the stairs and into her apartment. There she kept the lights low and stayed out of the room where her books were shelved. In a few minutes she was ready for bed and laid down in a mellowing darkness into which for the moment no words intruded. Tired as she was, she felt almost afraid to sleep, knowing how language could maraud through her dreams.

*

"What should I paint, Daddy?" Marinda asked. Spread around her on the concrete patio beside the pool was a set of sixteen different colors, some brushes, and several big pieces of white paper. She'd received the paints for her seventh birthday but hadn't been able to use them that day. Now it was days later.

"I don't know," her daddy said. "What would you like to paint?"

She could tell he didn't care about the answer. He sat stiffly in the patio easy chair, arms tense at his sides, eyes looking at her but not really. He asked her a lot what she would like. Most of the time he didn't want to know. He was either thinking about something else and pretending to ask, or wanted her to say what he wanted her to say and it was her job to figure it out.

"Tell me one of your dreams, Daddy. I'd like to paint dreams."

"That's a little silly, don't you think?" He frowned distractedly. "You're a big girl now. Paint something real."

"Okay." Marinda didn't know what he meant by real. Wasn't everything real, if you made it? She put blue on a brush and painted sky, put the blue down. She put green on another brush and painted grass, put the green down.

Over on the patio table, the backyard phone rang. Daddy sighed heavily. Usually he stayed near the phone but he'd moved away from the table to watch Marinda paint. He groaned his way out of the chair, went to the table and answered. He started saying things Marinda didn't understand. It was strange how adults became different people depending on who they were talking to.

Marinda looked at her painting, picked up a brush, put it down again. She liked to paint, but knew she was supposed to wait for her daddy to tell her what to paint so she didn't get it wrong. She didn't want to wait and started anyway. She put red on a brush and smashed it on the paper. She pushed harder and harder, flattening the brush against the paper so the bristles splayed out in a fan.

"I know it's not easy," Daddy was saying to the phone. "It's got to get done whether you like it or not."

He wasn't talking to Marinda, but she took him at his word. She painted one color, and another and another. She wasn't painting anything real. A breeze, bringing the smell of flowers, came through the palm trees that stood around the edge of the pool. Beyond the trees, the hills were outlined in crisp air. If she only painted real things, she'd have to paint houses and schools and cars and stores. There were a lot of those already. Wasn't it better to paint things that weren't real yet?

"That's all I have to say about this." Daddy hung up the phone.

"Come look at my painting," Marinda said.

He glanced in her direction, not really seeing her or the painting. "I'm glad you're having fun."

"Is something wrong, Daddy?"

"No. Just some adult things you wouldn't care about."

"Real things, right?"

"What? Yes, right. Real things." He looked away from her, out toward the hills.

Marinda put the first piece of paper aside. It was filled with color.

Even the sky and grass didn't look like sky and grass anymore. She put a second piece of paper in front of her and wondered what to do.

The glass doors to the patio slid back. Her mother stood there, moving from foot to foot, hands fidgeting. Marinda's mother never stood still. When she wasn't racing around, she was on the verge of racing around.

"We're fine back here," Daddy said without turning, his back to Marinda's mother. His tone of voice said he didn't mean it. "How's everything going?"

"Almost finished, if you can believe it," her mother said. "The party's not even starting for another two hours."

"It's already three?" Daddy looked disgustedly at his watch.

"Anything wrong?" her mother said.

"I just haven't had time to relax."

"You've still got a little while."

"I guess."

Marinda's mother disappeared into the house. Marinda still hadn't put anything on the new paper. What was the point? No one was paying attention, not this afternoon, not with the party coming. She would have fun at the party once it started. Daddy was still looking stiffly toward the hills.

Without knowing why, Marinda put a long line of blue paint directly onto the stone patio. Then she painted another blue line on the patio, making an X.

"Daddy," she said. "Something wrong happened."

He seemed not to hear, didn't even turn around. Quickly she painted four green dots in the spaces between the blue lines, one dot between each set of lines. "Daddy," she said.

"What is it?" He came over.

"An accident," she said.

"Marinda, what did you do?" He saw the paint on the patio and stiffened even more, if that was possible. "Oh no," he said. "Marinda,

I told you not to get any paint on the porch. We have guests coming, damn it."

"I didn't mean to, Daddy. It just happened."

Her father straightened up and pulled away. "It looks like you *did* mean it," he said. "But that doesn't matter. You did it; that's what counts. Nobody cares what you *intend* to do in life. They just care *what* you do." He said it seriously but it didn't make sense. Clearly, people didn't care what she did. They just cared when she did things wrong.

"Go inside and tell your mother to bring something out so you can clean this up," Daddy said.

*

The young lieutenant in full uniform held the leather folder tightly under his arm. Light was dim in the hallway and he walked down it tensely, looking straight ahead, as if he expected any moment to be challenged. He saw no one. In fact the building felt almost empty. He knew it wasn't, that behind this door or that, work went on, as it always had and always would. He didn't care how many years the trouble continued. Sooner or later it would end, and things in Mytros would go back to being what they had been.

He turned and went through a door, past a young woman at a desk. He nodded at her before going through another door into another dimly lit room. "General, Sir," he said. "You told me to come right through."

"Yes, absolutely. You have the material?"

"Of course, sir."

"Let me see it."

The lieutenant handed over the folder. The general took it and leaned forward in his chair to use the lamp on his desk, which was plugged in and had its backup battery visible nearby. These days blackouts, some accidental, others caused by vandalism, things now common across Mytros and its suburbs, were common even in the most secure government buildings. The general took no chances.

"Sit down, lieutenant." The general pulled a document from the folder. "I'm going to read this out loud, at least the key parts, so we can both hear it. You're an important witness, as I'm sure you understand. You're required to sign off that I read it in your presence."

"Yes, sir. I'm honored sir."

"Spare me," the general sighed.

"Sir?"

"Never mind. I appreciate your adherence to form, lieutenant."

"Thank you. It stands between us and chaos, sir."

"I guess it does." The general shook his head almost sadly. The lieutenant had no idea how such a fundamental truth could be sad. The general looked worn out, as if he hadn't slept much. He was in his early sixties, the lieutenant guessed, still strong. It wasn't clear how much longer he would be that way.

The general began reading, articulating every word clearly. "One of the shortcomings of our current effort in these troubles is the ability of our citizens to imagine other organizational systems than those currently in place. They do not rebel in any consistent fashion, yet there is a constant resource drain from all sorts of temporary, ill-conceived, and sometimes even passive resistances to current systems and policy. Under ordinary conditions, such independence of mind, however half-hearted, might be considered a strength of a proud, free, and independent people. In the present troubles, when all mental and physical energies require consistent direction towards the resolution of current conflicts, wasteful fantasizing may be the undoing of our whole way of life. Therefore, the imagination of our citizens must be reorganized for more positive social results."

The general paused, squeezed his forehead. "With me so far, lieutenant?"

"Yes, sir."

The general continued reading, pausing every so often to catch his breath and shake his head. "Our scientists have determined that it is possible, through a program of technological applications explained in greater detail later in this report, to redirect wasteful mental energies. The treatment involves tapping directly into the dream state of our citizens and reconditioning dream energies to be in tune with state needs. Each person's dreams will be temporarily shut down, then started up again in a manner more compatible with necessary ends.

"The goal of the treatment is twofold. First, to neutralize any mental energy that goes towards imagining that social organization might be different. Second, to enable creative problem solving on the local level that will not suggest large-scale systematic alternatives.

"Setting the stage for the treatment requires a massive information rollout. As many people as possible must volunteer to take the treatment. The media public information campaign must be both specifically concentrated and widely diffused and must operate in all major public arenas. The campaign must establish the crucial truth that the state's good makes the lives of people better. It must make clear that the survival of the state requires citizens to choose freely to participate in this treatment, which will improve their health in a number of specifically detailed ways. The message will be reinforced by on-the-ground agents in all social arenas, public and private, who will encourage others with speeches, inside information, suggestions, joking camaraderie, and a variety of small rewards.

"This program will lead the massive majority of the population, certainly 85 to 90 percent, maybe even as much as 97 or 98 percent, to undertake the treatment voluntarily. Nonetheless there will be small pockets of resisters operating for different reasons and with different potential adaptability to our goals.

"The first group of resisters, easiest to work with, will be those whose fear of medical procedures outweighs their instinct for social preservation. This group will usually not be ideologically opposed to our goals. Rather, their fears will be based in things they don't entirely understand. Intensive psychotherapy programs should change the attitudes of most of these people within a few weeks. Extreme cases can be handled through medication (given, if necessary, in their food) designed to make subjects pliable in the face of their fears. Hysterics can be drugged into calmness.

"The second group of resisters presents more complex problems. These are the individuals who, for whatever reason, do not understand what is happening but become convinced that state activities violate them in some way. We might call them the 'crackpot fringe.' It is impossible to describe in advance all the theories to which these resisters might subscribe. The majority will be motivated by deep confusions that they think of as religious, racial, isolationist, or related to misunderstood notions of individual rights. One can assume that a certain percentage of this group will respond with clumsy criminality. If convicted of crimes, they can be given the treatment without their consent. However, some reactions may exacerbate specific regional feelings related to the ideas mentioned above. Such reactions must be handled carefully and quietly, so as not to encourage group revolts of larger than several people or sudden martyrdoms that could have unpredictable ripple effects. Of course most of these people will be borderline lunatics. In most cases, no more may be necessary than public exposure of their beliefs, undoubtedly leading to ridicule and group defections. Still, one must expect that among this group there will be some semi-successful revolts. We must in such cases manage tightly any information about these revolts.

"The final group of resisters represents the most serious concern: those who do understand the treatment and information campaign and have well-considered and articulated objections. These people will vary in rank and standing, although the great majority will be concentrated in urban, church, and university environments. Our biggest advantage relative to these people is their small numbers. That many consider themselves intellectuals or religious leaders with a stake in the system may also make them unwilling to resist too vocally. If we are forced to undertake small police actions, we can expect that most of these individuals will respond with little more than ineffective outpourings of language regarding their shock and anger, sometimes perhaps in public gatherings. The likelihood of their being generally pacifist, introverted, depressed, and prone to feelings of sedate cultural superiority will make them unprepared to respond aggressively to any major action. Any that we arrest can be treated with the same psychotherapy program as those who resist out of unarticulated fear. However, it seems inevitable that a small number of these individuals will succeed in going underground and forming networks of various sizes and durations. Such groups must be handled with discretion and detailed care. Some few cases may become uncomfortably public. These will lead to tricky public relations exercises whose details cannot be foreseen.

"The policy we have outlined above is not only tenable but in fact certain of success as long as all officials handle their duties properly. While a few individuals may remain in resistance, there seems little doubt that 95 percent of the population will undertake the dream alteration treatment during the acceptable time frame."

The general put down the document. "There's a lot more information here, having to do with scientific details relative to the dream alterations," he said. "You should know that information by heart also, but I don't think we need to go over those details here. They'll be the concern of the doctors anyway." He slid the document across the table to the lieutenant. "Sign there, if you would."

"Yes, sir." The lieutenant signed. "It's an exciting time to be serving one's city, sir."

The general looked away from him elusively. "Yes, it's finally come to this, hasn't it?"

"Come to this, sir? I'm not sure I understand."

"Never mind, lieutenant. It's been a long day. Time for dinner and a drink, if you ask me. You're aware of your next steps?"

"Absolutely, sir."

"Off you go then. I appreciate your timeliness in bringing this material to me."

"My pleasure, sir. Anything for Mytros, sir. Anything for my city."

"Yes indeed," the general said wearily. "Anything for the city."

*

"I could use another, Tom," Ralph Briggs said to the bartender. "My head hurts."

"One coming up for what ails you," Tom said. "Long week?"

"One week and another, it's all the same to a man on a pension." Ralph was in his mid-sixties, muscular if a little paunchy, his face a blotchy red. He'd had a few too many rounds since his retirement from the Baltimore Police Department the year before.

"Miss the force, do you?"

Ralph shrugged. "I see the guys I want to see. The rest I can do without. Besides," Ralph looked out the window into sharp late afternoon sunlight, "all sorts of forces are floating around out there."

The bartender, unkempt short hair darkly colorless in the brown light behind the bar, frowned and flexed his forearms as if protecting himself or showing off. "You had your good years, Ralph. Don't want to forget that."

"I'm not forgetting it. It's just this headache."

"What's that about?"

"Damned if I know. Comes and goes. Couple weeks now.

Sometimes it's this buzzing and ringing. Like something that shouldn't be there has gotten inside my head. Had problems with my phone too."

"Maybe you're picking up somebody's wireless." Tom laughed. "Or the radio."

"Speaking of the radio," a balding man in a tee-shirt further down the bar said, "you listen to that Orioles game last night?" He was the only other person in the bar.

"They got some runs, Davey," Tom said to him. "Belle will start hitting better if he relaxes. And Baines, that guy's pure swing, you know? Surhoff's rocking it too but I don't know if that'll last."

"Belle's a stupid spoiled motherfucker." Davey's pointed face puckered disdainfully. "Yeah, he'll get the stats, but he doesn't make anybody around him better. He wants to win, sure, but he wants to do it by himself. It's not about hitting anyway. They don't have anybody can get anybody out except Mussina. What are you gonna do? Pitch him every day and have him relieve himself?"

Ralph lifted his drink, took a swig. The ringing went through his head again. It started near the top and came out his ear. Sometimes— at night, when it woke him from sleep, or when he was concentrating hard—it sounded like voices, although he couldn't make them out. He wasn't going to tell anybody that. He put his head in his hands.

"You okay?" Tom said.

"This fucking headache," Ralph said.

"Want aspirin?"

"Took some already. Too many."

"That beer a good idea?"

"It's that summer smog gets to me," Davey said from down the bar. "When the city's hot as all get out and the air starts to smell like an exhaust pipe."

"Yeah," Ralph said. "I…" A loud ringing crashed through his head and he couldn't see. The bar top felt cool against his face. He was staring down its wooden length. A few inches away, a beer spill spread out.

"Jesus," Tom said. "Maybe you need a doctor."

"No doctors," Ralph said. "All that poking and pinching. I just need to go home and take it easy." He stood woozily, put some money on the bar and headed out the door.

For a moment, he noticed that the spring afternoon was cool, a little clammy… then he wasn't noticing anything outside himself. Noise pounded through his head. Next came voices, a bunch at once. He couldn't hear what they were saying. He pushed his hands against both sides of his head, trying to relieve the pressure. "Get out of my head," he said. Had he said it out loud?

He staggered, reached to catch himself on the rough surface of a wall. The street around him was familiar. He saw it only a second before noise surged through him again.

Faces swarmed into his like insects. "I want you out of my head," he said. The faces fell back, startled. His hands still pushed hard against the sides of his head. That did no good. The ringing, the buzzing, the voices seared through him like someone had strung an electric wire through his ears.

He had to get home. When he tried to look around, he couldn't see. Then what he did see made no sense. Why was he in some room, where people lay sleeping, attached to some strange machinery? No, it was just his street, just another afternoon. He knew where his house was, two blocks ahead…What were all these people doing here?

Of course there was no one around. "Get hold of yourself." He was shouting, was he? The pressure was too much. When had he gotten down on his knees? If he could get up again, he didn't have far to go.

The voices were everywhere, metallic and distorted as if over some intercom gone wild. If only he could hear what they were saying, that might relieve the unbearable pressure, his head throbbing against his hands. Get them out of there; there were too many for his head to stay together. They had all gone into his head because it was the only way for them. They had no heads of their own anymore or something had gone wrong with the heads they had…

Here and there, he could feel the cool rough gravel of a driveway against his legs, arms, face. He hit his head against the gravel. He hit his head harder against the gravel. Then he couldn't find his head or the gravel and there was just the ringing, the voices. He followed them a long way down, then farther. Then he wasn't even following. Certainly he made no sign of recognition when, later that afternoon, a young neighbor on his way home from work found him in the driveway, on his back, body thrashing, eyes rolling, terrified by something nobody else could see.

TWO

In Washington, D.C., on March 12, 1999, at approximately 10:15 a.m., a man walked to the ground level, general public front entrance of the Library of Congress Adams Building. He came into the building, pulled out a pistol and fired, killing a guard, John H. Jenkins, 42, who in giving directions to a patron had momentarily turned his back to the door. The few people milling in the entrance area panicked and scattered. The man took a right, passed the metal detector, then a left, firing a few shots haphazardly, according to a witness who watched from under a table. One man, 25-year-old Reginald Chase, was hit in the leg.

The second security guard stationed near the metal detector, 31-year-old Stanford Rowe, was in the bathroom when the firing began. Hearing screaming and several loud pops, he looked out onto the chaos of the hallway and ducked back into the bathroom, where he immediately called for help. He later reported hearing about six or seven shots. After calling, he went into the hallway again. The gunman had moved onto a stairwell, headed, it turned out, for the second floor, the main floor of the library.

The main floor of the Adams Building has on one side of the central hallway a room full of computers which patrons use to search for books. A door on the other side of the hallway leads to the main rotunda of the library, after one passes through a small reception room. The gunman didn't fire any shots when he came onto the main floor, and the building walls were thick enough that no one on the floor knew yet that anything was wrong. The gunman entered the reception room, where several patrons sat at desks. The on-duty librarian, 47-year-old Sheila Murphy, stood behind the reception podium. The gunman fired a shot into the wall and grabbed the librarian by the shirt, dragging her around the reception podium while people erupted into screams and chaos and fled the room. The gunman pushed the librarian toward the door to the main rotunda of the library. People coming out of the rotunda were forced back into it. The gunman waved the gun around and fired a single shot, which cut the hand of patron Lucinda Dupree, 35.

After entering the main rotunda, the gunman closed the rotunda entrance doors and passed through a short hallway between library stacks into the open center of the rotunda. Some people managed to flee into the labyrinth of the back stacks. Others were running, or ducked under the heavy wooden tables surrounding the rotunda. At the center of the rotunda sat the round circulation desk where people turned in their book requests. No one stood there any longer, the on-duty personnel having dispersed through the room.

According to Sheila Murphy, the gunman pushed her behind the circulation desk and began a long, mostly incoherent rant. He made no attempt to seize more hostages or fire more shots. According to Murphy, the gunman kept repeating, "You'll never have dreams again; I've taken back the dreams you stole from me," and words to similar effect. In her testimony, Murphy claimed that his words made clear what he believed he was attempting. Somehow, Murphy reported, the gunman believed that by seizing the Library of Congress, he was cutting off people's dreams. He believed that his own dreams had been stolen from him and he was attempting to steal them back.

By this time, police in significant numbers had circled the front entrance and then entered it. First floor witnesses knew only that the gunman had disappeared into the building. After climbing the stairs cautiously, police came out onto the main floor, where panic was more pronounced. Yes, witnesses told police, the gunman had been seen to enter the main rotunda. Police found the doors to the rotunda closed, of course, although not locked. When they attempted to go through, several gunshots forced them back out again. They didn't know at the time whether the gunman had hostages and if he did, how many.

The standoff between police and the gunman lasted nearly ten hours. At 8:27 p.m., the gunman surrendered his hostage. Two minutes later he walked out of the rotunda unarmed and into police custody. According to Sheila Murphy, the gunman grew calm some half hour before surrendering. She stated that whatever he had been trying to do, he believed he had done it.

The gunman, 33-year-old Oliver Lowell from Bloomington, Indiana, was an unemployed truck driver and electrician with a history of erratic behavior but no prior arrests. His parents, Frederick and Minnie Lowell, were longtime, well-liked residents of Bloomington who had repeatedly tried to help their son, with little success. He had refused for some time to take medication or to continue psychiatric care. Because he was clearly delusional, after his arrest he underwent further psychiatric evaluation.

The incident captured significant media and political attention, mostly because of the location of the attack. The Library of Congress was used daily by hundreds of members of the public. There was immediate outcry about whether public buildings in D.C. were safe for tourists and other users. Calls were made for firmer security and more powerful weaponry in the hands of guards. Actual response included adding several more security guards to public buildings in the area and instituting new security routines that involved more movement between posts and more requirements regarding how guards checked on each other's whereabouts.

Funeral services for John Jenkins received national attention and extended local television coverage. Jenkins had twenty years' experience with government security organizations. He had served long and generally well, although his record was not distinguished. He was divorced. His administrative superior had been worried about a recent increase in his drinking, which perhaps had caused several absences from work in the last six months. His son, William Jenkins, 18, was currently working as an assistant manager at an area grocery store. Several congressmen complained that maybe Jenkins and Rowe had not been paying attention on the job. One was in the bathroom, for Christ's sake, although that was hardly against regulations. But if the congressmen and their allies suspected that the guards were part of a longstanding problem of D.C. and U.S. government employees failing to adequately do their jobs, they voiced these suspicions mainly as rumor and innuendo that reverberated around Capitol Hill for several weeks before fading away.

With only one dead security guard and only two people wounded, the incident did not stay in the media eye long. In a country in which random violence was increasingly common and frequently more deadly than what happened at the Library of Congress, the incident was for most Americans little more than a blip on the daily screen of media distraction, one that left no impression at all by the time similar, larger incidents hit the headlines. It wasn't long before the Library of Congress was doing normal business again, patrons coming and going, security guards at key entrances engaged in occasional watchfulness and chatting with those entering the building.

The incident did appear in the national media several more times in the months after Jenkins' funeral. First, about three weeks later, psychiatric transcripts regarding Lowell were released to the press. Those transcripts showed that Lowell, undoubtedly insane, had developed one of the most sophisticatedly paranoid scenarios of any random assassin in recent memory, a scenario which in its vividness and subtle twists and turns impressed his doctors as the creation of a first-rate, though murderously delusional and racist, imagination.

*

Marinda tried to paint all afternoon. Finally she gave up and called Jerry, who said he would come over. As far as the outside world was concerned, she had artistic originality, marketable talent and impressive potential. Her pieces had been displayed in a few significant shows, and several local commercial galleries featured her art. But the outside world didn't feel the lack of motivation that overwhelmed her lately when she tried to create new work. The moment she gathered herself and her materials to start, she'd suddenly need to stare out the window, run an errand, or turn on Oprah Winfrey.

She had never been a disciplined painter. Instead she painted in fits of rage, boredom, anxiety, or unresolved tension sexual or otherwise. Painting happened to her, she felt, more than she decided to make it happen. But if it had happened to her frequently in the past, now it seemed mainly to abandon her. Partly that was because she was older, had more things to do, more ways to distract herself. So she had been trying, for the last several months, to set aside an hour or two every day, at least, to paint. Maybe once a week she did paint something. They were usually just fragments of pieces, possibilities with no clear direction. Their unfinished, neglected skeletons lay scattered around the big back room she used as a studio.

The problem seemed to be that she didn't feel intensely enough about anything to push a painting through to a conclusion. Worse, sometimes she would be painting when it would occur to her that there wasn't anyone anywhere that she wanted to see her paintings. Why paint when there was no one to paint for? Often she painted because someone wanted to stop her from painting or made it clear they didn't approve. Then she would feel an anger and hostility that could push her all the way through several works, leaving her exhausted and victorious in the aftermath. These days there was no disapproval to play off, and no approval either. Was the goal of painting really to prove her genius to the void? Not that she felt she had any genius, but that wasn't the point. No one cared about her painting, herself included, and here she was pretending to be a painter.

Jerry took his time showing up. Marinda moved fitfully among her materials, opening this and closing that, then showered and changed into evening clothes. Eventually the bell rang.

"Where should we eat?" Jerry said when he was thoroughly inside and holding court from the couch. "No more Italian, please. I've had it with Italian." His shirt was wildly untucked. He was sweating.

"Are you going to open that wine or just sit there complaining?" Marinda said.

"I think I'll sit here complaining." Jerry flicked his hand imperiously. "Besides, you're hardly one to give orders. You forgot your money again last night. That's three times in two weeks."

"I know." Marinda opened the wine herself. "I'm trying to do better."

"Try harder," Jerry said. "It's a good thing I have extra."

When their glasses were full, he continued. "So you were painting? Your hands still look blue. Little Marinda has dirty hands and needs to clean her nose."

She grabbed a loose end of his shirt. "Aren't we the king of fashion ourselves?"

Surprisingly, Jerry's face beamed pleasure. "There's no type of king I'm unhappy to be."

Despite herself, Marinda laughed, though she cut it short. "What's the king been doing today?"

"I'm starting a magazine," Jerry said. He tried to look serious, his mouth tightening, always a bad sign. "Some articles on culture and entertainment but mainly just a lot of ads. We could give people advice on restaurants and nightclubs and fun little spots that nobody knows about. I talked to my Dad and he has no problem fronting me the money. I know a couple people who could write articles. You could even do some."

"That's awfully kind of you. I'd expect to be paid."

"Money's not the problem. The question is whether I feel like doing it. I felt like it earlier today. Now I feel more like deciding where to eat."

"Would this magazine cover the queer scene too?"

Jerry glared at her. "Would it have to?"

"If you want to do a foo-foo magazine successfully, maybe, yeah. Unless you're planning a how-to-do-the-city pub for outdoorsmen, the best duck-hunting spots in Manhattan, that sort of thing."

"I suppose I could hire someone to cover the queer scene." Jerry sniffed disdainfully. "I don't know anything about it though. Say, what do you think about this Asian mail order bride thing? She'd cook and clean for me and submit to my every whim because she'd be so happy to be out of servitude back home."

Marinda looked at him, stem of the wine glass between his fingers, stomach spilling over the front of his pants. "Why are you thinking about mail order brides?"

"Have a friend with a connection, that's all. It's easily done. I have needs."

"Why don't you buy a hooker? You know, as a sort of test case."

"Test case of what?"

"Oh…just that relationships based on money maybe aren't that fulfilling."

"Listen to you," Jerry laughed. "Come off it. Everything's based on money. Wow, you really have been painting today. You better watch out, or you're going to become some moony-eyed hippy romantic and marry a folk singer from Vermont who makes pottery."

"And that would be wrong because…?"

"Because you're spoiled. That's what we have in common, Marinda. The only difference is I don't fight it. I like having things my way. I like going to restaurants and drinking good wine and meeting chicks and…"

"…and staying up all night and sitting on the couch and planning to be famous," Marinda finished for him.

"What's wrong with that?" Jerry said.

"Nothing." Marinda sighed. She poured more wine, though her glass wasn't empty. "Where *are* we going, Jerry? If I hang around here much longer, I'm going to kill one of us, and with my luck lately it won't be you."

*

It had been a long week for Steve. He still had another hour or two in the office, then the subway ride out of Manhattan to his apartment in Williamsburg. I wonder where Marinda is, he thought. He turned back to the article he was writing, a stupid piece on frequent flier miles. He told people he was a reporter because that was his job title but as far as he was concerned, he was an ad writer. The magazine he worked for—a local entertainment offshoot of Playboy—published little articles detailing little things of interest to uninteresting people. Why couldn't he be somewhere exciting, doing something important, instead of putting up with a non-stop parade of bullshit that he couldn't even make himself angry about? About once a week, he would call a travel agent to see about flight prices to Paris, Tokyo, even places in Africa. I should just go, he thought. So far, he hadn't.

"Hey," Cynthia came over to him. Again he felt that sensation of wanting her. She was wearing a long skirt that looked good. Her hair bounced loosely, without the professional uptightness he hated. He even considered asking her out. But Marinda had ruined everything. If only her parents hadn't been such religious nuts. Between Marinda and her parents, nothing was left.

"Hey yourself," he said.

"What are you doing after work tonight? A couple of us are going for a drink in the neighborhood about seven. Just some low-key hanging out. Want in?"

"I was hoping to change out of my work clothes before I did anything," he said. "But I'd have to go all the way to Williamsburg. So maybe, yeah. Where are people going?"

She told him the name of the bar and said it was only a few blocks away. "Ever been there?"

"No," he said. "I'm not big on bars. I'll have one or two drinks at most sometimes."

"Really?" Cynthia said. "That's interesting. Everybody I know drinks, some too much. It's boring."

"It's bad for you, too." Steve felt an adrenalin surge at the chance to explain; a lot of people could have benefited from his explanations. "Besides, don't you think most people drink because they can't deal with their lives? They can't look things straight in the face so they need to get bombed."

"I don't know," Cynthia said. "That sounds a little harsh. But I know what you mean."

Steve shrugged. "I don't want to be the kind of person who

thinks other people or things can solve his problems. That's one of the reasons we *have* so many problems. People always want to blame somebody or think something can save them from themselves."

"You could be right," Cynthia said. She leaned against the edge of his desk, nearly touching his arm. The sweet smell of her skin floated around him.

"I mean that's what religion is, isn't it?" Steve said. "Something people can hide in so they don't have to look at the way things are? So they make up some little belief system and follow its rules and listen to what its little leaders tell them. That way, they don't have to know what's going on in the world."

Cynthia smiled. "You're kind of funny, you know that?"

"I don't see what's funny about it. Religion ruins a lot of lives. Look at those cults, the things that happen to the people who stay in them, and even the people who get out. My last girlfriend's parents were in a cult. It caused so many problems that things between us didn't work out."

Cynthia startled. "They were in a *cult*?" Her eyes looked into his as if trying to tell him something. Maybe she didn't mind that he didn't have a girlfriend. "That's too bad," she said, not sounding sorry.

"Had their own weird religious wacko preacher and everything. Big money in it. They'd have dinner parties and bring all this weird food and these weird little objects, then they'd pray some and he'd talk, spewing some bullshit they thought was wisdom. It was creepy."

"You actually went to these things?"

"Me? Oh no way. It's just that Marinda would talk about it all the time. Then she'd get to thinking she should be religious too, even though she wasn't. She didn't believe in God but she couldn't get it out of her head that she was supposed to."

"You don't believe in God, obviously?"

"Why, do you?"

"I don't think about religion much one way or another," Cynthia said. Her eyes floated upwards as if shooing the question away. "I know some people believe in it. It's life that counts, right? Not what happens after you're dead?"

"Sometimes you have to think about it though." Steve gave her his most reasonable, let's-be-fair voice. "I went out of my way to help her. I would have gone farther too, if she'd let me. She got too freaky for me. I had to get out."

"It's nice you cared so much. What kinds of things did she do?"

"It wasn't what she did really. It was just the way she was thinking. She would get it in her head that I was trying to control her thoughts."

"You mean telling her what to think?"

"No. Controlling her thoughts. Putting ideas in her head that she couldn't get out."

"That's crazy."

"Isn't it?" Steve shook his head ironically. "And she seemed like a regular girl. A little California-style flakey maybe, no more than typical for people out there. But she was nuts. Only you wouldn't know it. That's the thing I learned from the two years we spent together. It's not even that you can know people casually and not see their deep weird problems. It's that you can know them *well* and not see their deep weird problems. How many people are walking in the streets, holding down jobs, eating in restaurants, seeming more or less ordinary but when you get down to it, they're out of their minds? It's made me cautious. I wasn't ever the kind of guy who goes out with girls just to fool around. I'm in it for serious or I'm not in it for long. But now I think more about it. I'm not going to fall for somebody again until I know a lot more about her. I want the next woman to be the right one."

"I think that's admirable." Cynthia smiled. "I know too many guys who just think about how many women they can sleep with."

"I'm not like that," Steve said.

"So are you going with us? It should be fun."

"Sure. As long as it's not one of those things where everybody drinks until they can't see straight."

"It might be for one or two of them. It doesn't have to be for you and me. If we don't like the way things are going, we can take off for somewhere else."

Steve looked at her. Maybe Marinda had sent Cynthia to distract him? It seemed unlikely. Besides, Cynthia was nice and maybe he could have some fun with her. Sure, Marinda had ruined everything, but he'd show her she wasn't completely in charge.

"Sounds good to me," he said.

"Great," Cynthia said. "I'll come get you when it's time to go."

Steve nodded. "I'll be here." He turned back to his keyboard.

A moment after she was gone, Steve had second thoughts. This was the kind of thing Marinda might use against him. Maybe she had gotten Cynthia interested in going out with him so she could later say he was running around behind her back. But even though she'd ruined everything, he knew she didn't mean it. It was just her parents' phony religion manipulating her. It was pathetic how religion could turn someone into a sick puppet motivated by obsessions she had no control over, believing things that came out of some insane fantasy world. It was amazing he still loved her, given her foolishness. Ah well. It just proved he was the one who could make her well again. It was only a matter of getting her to listen.

"If you're tired of the food on these odd-hour flights that are the only ones the airline will honor for frequent flier credits," he wrote, "here are several easy tips on how to make the service work for you."

*

If you ask me what it was like in Mytros, after the dream alterations, all I can tell you is what it wasn't like. It was nothing like waking from a long dreamless sleep. It wasn't like going from a place to a place, a past to a present, a present to a future. It was nowhere to have been and nowhere to arrive. It wasn't like being able to compare. Experience is always elusive, so present when it occurs that one can feel utterly absorbed and understand nothing of that absorption, yet so gone later that even the most serious reflection can't bring back even one small piece. But it was nothing like experience, not in any way I understood, and it was nothing like memory.

I know I walked a lot. My body moved around, doing its routines. The presence of any place, the actuality of things, had about them an unbearable drone. I would say that the presence of other things *burned,* if it weren't that such a description has too much passionate connection, even if only with despair.

Nor was it grief I was feeling, although sometimes in lucid moments I could remember that grief was something I knew. Grief is a kind of body, a living presence that can't take the place of the living presence that has gone, but nonetheless becomes a marker of one's own realness. Look in that corner and the person isn't there; look out the window and the person isn't there, look in the sky, the bed, the kitchen, the street, and the person isn't there and never will be. Everywhere you look, the person isn't there, but the person's shadow is, because you *are* their shadow. But if I was the shadow of something, I didn't know what it was.

Mytros was still there, of course. People, restaurants, clothing stores, book stores, office buildings, corner vendors. Parks and trees and sidewalks and streets and cars and traffic lights. It had once been my city. Now, none of it meant anything.

If I can't explain how the dream alterations moved me around, how they became me so much that I didn't exist except inside them, how can I explain what things must have been like for so many other people who (I can only guess) must also have succumbed? Who am I to say what anyone felt when the world stopped dreaming, or how or why they felt it? Certainly there was fighting and shooting and frenzied outbursts and dramatic public suicides. Do I recall correctly? Do I remember cars burning in the streets, people screaming at each other, beating each other, rocks being thrown and riots beginning? Do I remember quiet ordinary days in which I couldn't tell whether anyone besides me felt hopeless beyond sickness?

One evening, I found myself in a basement meeting hall in an old decaying building in an abandoned part of the increasingly abandoned city, talking to members of the underground. They gave me some kind of drug to clear my mind temporarily, and I knew who I was. Before the dream alterations, I'd had some connections to protest politics in Mytros, though like many people, my inklings of fear about the coming dream alterations didn't trouble me enough to really resist. Now the people I hadn't paid enough attention to, before, had found me. There were others like them, they said, who hadn't submitted to the procedure. Even though those people had become outlaws, they walked with a clear head through the streets of a city fogged with delusion. In fact, although the outlaws had to be careful, the government that had made them outlaws was in careening disarray.

Still, they were under constant if erratic threat. They didn't yet have anything that could reverse the alterations in others, although there were odd, incomplete, and conflicting ideas about various possibilities. Certainly they didn't have the strength, militarily or with propaganda, to fight back against the government, which despite its disarray still had on its side money and weapons and television and radio stations, with enough coherence among its police and military forces to round up any still suffering from the "disease," as it was everywhere proclaimed and as most people believed, when they were coherent enough to believe anything. Nonetheless there were secret networks of informed resisters, and their ranks were growing.

"What about those of us who haven't escaped?" I asked them, a fog coming over me again. "What are you going to do, shoot me up with drugs forever?"

"How much are you willing to risk?" one said—I wasn't aware enough to ask names.

"I don't have anything to risk," I said. "I have nothing."

"Then you could hardly object to leaving not just the city, but the whole world, behind?"

"There's no world to leave behind," I said.

"And if I told you there was some other world you might go to? Some other world where your condition might—I can only say might—not exist?"

"I wouldn't even have to consider it," I said.

As simply as that, I became one of the first subjects of a new, risky experiment. I didn't know much about how it worked—why ask? Even if it killed me, that solved my problem too.

*

"Are you going to ask Geena on a date?" Marinda demanded of Jerry as soon as they were seated, drinks in hand, at a table near the bar. The place was crowded, although there was an empty table here and there. A lot of people were choosing to stand. It was considered a place to see and be seen, as the phrase went. Marinda didn't want to do either. She was here anyway.

"She's hot for me, isn't she?" Jerry said.

"I didn't say that. She does seem to like you. Beggars can't be choosers, dear."

"There's no way I resemble any kind of beggar," Jerry said, "even metaphorically."

"You're not answering my question." Marinda saw, out of the

corner of her eye, a small knot of people hovering awkwardly near her.

"I don't know. Should I?"

"Yes. She's nice, she's pretty, and she's smart, although for some reason she's not smart enough to see through you."

"You just can't accept that other women might find me interesting." Jerry grinned. "It's because you love me."

"Please," Marinda said. "Are you going to go out with her or not?"

"I don't think so. She's not my type."

"That's the most ridiculous thing I've ever heard." Marinda put her hands on the table and pushed, for emphasis. Her chair slid backwards. "If you're going to turn down everyone who…"

One of the men from the pack standing close beside her tripped over Marinda's chair. She shrieked. "Oh hey," he said, falling. He floundered, sitting, into her lap, while his head dipped back like he might turn upside down. She reached out to steady him. Jerry lurched away from the table, frowning disdainfully. The man's legs flopped upward into the air for a moment. Aided by Marinda catching him, they found the floor again.

Stunned, he stayed sitting in Marinda's lap. "That's the first unexpected thing that's happened to me in weeks," he said.

The skin of his face, so close to hers, was pale. There were brown rings around his eyes. She tried to help him to his feet. "Up you go."

"Then life will be ordinary again," he said, "and none of us will notice anything." He grabbed the table and stood. He was tall, lanky, and awkward. "And that's better, because noticing things is always annoying."

Marinda laughed. "I think I'll keep noticing you for a while, seeing as you've probably broken my knee."

"An actual injury!" The man laughed also. "I wouldn't want to say that's good, but at least it reminds us how to be in pain. Otherwise we might almost be happy."

Marinda looked at Jerry who, still frowning, had not yet moved back to the table. "Pain reminds me of everything I know about," she said. "And gives me something to do on weekends."

"I've given up caring that weekends exist." The man's hands gestured wildly as he spoke. "Once I realized that the calendar was an arbitrary trick, I decided to ignore it. It's a game that somebody made up because they didn't know what to do with themselves. Now everybody else plays too because we can't think of any other game."

Jerry cut in, "It's been real, but if you're done falling down…"

Jerry's obvious desire to get rid of the guy spurred Marinda on. "What other game could we be playing?" she asked.

The man's face lit up, then settled back into the expression he'd had since he stood, an expression, Marinda decided, that had elements in it of amusement, confusion, exhaustion, and something she couldn't identify. He was handsome in a way, if too skinny; long chiseled face, eyes retreating behind the brown rings. His slacks and shirt were fashionably casual. "The thing about games," he said, "is that nobody knows how many of them there are to play. The only limit is how many we make up. Sometimes I think we could live in a world where people made up new games all the time. As it is, everybody's so busy thinking they already know what the game is that it never occurs to them there might be others. Saves effort, I suppose."

"You play games?" Marinda asked.

"As consciously as possible." His eyes twinkled. "I'm not, sadly, all that conscious. I'd rather be distracted by circumstances that leave me empty and upset. There have been times when I wasn't upset. They scared me. Give me a problem I can't solve, a love I can pursue but don't want to have, in fact any small thing to keep me disturbed, as long as I don't have to confront the possibility of having no immediate crisis. When I'm not having a crisis, I freak out."

Marinda laughed again. "I'm not sure I can remember the last time I wasn't having a crisis."

"You're a lucky woman," the man said.

"I don't feel lucky. I feel like I don't know what to do with myself."

"Have you tried long hours of boredom and insecurity? They can fill your days beautifully if well matched with the occasional moment of blinding agony."

Jerry frowned into his drink. "I can't believe we're having this conversation."

Marinda pointed at him. "This is my friend Jerry. He represses a lot."

Jerry snorted.

"And I'm Marinda," she went on. "Who are you?"

"Call me Herbert," the man said. "It's not my name."

Marinda stared, fascinated. "Why don't you sit down and join us, Herbert."

"Would I be interrupting something?"

Jerry said, "Actually…"

"No," Marinda said.

"I'll sit down anyway. It's not as good if I can't interrupt something. But if you promise to keep forgetting the subject, I'd be more than glad to join you." He took a seat. His lips flared out as if he was pleased with himself.

"Aren't you here with friends?" Jerry pointed at the group of people Herbert had been speaking to a moment before. After briefly watching Herbert fall, they had gone back to talking among themselves.

"I never go anywhere with friends," Herbert said. "It's why I have so many."

"So the people you're with are…?" Jerry pressed.

"At first I thought of them as suggestive shadows. Or perhaps small farm animals. Just a minute or two ago, they started to sound like people. Upsetting."

"What do you do?" Jerry asked. "For a living, I mean?"

Marinda said, "What do *you* do, Jerry?"

"I'm in the beginning stages of running a magazine," Jerry said.

"There aren't any issues yet?" Herbert asked.

"Not yet. There will be."

"Why? What could be better than a magazine without issues? You know everything it says without reading it."

"You have a job here in the city?" Jerry insisted.

"I do this and that, yes. All of it unnecessary. I'm an expert at doing unnecessary work. It gives me constant opportunity. I used to want to do something important and found myself unemployed all the time." He looked at Marinda. "You're an artist of some sort, aren't you?"

"Painter. I guess. Lately I can't get anything done. How did you know?"

"Because you're not pretending to be stranger than you are. On the other hand, you're not pretending that you're not strange. I hope you're not acting like yourself though. People who act like themselves are almost always wrong. Besides, it's New York. We're all artists. We know that because television tells us."

Jerry looked at Marinda. "I need another drink. I may go check out who else is around, so if you want something you'll have to get it yourself." He stood up. "Have money tonight? Don't want to worry about you when some other woman's all over me."

"Got some right here," Marinda pulled some wadded bills out of her pocket. "I walked out without any, then found I'd left some twenties in these clothes."

"At least you've got the habit down," Jerry said.

"I don't want to break up the…" Herbert began.

"You're not," Marinda said. "At all."

"Shame," Herbert said.

*

Sarah never stopped being amazed how different words could be. At some moments—like much of yesterday—they mainly seemed labels, at others like casual side comments or intentional non sequiturs. Still other moments they were intensely angled, related to their sources tangentially in ways difficult to decipher. Sometimes at poetry readings, like this one, which had just ended, she would be overwhelmed with the physical thickness of words tossing themselves around and would have to leave. Other times, the words were restrained, suggestive, or moody in unexpected ways.

Tonight, at the well-known Soho gallery where the reading had been held, the main thing that saturated her was people's attention. She hadn't been to a reading in six months. Everybody's concerns, good and bad, seemed transparent. None were too insidious, although she was surprised, as she often was, that people at these readings weren't aware of their own auras, at least not any more than people who didn't care so much about language. She had to remind herself frequently that other poets didn't *see* words as literally as she did, although sometimes at least they would believe that *she* saw them.

"Sarah, I'd like to introduce you to…" "Sarah, what do you think about…?" "Sarah, I loved your piece in…" "Sarah, I'm editing a book and I'd love to have…" She went through it all more or less gladly, although her shoulders and back felt tense.

One prominent male poet on the scene, who alternately gave off the words "protective" and "I want to be a leader" in between strings of more disjointed phrase, took her by the shoulder over to a comfortable chair, sat beside her and asked how she was. He was slender and refined in his shiny, dark blue, business-like shirt, although a bit sweaty from the warm gallery. He was "genuinely concerned" but "wanted information" too badly. He opened a notebook and set it on his knee.

"I hear you've got a new book coming out," he said. "I can't wait to read it."

"I was having trouble channeling everything," Sarah said. "But I finally finished."

"Could I get you to give a reading?"

"I don't know," she said. "There's a lot going on. Some things I don't understand."

"I'm not sure anybody understands more than you," he said. "But what do you mean?"

"The words I'm seeing recently are strange," she said. "They're suddenly coming from… well, that's the point. I don't know where they're coming from."

"Isn't that part of how it works for you?"

"Not usually." Sarah paused, considering how to explain. "People commonly believe that words come from them, right? But we both know that's not true. Words make people as much as people make words. People are stuffed with language. Words control us more than we control them."

"I buy that 100 percent." He nodded knowingly. "So what's different?"

"Lately I'm seeing words that aren't coming from anywhere. I mean, anywhere that's 'here.' They're coming from somewhere else."

His eyes focused on her hard, as if trying to solve a mystery. "Where else could they come from?"

"I don't know. But they keep coming. They tear little holes in 'here' and force their way through."

His eyes brightened with mischievous understanding. "It sounds, uh, pretty sexual and violent, the way you're describing it."

"Yes," Sarah said. "Of course." Then she stared at him. "Oh," she said. "Oh, I think I…"

"What?"

"I get it," she said.

"What?"

Newly energetic, she stood. "They're sexual. That's it. They come from elsewhere but they're trying to be born again. Here. Wherever they're coming from, they can't be born there anymore. That's why they keep appearing in the wrong places. They need to be born here but they don't know how."

"I'm sorry, you're losing me."

"Even if you cover a building with words," she said, "you can't make it pregnant."

"That's just fabulous." He wrote something in the notebook. "It's like a whole new stage in your thinking."

Sarah shook her head. "It doesn't have anything to do with me."

"Well…no, I understand that. But you're the one who sees it."

"I need to go," she said.

"Some of us are walking down the block for a drink. I thought you might like to come."

"I can't. I've got to find out." She squeezed his wrist gratefully and started walking towards the door.

"It was nice to see you." He tossed out the words at her back.

Out on the street, she breathed deeply. It was a warm night in the city. The density of language at the gallery began rolling off her shoulders. Then, as she expected because it was often like this, the streets were thick with her own realization. Her realization didn't create the thickness. Instead, it allowed her to sense some key element that had been there all along but which had now become blatant.

And oh, the streets were dense with it. Sex everywhere. It left nobody free of its pull, whether they understood it or not. Couples of various ages, gay and straight, walked by with ripe readiness, or a quiet fulfilled glow, or with energy bouncing off each other in convoluted knots and tangles, or with a powerful repressed fertile rage. Groups of college-age young men threw it outward in all directions, directly and unambiguously yet without focus, as though if they threw a thousand balls in a thousand directions, sooner or later one would hit something. Young women threw it too, often at angles, indirectly, under and over, to the side, glancing off this or that—or they'd throw something directly then look the other way, as if someone else had done it. Nor was it gone from the middle-aged and older people who walked the streets together or alone, aimlessly or full of intention. With them, the angles and degrees and moments of focus and low simmering burns and sudden flare-ups that vanished just as suddenly could be impossible to follow. The energy burned in her too, thrilling, terrifying. To realize that the words she was trying to find, the words desperate to be born here, or born again here, were appearing in her world, in her city, in so many ways, frequently, with no warning or indication to anyone other than herself—unless, that is, there were others who could feel it too—she was stunned by it. She had no idea what, if anything, to do.

Because one didn't need to be a scientist to calculate the odds of something this basic. Even in the worst-case scenario—if all the words came from the equivalent of alienated, introverted male adolescents who threw their endless energy in desperately unfocused ways—sooner or later some words would find a destination they could use. And if, as was practically certain, the source of the words was much more complex, even if far far away, when those words did at last find a destination, how could she know even the first thing about what they'd give birth to?

THREE

"It's a lovely night," Cynthia said. "I don't think there's anything more beautiful than New York on a spring night."

Steve walked beside her. Every so often he slowed his pace, trying not to walk with the rest of the group, two men and a woman. At work, he spoke to all three of them now and again, but he didn't like knowing people from the office. It was a waste of time because he didn't intend to stay. Besides, if they could be satisfied doing their stupid little jobs, they were too shallow to bother with.

"I know what you mean," he said. "But the city's so crowded. It's a great place to be for now, but I'm not sure I'd want to raise a family here. Kids need space."

"You want to have kids?" Cynthia pushed in a little closer to him.

"Sure. It's an important responsibility. Too many people who have kids shouldn't have them. So if mature and responsible people get so caught up in their careers that they don't have children, who *is* going to? Only people who shouldn't. That doesn't seem right."

"I agree," Cynthia said. "I really respect you, you know that,

Steve? I like what you have to say."

Steve nodded; he appreciated that Cynthia was sensible. "I've had a lot of experiences. Not all ones I wanted to, but sometimes you learn most from those."

A little while later the group was settled in the bar. Their table was just large enough to fit all five. They ordered a pitcher of beer and started it quickly. Soon they were on a second. Cynthia sat next to Steve, who sipped his beer slowly, frowning when he noticed the other men, Joseph and Daniel, draining their glasses quickly. He had no time for men like that. If they weren't literally the same office guy, distinctions between them still weren't worth making. Ties and rolled up shirtsleeves, etc. The conversation was mainly about work. Steve didn't pay much attention. He spent more time looking at the old photographs of the city that hung on the walls, shots of apartment buildings and crowds from long ago. Bits and pieces of the chatter came through anyway.

"I can't believe he lied to my face, twice," Daniel was saying. "There wasn't even a reason to lie. It's not like it did anything for him, and all it did to me was I had to go find out he was lying. So what was the point?"

"He's afraid of you," said the other woman at the table, Renee it seemed her name was. Pretty enough in her ordinary short-brown-hair, office-worker way, with a small perky nose and conniving eyes. One of those women who wanted to know everybody's business. Steve shook his head, quietly disgusted. "He knows you do better work," she said. "He's afraid everybody else knows it too."

"I understand," Daniel said. "I even understand him trying to figure out some way to screw me over. You can bet I'm watching for it." He downed the rest of his beer—his third glass, Steve noted—and poured himself another. "What I can't understand is why he'd tell me a lie that didn't do him any good and didn't do me any harm, but was just an annoying pain in everybody's ass. Then he did it again." He gestured to the waitress for another pitcher.

"If he's as incompetent as you think," Renee said, "maybe he's incompetent at trying to screw people over."

Everybody except Steve erupted into laughter.

"Steve's sure not saying much," Joseph said, glass raised in front of his face, dark blue tie dangling from his white and blue striped shirt. "Maybe this character's a friend of yours, Steve?"

"No," Steve said. "I've got no use for liars. But I'm not sure I see the point in worrying about work all the time. I just go in and get things done so I can go back to doing what matters."

"Kind of above it, are you?" Joseph said. His smile might have been mocking, to the extent that office guys like him had expressions at all on their bland, photo-ready faces.

"You can put it that way if you want," Steve said. "I wouldn't."

"What way *would* you put it? Enlighten us." Joseph tossed the rest of his beer back into his throat.

"I'd say the job we do is pretty much a waste of time," Steve said. "But hey, we need enough money for beer, right?"

"Damn right," Joseph said, pouring himself another. "I didn't realize you had so many better things to do." He was glaring.

"I really like New York City in the spring," Cynthia jumped suddenly into the conversation. "It's my favorite season."

"A wonderful season to waste your time," Joseph said.

"There's just so much to do," Cynthia went on, trying to ignore Joseph's hostility. "The other night, a couple of girlfriends and I..."

Steve didn't listen to her story. Asshole, he thought, glancing every so often at Joseph's guard-dog head. Joseph stared at Steve a moment more, then turned away, getting absorbed in Cynthia's story, something about a nightclub, Steve gathered, and some guy who kept buying rounds of champagne. Damn it, Marinda, Steve thought, it's your fault I have to put up with conversations like this. If you weren't so twisted with religion and so convinced you're mad at me, we'd be together right now and I wouldn't have to be here.

Still, Cynthia was pretty, however dull. She filled out her shirt nicely and she definitely seemed to like him. Her face was lively and animated in a healthy way Marinda's had never been; Marinda's face had grown bright mainly when she was anxious. It seemed likely that Marinda hadn't sent Cynthia to distract him, although it was still possible. Of course she wasn't the kind of woman he could take seriously. Maybe he'd have a fling, to prove to Marinda that he had options?

"So there we were at four in the morning, god knows in what part of town, and we can't even find a cab. And oh my god, we were just so drunk…" Cynthia saw Steve's frown. "I mean, I don't really drink much, but the guy had been buying us all this champagne."

"Reminds me of a night right after I got my first job in the city," Joseph said. "Me and a couple guys I met at work headed out…"

Steve turned away and looked around the bar again. He liked the photographs: the buildings, cars, people. The photos showed a young, energetic, hard-working New York, one that was moral and good, not like today when people were screwed up by religion, money, alcohol, or their own shallowness, and often enough all at once. Steve looked at the other groups of people around the bar, most young office workers like the people he was stuck with. Pathetic. The bar smelled of beer and pointlessness.

Cynthia leaned close to him and whispered. "I hope you don't think I'm some kind of lush. It was just a one-time thing. I don't even really like champagne."

"Don't worry about it," Steve said. "But I'm not sure how much longer I can take being here. I'm not into these kinds of places."

"We can go, if you want."

"…so what do you think about that, Steve?" Joseph turned sharply in his direction.

"About what?"

"I'm sorry. Wasn't I saying something worth your attention?"

"I was talking to Cynthia," Steve said. "What's your problem?"

"I don't know," Joseph said. "Maybe you're my problem."

"Why would that be?" Steve said. "Do you resent people who can leave a bar not seeing double?"

Joseph stood up.

"Guys," Cynthia said. "Cut it out."

"Yeah Joseph, come on," Daniel said. "What's the big deal?"

"Steve here thinks he's better than everybody," Joseph said. "It pisses me off."

"If the shoe fits," Steve said.

"I'll fit the fucking shoe," Joseph said, "right down your fucking throat."

"Hey," Daniel shouted. "Everybody stop it. Jesus."

"You're acting like a couple of children," Renee said. She was smiling.

"Don't worry about me," Steve said. "I'm not the kind of guy who gets into fights in bars so I can have something to think about."

"See," Joseph said, looking at Daniel. "It's that kind of shit."

"Just calm down, all right?" Daniel said. "Everybody."

"Steve and I were about to leave," Cynthia said. "We just wanted to stop off for a quick drink is all."

"Maybe you better do that." Daniel looked at her and avoiding eye contact with Steve.

"I'm ready to go," Steve said. "Any time."

"Okay," Cynthia said. "Look, it's been a hard week."

"I feel fine," Joseph said.

Cynthia stood, took her jacket off the back of her chair. "Let's go for a walk," she said to Steve.

"Sure," Steve said. "The smell of all this beer is getting on my nerves." He stood too, reached into his wallet and dropped a ten on the table.

"No no, hey," Daniel shook his head. "You barely had any. Just a buck or two is fine."

"Consider it on me," Steve said. "I don't want you to think I waste my time holding a grudge."

"All right, sure," Daniel said. "Thanks. See you both in the office Monday."

Joseph sat next to him sullenly and silently. Renee still had an amused smile on her face.

"Great." Cynthia forced an exuberant smile. "You guys have a good evening."

"Yeah," Steve said. "Have a good evening."

*

"I wanted to be a musician," Marinda's father said. They were driving in his red convertible, coming back from picking up her prom dress. His light blue shirt was buttoned at the wrists, protection against the wind, his silver hair flashed in the sun. He glanced over at her occasionally, his jaw tight. "Sometimes you have to be practical and give up what you want. You're going to have to learn that. Except I've spoiled you so much I'm afraid you'll learn the hard way."

Marinda was looking at the dry clear sun lighting the hills and the houses on them. The sun was warm, the breeze cool. Hidden beyond the hills, for the moment, was the ocean. She could have been at the beach in a new bathing suit instead of running errands for a dance she barely cared about. The breeze across the convertible chilled her skin and she shivered.

"It's nice out," she said. "Do we have to talk about this?"

"I'm sorry, but we do. You'll be leaving home in a couple months and I want to make sure you understand me."

"I do understand you," Marinda said. "Really."

"The band I was in was good, you know? If we'd stuck it out, we might have had some hits."

"I know."

"We were playing every Friday and Saturday night, at clubs by the beach or in the city. We'd get good crowds, people would dance. We were even playing some of our own songs—and people would actually sing along. That may be the thing I'm proudest of, that people sang my lyrics."

"They sometimes do that now."

"It's not the same." Her father sighed. "I mean, it shows I know what I'm doing. But people signing your jingles is not the same as being the Beatles."

Marinda's father was a Beatles fanatic. Not only did he have all the albums and many singles, he also had lots of memorabilia: photographs and books, plaques and trinkets of all sorts. His most prized possession was a guitar George Harrison had played for a few weeks in the summer of 1966 on the Beatles' final tour of the U.S. "Nobody's the Beatles but the Beatles," she said.

"That's what I'm trying to tell you." Her father glanced at her suspiciously. "It was a wonderful fantasy but nothing more. I guess," he smiled, "it was also a great way to meet girls."

"I just want to take a few painting classes," Marinda said. "I don't see the problem."

Her father ran a hand impatiently through his hair. "The problem is I'm sending you to an expensive school. I don't want you throwing away money on fantasies, even wonderful fantasies. And I know they're wonderful. I had them too. But they'll end up hurting you. I don't want you to get hurt like I was."

"I'm not you. Don't I get to find out some things for myself?"

"I'm not saying you can't keep painting. I'm just saying it's not a good thing to go to school for. It's a hobby, Marinda. It'll never be anything else."

"Oh," Marinda said.

"All I want is you to be happy. That's what I've been doing this—all of this—for. So your mother and you could have a happy life and never have to worry. If it weren't for the two of you, I might have followed those fantasies to the bitter end."

"Oh," Marinda said.

"What I'm trying to say," her father straightened proudly in his seat, "is that it's a good thing I didn't. Sure, I haven't always liked my job, but I knew I was making a nice life for all of us. Now here you are, in a great position to do something worthwhile. You've had advantages I wish I'd had. But I don't want you to think that just because that's true, life is some playground. Sometimes, in order to be what we have to, we have to give up our dreams, at least the unrealistic ones."

"Why is painting unrealistic?" Marinda said. Angry tears started in her eyes. She forced them back.

Her father was still looking at the road. "Because you can't make a living at it. I'm happy to support you now but I can't do it forever. I wish it wasn't true, Marinda, but the only people who get any respect are people who make money. I want you to be someone people will respect."

"I don't want to do anything except be a painter. I don't care about money."

"I didn't want to do anything except be a musician. Don't you see how alike we are?"

"I guess."

"Sure we are." Her father smiled a big charming smile. "We're both dreamers, you and me. That's why you don't have to go through some of the things I had to. You can learn to be practical now, instead of later, when it might tear you apart."

"I don't want to be practical."

"I know, but you have to be." He shook his head benevolently, as if they were sharing a profound family secret. "Better that the message comes from me than from some stranger. At least this way, you know you're being told the truth by someone who loves you. And I do love you. You know that, don't you? You know everything I've done has been for you and your mom?"

Marinda looked again at the hills. For a moment she imagined what might lie beyond them. Terraced palaces maybe. A place where people sang to each other and painted all night while watching the stars. There weren't such places, of course. The only thing on the other side of the hills was the ocean, the one she loved, which was, now—like the rest of her dreams—lost to her.

"Yes," she said. "I know everything you've done for me."

*

Jerry couldn't believe it, but Marinda was still talking—really totally talking—to that weirdo who had tripped over her. What a jerk. He could babble about nothing for hours, probably did it all the time. It was clear he didn't have much money and maybe not even a job. Just like Marinda to fall for some worthless guy whose only talent was talking. Jerry was amazed, sometimes, at the ridiculous problems Marinda created for herself then expected him to solve. It was a good thing he was there to protect her, the very thing her father said to him when he and Marinda were in California seeing their families at Christmas. The families had known each other since Jerry and Marinda had been children. I appreciate how good you are to Marinda, her father had said to him many times; she's not very practical and I know you'll help keep her on the right path. Still, it was frustrating that Marinda couldn't see the situation clearly. If she had any sense, they would have been married long ago. Not that he minded being free. There were so many hot chicks in New York. If sooner or later he was destined for Marinda, that didn't mean he couldn't do the nasty a few times before she figured things out.

There were certainly some babes here tonight. The crowd was a mixed one, though, including a few guys who—there was no other way to say it—weren't really guys. There was one in particular—beefy, with big shoulders, and a big beard too—who kept looking Jerry's direction. Jerry often wondered what it was like to be gay. Men, undressed, touching and grabbing and even putting their mouths on each other until it was hot in the room… he shuddered, felt his stomach turn from the sweetness of his drink. He looked at a blond sitting with a friend at the end of the bar. She had big hair and serious cleavage and leather pants that he could see were tight, though she was sitting down and he couldn't check out her ass. A big girl, the right kind of big. He moved down the bar until he was standing only a foot or two away. She looked at him briefly. Her friend, a brunette and too thin, didn't even do that much.

"It's a shame a beautiful lady like you isn't getting all the attention in the bar," Jerry said to the blond. "People have no taste."

She looked at him again, in his face then down at his stomach. Disdain curled in one corner of her lip. "You're not actually hitting on me, are you?"

"Hitting has nothing to do with it, unless you'd like it to."

"Oh my god." The woman's eyes grew large and unbelieving. Her brunette friend looked over blankly. "You actually believe I'm going to let you buy me a drink or something."

"I could buy you a house if I wanted." Jerry smiled at the challenge. "I could buy you a couple of houses."

The woman laughed. If her tone was mocking, that was only, he knew, because she didn't get it yet.

"Don't you want to find someone who plays on your team?" she said.

The comment startled him only for a moment. "What are you drinking?" he asked. "It looks tasty."

"Oh my god," the woman said again. She looked at her friend.

"Should I let him buy us a drink?"

"I don't care," the brunette said. Her mouth hung open a bit.

"All right," the blond woman said. "We'd like a couple of strawberry daiquiris." She looked at him closely. "I bet you drink those too, don't you?"

He wasn't sure what she was implying. "I've had a lot of drinks in a lot of places." He motioned to the bartender.

"Really," the woman said. It wasn't a question.

"My businesses keep me moving around," Jerry said. "I travel a lot for pleasure too."

"Your businesses?" It was her first question that was really a question. Jerry ordered the daiquiris and a gin and tonic, then turned back to her.

"Yes. I'm here in New York starting a magazine. It's just an offshoot of the work I do in film."

The woman was smiling scornfully again. "Oh yeah?"

"Yes. My family owns a major share of one of the biggest companies in Hollywood. My father heads the board, for now that is. He'll probably retire in a few years and let me take over."

"What studio would that be?"

He told her. Her eyes grew larger, less scornful. "Are you fooling me?" she said.

"No," Jerry said. The expressionless brunette's mouth fell open a little more. She looked like a horse.

The drinks arrived, and the blond took hers. "Why don't you tell me about it?" she said.

The challenge he'd been feeling slipped out of Jerry's chest. Now that he knew he could conquer her, what was the point? The bearded guy was staring at him again. For a moment Jerry couldn't focus. He tightened his back as if shaking something off.

"I'd be glad to tell you anything you want," he said.

"I'm really really sorry," Cynthia said when they were out on the street. "I didn't know he could get like that."

"Don't worry about it," Steve said. "It wasn't your fault. Seems to me he's a guy who lets beer do the talking."

"You must be right," Cynthia said. "I never noticed it before."

"I wasn't going to fight him," Steve said. "I don't have time for stuff like that."

"I feel a little embarrassed, that's all," Cynthia said.

Steve didn't reply; they kept walking. He pulled his shoulders towards his neck as if trying to protect himself from the cold, even though it wasn't cold. He wondered where Marinda was.

"I do the best I can," Cynthia said as if she wanted him to understand. "New York's a great city, but it's not that easy to meet good people. Most of them are just so much out for themselves. I don't mind ambitious guys, I really don't, but I like them when they're like you. You know, balanced. You want a good job but you want a life outside that too. And not just a life of running around and getting drunk and trying to see if you can trick women into sleeping with you. I admire that."

"Thanks," Steve said.

"You want to go somewhere else?"

"I don't think so. I need to head out to Williamsburg. Where do you live? I'll get you there."

"You don't have to," she said.

"It's the way I do things," Steve said.

"Maybe we can go out another time?"

"You bet," Steve said.

"When?"

Steve looked at her. Was he sure Marinda had nothing to do with this? Maybe he should just forget about it… on the other hand, maybe he needed to know what it was about. "Anything wrong with early next week?"

"That would be great." Cynthia smiled. "You know, other than what happened, I've had a really good time with you."

They reached the subway entrance. Steve put his hand on Cynthia's back and led her underground.

*

"Your friend Jerry seems quite the ladies' man," Herbert Rupert the Third and a Half said to Marinda. That wasn't his name of course, but it was the only one she'd been able to get out of him. "I can be a flirt myself, especially with people who would never go home with me."

"Actually, you and Jerry are alike that way." Marinda looked over at Jerry, who was fervently in conversation with some blond of exaggerated body parts.

"He seems to be having luck at the moment."

"He sometimes does when women find out how rich he is. Not that he made a penny of it. Still, the moment he senses they like him, he usually backs off."

"Sounds smart. I have enough trouble going home with myself. Imagine trying to bring someone with me."

Marinda laughed. "The talking just goes on and on with you. There's no end to it, is there?"

Herbert smiled as if he was doing her a favor. "I talk mainly to reassure myself I'm not saying anything important. The more I talk, the more I'm aware of my own inner silence. It's comforting."

"What is? Inner silence?"

"Yes. It reminds me I don't exist, which is a great relief from the turmoil of being me. It's amazing the pain people go through trying to be themselves."

"You don't try to be yourself?"

"I try as much as possible not to. In things that matter, it's crucial to realize that I'm no one."

"You're making my head spin," Marinda said. "Feel like getting out of here?"

"What about your friend?"

"He's capable of making a fool of himself without me."

"Where should we go?"

"I have no idea."

Herbert stood. "Perfect."

It wasn't much longer before they found themselves in another bar of a similar sort.

"This looks like the place we just left," Herbert said. "I was hoping that when we went somewhere else, we wouldn't really have a change of scene. I'm most nostalgic for places I can't stand."

Marinda smiled. "So… you're single."

"Sadly, I'm multiple. But not the slightest bit schizophrenic. Despite my best intentions, I'm well integrated."

"That's not what I mean," Marinda said.

"You aren't going to suggest you like me in some way, are you? I get disconcerted when people like me. I'm hopeless, you can be sure."

"I *am* sure." Marinda laughed. "I was just curious. Prying is one of my most developed arts. Then again, I already knew."

"I'm always most curious about things I already know," Herbert said, "and I appreciate you asking. I started out with girlfriends, mainly because it was what the boys around me were doing. Later I switched over to boyfriends, which is more my style—mostly. But boyfriends, it turns out, are human too, despite their long history of denying it. Lately I've preferred brief involvements with men I barely know, since that most mirrors my relationship with myself."

"Whatever makes you comfortable," Marinda said.

"Comfort is usually just a bad habit we've gotten used to. I feel free to change my mind about everything. That it can be changed is one of the few good reasons to *have* a mind."

"All right," Marinda said. "You think your answers are so original. Why don't you tell me this then: what's wrong with everything?"

Herbert looked at her. "I don't know what you mean."

"Why is the world so dead? Why isn't there any reason to care about anything? Why is everything everybody says a lie, and not even a conscious one at that?"

"Because the truth is always preferable to a lie, and nobody wants anything preferable."

"No," Marinda said.

Herbert startled, recovered quickly. "Because certain people always get what they ask for and so never have what they want, because there's always something else to have, and knowing they can have it makes them unable to want what they do have. So having everything and not wanting it, they kill whatever they get their hands on."

"That's better," Marinda nodded. "Still, you know, just a quip."

"Okay, try this: the world is so dead because we know we have to die. Once we know that, we can't wait to get there."

"Wow. You're warming up."

"How about this then?" His hands flourished in an elaborate circle. "The world's not dead at all, and that's what you hate about it. Your question is a false one, which is, of course, what makes it possible to answer. The world's not dead—you are. The fact is, you *want* the world to be dead, you want not to care about anything, and you can only stand it when everybody lies. Because if they tell the truth, you're afraid they'll tell you what a mess you've made."

Marinda smiled, sat back in her chair. The waiter came by; she ordered a gin and tonic and Herbert ordered a Manhattan. "I think I'm going to spend some time with you," she said. "If you looked at me, would you guess my parents were into mystical New Age religion?"

"I would guess that because they have lots of things, they have no idea what those things are."

"You don't miss much, do you?" Marinda's face tightened uneasily. "It started a couple years ago. They'd always gone to various churches, mainly for show. Taking it more seriously was my father's idea. My mother seems to go along cheerfully with whatever he says, although when she closes her own door she's nothing but resentment. He said he was tired of feeling empty. But it's not like becoming a mystic really changed his values. He still believes that what he calls his "practical" ideas are the right ones. Just, now, he wraps them in mystical faith and he's found a church to back him up. It's not Christianity, not an eastern religion either, just a sort of feel-good and make-other-people-pay-for-it, cash-and-carry invention."

"He has his own church?" Herbert said, clearly impressed. "I've always wondered whether I could start a church myself."

"It goes something like this," Marinda said. "The world is a ball of floating dreams. There's a dream out there for each of us if only we can find it. Finding it is the problem. It's hard because a lot of dreams that aren't good for us are floating around also. A lot of dreams are 'unpractical'—and yes, he says 'un' and not 'im'—and so all the more attractive. We've got to deny ourselves unpractical dreams and find the practical one that's meant for us. There's a big cosmic war going on, a war of good dreams and bad ones. I get phone messages from my father, reminding me to watch out for bad dreams."

"Some of my best friends are bad dreams," Herbert said.

"*I'm* a bad dream." Marinda's eyes flitted like she was trying to avoid a trap. "I've never been able to accept the idea that one should get rid of negative feelings and live some cheerful and bland—my God, you have no idea how bland—life of good dreams and good energy. Okay, it's true, half the people I meet I want to throttle, and most things don't seem worth doing, and I can't hold a job or make myself get up before noon, and even if I have good reasons for the ways I feel, a lot of it is just my own weakness. But the thought that I would just get rid of all that, that I would even want to…the idea that one should approach life with a cheerful untroubled smile, or as some war between good and evil in which one is committed to some weird notion of good, it just about drives me crazy."

"Just about?"

"Fine," Marinda said. "I'm a total fucking mad woman."

"We can never be as mad as we'd like to be."

"Herbert," Marinda said. "You'll be twisting phrases in your grave."

"I'm already twisting phrases in my grave," Herbert said.

*

Subject: Oliver Lowell
First Psychiatric Interview
Lorton Prison
March 20, 1999

Dr. Rudolph Stein and Dr. Henry Whitlow

Q: Are you comfortable, Mr. Lowell?

A: At least there aren't any windows here.

Q: You don't like windows?

A: No.

Q: Why not?

A: Windows are open spaces that can be used to get inside your head.

Q: Used by whom?

A: Anywhere there's an open space, they can get a dream

inside your head.

Q: Who is "they"?

A: The people from the other planet. I don't know its name.

Q: Did "they" have something to do with what happened at the Library of Congress?

A: No, not them. The others, on the other side.

Q: There are two sides then?

A: Are you guys stupid? That's the whole problem.

Q: What were you doing at the Library of Congress?

A: I had an assignment to shut down the escaped dreams that are arriving from the planet. It's my duty, a matter of life and death. If I don't get them, they'll get us.

Q: The escaped dreams, you mean?

A: And the people who sent them.

Q: You went to the Library of Congress to stop the escaped dreams and the people who sent them?

A: Yes.

Q: Why the Library of Congress?

A: It's where the books are kept.

Q: What do books have to do with it?

A: Books store dreams until the dreams are ready to burrow into someone's head. You know that. Books are soaking in bad-dream germs. All those infected people! Hundreds come in every day. I wanted to save them but I think I was too late. Once you get infected by bad-dream book germs…you've got to round them up, quarantine them, you hear me? They can just walk around and touch other people, and they're covered in endless bad dreams.

Q: You say the idea to do this wasn't yours?

A: I have my duty, and I did it.

Q: Who gave you this duty? Why did they give it to you?

A: Because they're at war. They tried to stop the bad dreams on their own planet, but they couldn't. They caught a lot of the dreams, sure, but some escaped. And the ones that escaped are trying to come here. If they have a chance to infect us, our world is going to end up like theirs, a world consumed by bad dreams. They even get in me sometimes. So far, I'm winning, I'm fighting them off.

Q: Can you describe why you chose the Library of Congress rather than any other library?

A: It's the official dream center, isn't it?

Q: What do you mean?

A: I love my country; you're trying to trick me.

Q: We just want to hear what you have to say. We're very interested in what you're telling us about the Library of Congress.

A: It's the official dream center, where they store the books and the dreams. All the books are there. I'm sure some are good books too, but the librarians haven't been cautious. Ever since the Liberal Jews took over the country, all sorts of bad-dream books have been let into the library and almost no one knows. The library's the perfect place for escaped dreams from the other world to land and hide. Some are there already. I slowed them down, maybe, but that's all. I can only do so much. I'm just one man.

Q: What do you mean, "liberal Jews"? Tell us about them.

A: They run the country now, although people don't know it.
They look like everybody else, but you can tell who they are
if you grab their hair. They all wear wigs. If you're a Liberal
Jew, your hair falls out.

Q: And the Liberal Jews are responsible for the bad-dream
books?

A: They're responsible for the bad-dream books in this world
anyway. But even the Liberal Jews aren't prepared for the
escaped dreams of the other world. They're evil and bald,
but they still don't understand what they're up against.

Q: Which is the other world? And its escaped dreams?

A: Yes.

Q: What can you tell us about this other world?

A: There's a war going on there, over good dreams and bad
dreams and who will control their power.

Q: How did this war get started?

A: The bad dreams started taking over, so the people in charge
decided they had to shut those dreams down. It's not safe to
dream anything you want. But that's what was happening.
So they took steps to close down the bad dreams, and to
some extent it worked. But some bad dreams got away and
went underground. And now those dreams are being sent
here.

Q: The bad dreams from the other world figured out how to
send themselves to our world?

A: Yes. And it's happening right now! Why are you holding
me hostage?

Q: We understand why you're concerned, but we're not the
ones holding you. You're under arrest, and we don't have

any control over that. If you tell us your story thoroughly, we'll see what help we can give you. How do the bad dreams send themselves to our world?

A: Through the Crab.

Q: We don't understand.

A: It lays an egg in your eye. The egg allows a person and his bad dreams to escape his world and come here.

Q: A crab lays an egg in somebody's eye?

A: What? Am I not speaking English?

Q: An actual living crab?

A: No. It's a mechanism. It looks like a crab because it's got to crawl up onto you before it can infect you.

Q: How does the egg work?

A: The Crab makes an incision in your eye and places the egg there. The egg produces some chemicals that move out from your eye and into your brain, and somehow the chemicals manage to connect up the brain and eye again, which reverses the operation which stops the bad dreams. The Crab allows people to project their dreams outward, through time and space. That's how the escaped dreams are coming here.

Q: How did you discover all this?

A: I was contacted.

Q: By the escaped dreams?

A: They tried, yes. But I resisted. Then the other side contacted me. They knew I loved my country. They recognized I would help their cause if I could.

Q: How did the other side contact you?

A: Oh come on, how stupid are you guys? How does anybody contact anybody? They called me on the phone.

Q: You talked with these people from another world on the phone?

A: No. They're not from our world, remember? It's a pretty damn long distance call. They type in a code over the phone, and the code translates into messages in my head.

Q: What does this code sound like?

A: Beeps of different durations. At first I just take it in and don't know what it means. Like I said, the code translates into messages in my head.

Q: Can you explain how that works?

A: I hear the sounds for a while, and slowly but surely they turn into meanings, although they don't usually do that until I sleep.

Q: What do you mean?

A: The beeps turn into meanings when I dream.

Q: Could you explain? It's not clear.

A: Look. I'm not an expert, just a foot soldier. I've never claimed to be anything else.

Q: Yes, but from your point of view, how does it work? Don't worry about being technically accurate.

A: There are the beeps, see. They play themselves over in my head, and usually they make me sleepy, sometimes right away. Then when I go to sleep, I feel like I'm starting to understand things I didn't before. Do you know how, in a dream, sometimes things will happen that have something to do with your waking life, only you don't know what, and then you wake up thinking about it? Sometimes you get nothing. Sometimes you wake up and understand something you didn't before. That's what the beeps are like. I almost always understand them when I wake up. I'm meant to.

Q: In this case, what did the beeps tell you about the Library of Congress?

A: I already said, right?

Q: But how specific were the directions?

A: Pretty specific. Not that some of the initiative wasn't my own. I don't want you to think I'm some fucking puppet. I don't have to do what they say. I do what they say because I believe in their cause.

Q: So they told you to do what, exactly?

A: They pointed out that a lot of escaped dreams were stored at the library. I had to clear people out and wait for further instructions on how to destroy those dreams.

Q: Did they tell you to shoot anybody?

A: I've got standing orders to kill anyone whose dreams seem infected.

Q: Are you saying you can see whose dreams have been infected?

A: Not all the time. I can only see when the infection has gone pretty far. It's a problem I don't know what to do about. I can't catch people in early stages.

Q: And the people you shot at the Library of Congress? Were they infected, or just people in your way?

A: What do you think, I'm a murderer? I only shot infected people, and even then, only ones who were too far gone. I'm hoping that in some cases, the problem is reversible.

Q: So the security guard you shot…?

A: I wish I didn't have to. The people who work there every day, they were the worst off.

Q: Yet you didn't shoot the librarian—and she must have absorbed a lot of escaped dreams.

A: That threw me, I admit. I expected her to be practically glowing with them. She wasn't. She was clean.

Q: Any idea why?

A: Not for certain. I have a guess.

Q: Which is?

A: I think maybe she's on my side already and has taken precautions.

Q: We'll come back to a lot of these things later. For now, we just want you to be clear with us, again. You received orders to seize the Library of Congress, but you didn't receive specific orders to shoot anybody. However, you have general orders to shoot anybody infected with escaped dreams.

A: Right.

Q: And would you continue to have such orders, were you set free?

A: I may be the only person standing between us and total destruction. Yes, of course I still have them.

Q: And you would continue to carry them out? That is, you'd keep killing people whose dreams are contaminated?

A: I would consider it my duty, and a sacred honor.

*

Steve headed up the stairs to his apartment. From outside his door he could hear his phone ringing. He came in quickly and reached the phone on the fourth or fifth ring, before his answering machine picked up. The machine was set to pick up after the sixth ring. He only wanted messages from people who were serious enough to take the time.

He yanked the phone off the receiver. "Marinda?" He waited a moment, ready to hear her apology.

There was no voice on the phone. He stood silently, waiting.

Over the phone came an electronic signal, a number of beeps in a pattern that repeated itself. He had gotten this pattern a lot recently. It was somebody's fax machine, maybe, although it didn't have the usual harsh grinding whistle. He could have hung up right away, but found himself listening to the pattern awhile—as he usually did—as if it was a secret code he needed to decipher. He wondered sometimes whether the beeps were trying to tell him something about Marinda. Maybe they were even a subconscious message from her, a way of saying she needed his help. It was hard to be sure…of course he didn't really think they were from her. Did he? Of course not. On the other hand, she was capable of outrageous things.

Eventually he put the phone down, the pattern of beeps still repeating in his head. It had been a long day, then a long evening. What a jerk that guy Joseph was. The city was full of jerks like that… hell, the whole world was. He had to be careful all the time. It would have been nice to hurt that guy. It was too bad his principles didn't permit it. Steve went over to his dresser, opened the top drawer and for a moment held the small pistol he kept there, feeling its weight against his palm. He didn't believe in guns. It was sad he had to buy one. But what was he going to do, let people abuse him whenever they felt like it?

Cynthia was nice in her way. Assuming—he thought it seemed safe to assume—that she wasn't a friend of Marinda's trying to distract him. Even if it was likely that she was a little more wild than she let on, she seemed a smart, decent, young woman. They'd had a good conversation, though he couldn't remember any particular thing she'd said. But she'd understood what he told her. There was a time when Marinda had also understood him, when she wasn't being distracted by the bad influences that contaminated her.

Steve yawned. He got out of his clothes and into the gym shorts he slept in. It was warm in the apartment. He never put his air conditioning unit in the window before June, so he turned on the fan, turned out the lights and got in bed. His apartment faced an alley. It was amazing how quiet the alley could be even when the street was noisy. He yawned again. He thought about Marinda, Cynthia, that asshole Joseph. Maybe he should have hurt the guy, set him straight…set them all straight…it was interesting, the way he could still recall the odd beeping pattern on the phone…

His father was at the dining room table. "Just my luck," he said, "to have a son who can't stand up for himself. What a girl. Maybe I should start buying you dresses."

Was his father drinking? It was hard to tell in the room's odd light. Yes, there seemed to be a glass of something in his hand. Whose hand? His father's?

"What a pussy," his father said.

That asshole Joseph shouldn't have talked to him that way. But Joseph *had* talked to him that way, while Marinda watched. No, it was Cynthia watching…wait, who was Cynthia? He'd been out with Marinda and things were going well until that asshole Joseph started mouthing off. People always thought they could do or say whatever they wanted and they wouldn't get in trouble.

Marinda smiled. What kind of smile was it? Maybe she was smiling to hide her anger at the fact that he wasn't standing up for her. She could see right through him. She thought he was a girl. Why did everybody always think he was a girl?

"That's a tasty mother, yes?" his father said.

Joseph sat at the table, leering. Was Marinda sitting on Joseph's side? They were all sitting on Joseph's side, weren't they: Marinda, his mother, his father. "You're only faking it," Joseph said. Joseph was his father…no, that wasn't right. It was hard to see in the darkness of the bar. "You've got nothing," Joseph said. "You never did. Marinda dumped you, get it? Fucking girl."

"Are you talking to me?" Steve said.

"I'm talking to the girl," Joseph said.

Beep. "I'll show you who you're talking to," Steve said. He kicked the table and Joseph jumped back, surprised. Joseph lunged for him. Steve hit him hard with one of the table legs. What was his family's kitchen table doing in the bar? Never mind; he'd torn up the table, had the leg in his hand. He hit Joseph across the face with it. Joseph's face snapped back into darkness.

He held the leg in his hand. It was Joseph's leg, wasn't it? He took the leg, twisted it, hit it and broke it at the ankle. Joseph howled. Only who was howling exactly? He kept breaking the ankle. He kept howling. "Why are you making me do this, Marinda?" he said to the darkness.

He leaned forward. Joseph lay in shadow, ankle snapped in two. Now that his ankle was broken, Marinda wouldn't want him. She'd stop acting foolish and come back where she belonged. Beep. His father wasn't there, just Marinda and darkness and some guy crying because his ankle was broken.

*

The next morning, Sarah was exhausted. Evenings like that, when more sensations came through than she knew what to do with, often led to mornings when her whole body felt wrecked, out of shape, like she had put herself through a demanding physical workout. It was another sunny spring morning. She opened the curtains a little, letting light into the apartment, not too much.

She went to the kitchen to make coffee and discovered, to her annoyance, that she had none. Recently she hadn't been attentive to her daily needs. She had to have coffee. She found her sunglasses on the table by the front door and headed out.

The sunglasses shielded her not only from the sun but from most unwanted verbal auras. God, she was sick of words. She'd never shared the love of words that some of her poet friends professed. Although she understood why they felt that way, she could never agree. For many poets she knew, words were protection, a source of comfort or a way of fighting back in a world in which the poet often had little but words. Often, poets were dense balls of language, twisting themselves this way and that in unique protective rituals.

Of course, most of them also understood the danger of words. But because they weren't her, it could be difficult for them to feel the absolutely shocking weight of language, its physical and violent history, which could overwhelm her if she wasn't careful. If words weren't quite a deadly virus—one could survive them after all—they were hardly a clear advantage for the body either. They held it down so firmly, made it so much what it was, that without words the body would have been something far different. When, in her teens, the gift had first appeared to her and language began flying off everything, for a while it seemed like words were her veins, muscles, nerves, bones, that she was bound as tightly in language as her body was bound by its ligaments. Then she realized that such an understanding of her body revealed only another layer of language, for what were veins, muscles, nerves, and bones but words? Yes, the body was there, more than a displacement of language, but how did one feel it without translating everything back into words again? Some people claimed they could, and sometimes there was truth in that. But it was hard to put much faith in those claims when they came from the mouths of people from whom words were exuding like froth.

On the street, she hoped no one spoke to her. Even a momentary eruption of language might send her reeling. There were cars on the street, of course, and people, going through their morning rituals. She kept them all at a safe and silent distance.

The coffee shop's tinted windows and the otherwise dim light inside made it too hard to see. She took off her sunglasses although she had intended to keep them on. The shop had its usual assortment of morning customers at tables or in easy chairs, sipping coffee, eating muffins or bagels, reading the newspaper or staring off in a morning daze, not ready to accept being awake. Others got their coffee and left hurriedly. The place smelled creamily comforting. A few seats were hidden around a corner at the end of the counter, a sheltered spot where she herself sometimes huddled. She noticed, and turned quickly away from, an aura pressing forward from that corner. She couldn't read it and didn't want to.

"Large coffee please, one blueberry muffin," she said, trying not to look at the girl behind the counter. The orange-rimmed menu blackboard didn't give Sarah too much trouble as long as she didn't stare at it directly. There was still an aura pushing out unmistakably from around the hidden corner. Nowhere else on the street or in the store was there any aura at all. She took her coffee and muffin and paid quickly, determined not to see where the aura was coming from.

But what harm could it do to look, except to give her a bigger headache than she was already about to have? The aura was strange, a dim glow so out of place with her own sense of what was otherwise there that she couldn't make sense of it. Especially in her dulled condition, its oddity seemed a warning. Whether that feeling was coming from her overtaxed imagination or not, it might be better to resolve the uncertainty.

A moment later she was on the street, leaning against a car, gasping, her body shaking. She didn't remember going out the door. She had turned the corner, and there, against a back window, sat a large man, bewildered, disheveled and stained. She registered all of him only briefly because his eyes were on fire. The words "I'm not me" burned off his eyes, into her, crashing her out into the street as surely as if they'd thrown her through the glass. He had no control over his eyes, she could tell. The words flashing out of them practically scorched her. She huddled against the car, her body still shaking, foreign. The words had been coming from him, but they weren't his words. They were words from that other place, and they were burning him up. She couldn't lean against the car anymore and sat abruptly, nearly falling, on the sidewalk.

A hand grabbed her arm. The aura was there again, flattening her. "You know who I am," he said.

"Get away from me. Don't touch me."

His hand let go. "You know who I am," he said. "You've got to help me. Tell me who I am."

"What?"

"Tell me who I am. Please."

Sarah looked up, but not so much that she would see his eyes. She couldn't bear to see his eyes. "You mean…?" She stopped. People passed them on the street as if nothing surprising was happening.

FOUR

"Have you been adding to your checklist?" The Reverend Roderick Domville, sipping a glass of wine, smiled broadly. From the table beside him, he pinched one of the small cucumber sandwiches firmly between swollen fingers.

"I sure have," Fred said. "It's been keeping me focused on the proper dream path." Fred was a tall man in his early fifties, silver hair with streaks showing it had once been black, and a crafted tan on his smooth skin. His silk button-down shirt glistened in the sunlit conference hall. The glass wall behind him stretched across the whole room and looked out above the houses covering row after row of dry Los Angeles hills, their brief spring green already faded. A mix of therapeutic floral aromas floated through the conference hall air.

"You're making progress, Frederick," the Reverend said. "I have nothing but admiration for your spiritual discipline." He took a bite of the sandwich.

"Thank you." It was Fred's turn to smile broadly. "I can't tell you how much it means to me that you think highly of my path."

The Reverend bowed. He wore a stylish white collar and cravat above a long black robe. His face and hands were reddish, with sun-thickened skin. His father, a British Naval Officer in World War II, stayed in India after the war and made a fortune buying and selling goods legal and illegal, then settled down on his Indian estate to become absorbed in local lore and indulge his ultimate interests in plants and medicines. As the Reverend often told members of his church, his father was a grasping, conniving man whose practical skills were nonetheless valuable. The Reverend, finding his father spiritually dead, wanted to explore his own yearning without denying the importance of commerce. The result was that after some years of intensive studies in the mysteries of many religious traditions, eastern and western, he came to Los Angeles to open the Church of Good Dreams and pass along the wisdom of the New Way. "Perhaps at today's meeting," the Reverend said, "you'd be willing to read from the list?"

"I'd consider it an honor," Fred said.

"How is life with you otherwise?"

"Okay. Worries, but nothing unusual."

"And the lawsuit?"

"It's all right." Fred waved a hand dismissively. "They're making lots of accusations, but they don't have the evidence."

"I'm glad to hear that. And your family? Especially your lovely daughter?"

"They're fine. Sort of. I never know what to do about Marinda."

"I take it, then, that despite the excellence of your list, you haven't been able to help her give up her impractical dreams?"

"She still says she's a painter, if that's what you mean."

"Yet you continue to support her?"

"What can I tell you, Reverend?" Fred sighed. "She's my daughter, and I love her. I can't bring myself to cut her off. I realize it's an essential part of my path, but I can't, not yet."

"I understand." The Reverend smiled, if more thinly and reprovingly. "All in due time. Let me remind you: no one who is financially dependent can achieve the Way. More importantly for you, no one who allows others to depend on him can achieve the Way either. The Way requires not only that one guard one's own dreams, but also that one does not become contaminated, or even distracted, by the false dreams of others. Sooner or later, Frederick, you must require your daughter to rely only on herself, not simply because you wish her to follow the Way, but because you wish to follow it also."

"Yes, Reverend. My weakness is regrettable."

"It is, Frederick." The Reverend put a large hand gently on Fred's lithely muscled arm. "There is also forgiveness to be found in the Way, although ultimately one must transcend the need for forgiveness. I understand that as a father you feel conflicted. But you are making remarkable progress nonetheless."

"Thank you, Reverend. I hope you'll allow me to ask how *you* are?"

"I feel a great harmony, despite the petty concerns of this life."

"And *your* lawsuit?"

"They cannot win, given current licensing regulations."

"Every time I think about what they're doing, it makes me furious." Fred's upper lip bristled. "The very idea that someone could sue you for inauthenticity."

The Reverend shrugged indifferently. "Those choked on false dreams can only try to destroy the true dreams of others. That's what the Way shows us. From their position, of course, they have their reasons. In their diseased state, it seems to them that I am violating sacred religious and cultural traditions that I claim to teach but have no right to."

"But don't they understand that tradition must be changed in order for the Way to be followed?" Fred's eyes flashed. "Don't they understand that the true dreamer must not live anyone else's dreams but must create his own?"

"Sadly, they don't understand the Way. They see me simply as a thief."

"No one can own a cultural tradition. Any good businessman knows that."

"They don't understand business any more than they understand the Way."

"It upsets me, that's all."

"I appreciate your concern." The Reverend gripped Fred's upper arm with one large hand. "But there's no need to be upset at false dreams. One must simply transcend them."

"Yes." Fred nodded, his aggressive excitement subsiding.

By this time, other members were coming into the conference hall, on the first floor of the Church in one of its several main buildings. The members bowed to the Reverend, shook hands with Fred and each other. The table of food and drink by which the Reverend and Fred stood soon swarmed with lively, chattering, fashionably dressed people, most in their thirties, forties, and fifties, although a few were younger. At the center of the room sat a large circle of chairs. Slowly, still talking, people gravitated towards the chairs, food and drink in hand. The Reverend's Throne of Wisdom, a long white chair embossed with gold, stood in front of the long tinted window, the circle extending out from the throne on either side. The symbols painted on it were a hand reaching upward and an eye that looked like the sun.

When the Reverend finally moved towards the throne, the people in the other chairs quickly hushed. He sat down.

"Welcome to you all," he said. "The Way stretches out before you."

"We accept the lessons of the Way," everyone said from their chairs.

"I hope that many of you will stay for this evening's telling of the Story of the Mysteries," the Reverend said to nods and murmurs of approval. "It's a story you've heard before. It is good to hear it again, especially in the company of those who are also discovering the Way." He smiled at further rumbles of approval.

"As you know," he went on, "we meet on these afternoons so that any of you who wish to can bring me your stories of success or failure in your pursuit of the Way. Our goal is not to accuse those who have slipped on their paths. Rather, the goal is to find solutions to our difficulties and to remind ourselves of the reasons for our successes. Anyone who wishes to speak may speak, but please stand so that others can recognize you."

A man in slacks and a polo shirt stood. "Reverend," he said, "I can't help it, but I still feel guilty sometimes about how much money I've made in a world where so many are poor. I know I should feel my success is evidence of having chosen the proper dreams, but if that's true, why do I feel bad?"

The Reverend nodded. "I understand your conflict. When we are successful and others are not, we sometimes wonder if we are worthy. The mistake you've made is this: everyone on the dream path is responsible for their own happiness or misery. We have no right to be responsible for others, who must all create their own path, for good or otherwise. Still, when you witness poverty and pain, it's hard to avoid believing sometimes that you are responsible."

"Yes," the man said.

"Do you see," the Reverend said, "that you are not suffering from guilt, but from arrogance?"

"I don't see," the man said, his eyes squinting, confused. "Can you explain?"

"Your success in the world has led you into arrogance," the Reverend said calmly. "You now believe your success means that you can be responsible for the success of others. But you have no right to be responsible for them. They must be responsible for themselves.

Those who are suffering have chosen to suffer, even if they do not know it. They have chosen a world of false dreams. If they chose their dreams wisely, they would not suffer. You are suffering equally from a false dream. In your arrogance, you have been dreaming that you have the right to control the dreams of others. You are not content to dream your own dream. That false dream is the source of your pain. Do you see?"

"What do I do?" the man said.

"You continue to make money in whatever way suits you," the Reverend said. "Your success shows you have chosen your path well. But you must not give in to your arrogance regarding others. You have no right to control their lives or even to wish to."

The man bowed and sat down. A woman stood up. Her floral print dress was sashed, and she was wearing a wrap-around headdress pinned by a large brooch. "Reverend," she said. "I'm thinking about divorcing my husband. I'm in love with another man. I don't know what to do."

The Reverend stared at her a moment, considering. "Those who follow their own true dream paths," he said, "can never be bound by the false laws of this world. So you understand that the law is of no concern to me?"

"I understand," the woman said.

"Why do you wish to divorce your husband?"

"We don't have anything in common anymore," she said. "Except for our daughter, and she'll be going off to college in two years."

"None of us can share anything in common," the Reverend said, "other than our willingness to seek our own true path and our willingness to let others seek theirs also. You must put the question to yourself differently. Is your husband allowing you to achieve your dreams?"

The woman thought for a moment. "No, I guess he isn't."

"Then you will leave him, if you wish to follow your own path.

Staying with him would be to submit to his path. You say also that perhaps you love another. Why do you feel that you love him?"

"He just lets me be myself. I'm not sure I can explain."

"Only you can let yourself be yourself. Are you sure you're not expecting him, as a man, to be your guide?"

"Maybe I didn't express myself well. He doesn't try to stop me from being myself."

"That sounds better. It sounds like he is not trying to impose false dreams on you. If that's true, then there's no reason you shouldn't be with him, as long as you remember that you and only you can be responsible for your path."

"Thank you Reverend," the woman said and sat down.

Fred stood up. "Reverend, I have continued my checklist of unpractical dreams. I want to present them for your consideration and that of the others gathered here."

"This is an excellent project for your pursuit of the Way," the Reverend said. "We would be glad to hear more about your progress." His hand made a benevolent gesture of welcome.

Fred glanced around at the circle of people and began. "Unpractical dream number 43. The dream that refuses to believe that there's a dark side. Unpractical dream number 44. The dream that the dark side must inevitably win."

"Very interesting," the Reverend said. "Can you tell us what brings you to these reflections?"

Fred smiled, pleased to be asked to continue, and smoothed his shirt. "I know too many people who believe that no matter what they think, the dark side, the world of evil dreams, can't touch them. They think that whatever they dream is okay, and they can't face the fact that their dreams may destroy them. Yet there are also those who believe that human life is inevitably about suffering, that suffering must prevail. They think there are no dreams that can overcome pain and darkness."

"And in opposition to these people, you believe what?"

"That a person must choose a practical dream, that there exists a right dream for every person. But equally that we are always surrounded by dark dreams, and if we choose those dreams, we can be destroyed."

"You have philosophized very carefully on the truth of the Way, Frederick," the Reverend said. "Have you been as successful in your practical pursuit?"

"No, Reverend."

"Can you tell us why?"

Fred lowered his head, contrite, and spoke more quietly. "I've continued to financially support my own grown daughter. I know it may lead her to the world of evil dreams, but I can't help myself. She's my daughter, and I love her."

"I'm sure you do, and I'm sure we all admire your love for your daughter. It's the way you love her, Frederick, which may cause her destruction. It can't be true that destructive love is really love, can it?"

"No, Reverend."

"Then what do you need to do?"

"If I really love my daughter, I need to stop supporting her."

"That's good, Frederick. Thank you."

Fred returned to his seat, and another man stood. He was somewhat older than Fred, muscular and hearty. He wore an expensively casual light blue shirt and dark blue slacks. The Reverend acknowledged him with a nod.

"Reverend," this man said, "I've been considering whether I should donate some of my fortune to a worthy cause. If I make the donation to medical research, I'll be advancing human knowledge and helping the sick. But I can't figure out whether I want to do this in the proper path of the Way."

"I understand," the Reverend said. "Of course, no action is good or bad in itself. The issue is its motivation. You have to ask yourself why you wish to donate this money. If it is simply in the belief that you must do good for others, then clearly it is unconscionable arrogance, and you must not. If, however, doing this constitutes a gain for yourself, and you recognize that you're doing it for this gain, whatever it might do for others, then it would be acceptable. When you donate money to the Church of Good Dreams, for instance, you are doing it to obtain your own spiritual guidance in the Way, and so no investment goes wasted. But there are other occasions when we act differently. So I must ask you, why do you wish to donate this money?"

"I just feel that if I share with others, I can help make the world a better place."

The Reverend silenced him with a raised palm. "You are confused," he said. "Remember, there is no such thing as an action done primarily for others. All things we do are always, first, for ourselves. Some are conscious of this truth; others deny it, sometimes desperately, but their denial doesn't make it less true. When you use the word 'sharing' as you're using it here, you misunderstand the Way. You are attempting to pass off something done for yourself as something done for others, which is, as I say often, and have already said this morning, only an attempt to control them. You must ask yourself, what is your desire doing for *you*? Have I not taught you this lesson before?"

"You have, Reverend."

"Then let me say it again. All things we do are for ourselves." The Reverend's eyes swept the room. "I want everyone gathered here to say it also, to repeat after me. All things we do are for ourselves."

"All things we do are for ourselves," the gathered group said, sheepishly.

"Say it as though you mean it," the Reverend said. "For the good of your soul."

"All things we do are for ourselves," they all said forcefully.

"Muse upon that truth," the Reverend said. "It is central to your pursuit of the Way." He looked at the man who had asked the question. "Do you understand what you must do?"

"I'm trying to," the man said.

"You must not donate this money in your currently perilous spiritual condition. Until you recognize exactly how donating this money will benefit you, you must not donate it."

"Yes, Reverend." The man sat down.

No one else stepped forward. After a moment, the Reverend stood and looked generously upon the group. "Now we will adjourn for the Social Hour. I hope you will all stay afterwards, and join us in the Dreamatarium for the Story of the Mysteries."

*

Jerry buzzed Marinda's apartment intercom not long after noon. He hadn't bothered to call first. Ridiculously early, Marinda thought, looking at the scattered state of her apartment, clothes on the furniture and floor, empty wine and beer bottles tossed about, a few dirty dishes on the coffee table, painting supplies in stacks that hadn't yet made their way into her studio. She opened some windows to air out the mustiness and the odor of alcohol. Jerry knocked on the door, three quick demanding raps like always. She pulled her bathrobe tight and let him in.

He bustled into the center of the room. "So you went home with that guy who wouldn't shut up?"

Any intention Marinda had of telling him about her evening evaporated in his withering tone. "I didn't," she said, "since I seem to be here. Didn't yet, that is. Maybe later. What about you and the chesty blond?"

"I get bored when they're so eager," Jerry said.

Marinda didn't pretend to look surprised. "What's going on,

Jerry? You're here early."

"He's a total loser, you know. It's amazing you can't see that."

"Is this why you're here? To keep me from falling for Herbert?"

"Is that really his name?" Jerry frowned. "He said it wasn't."

"He said a lot of things. Some were funny. I felt entertained. I haven't felt that for a while."

"Thank you very much."

"You know what I mean. Don't be a brat."

"I don't know what you mean," Jerry said. "I don't know why you even started talking to the guy if you were already with *me*."

"If I hadn't started talking to him," Marinda smiled, "you wouldn't have had the chance to be a big man for that blonde."

"Does he even have a job? I could tell he doesn't have much money."

Marinda sat in a chair beside the coffee table. "He must do well enough to keep his own apartment in the city. Besides, is money the only reason to become somebody's friend?"

Jerry guffawed. "Come on, Marinda, listen to yourself. Money is the only thing that matters. Where would you be without Freddy's monthly checks?"

"You better calm down," she said. "I'll kick you right out of here."

Jerry sighed and sat on the couch. "You don't see it."

"What?"

"That money is what you're about. Money is what makes you possible, Marinda. You wouldn't be you without it."

"What if I do see that? At least I'm not like you, obsessed with it. At least I think about other things."

"Like what?"

"Like art," Marinda said. "And love."

"Oh God," Jerry said. "Spare me."

"Spare you?"

"Look," Jerry's face tightened with purpose. "At least I don't deny what I am. I'm selfish, and I'm spoiled, and I have a ton of money and haven't made any of it. I do what I want, mainly with no restrictions, and I don't have to care about anyone so I don't. I even lie sometimes. But what I never do is pretend I'm about anything else. I *am* money, Money's made me, there's no doubt, and I'm what money looks like when you've got it. But at least I know that. You, and everybody else really, money's making you too, only you don't want to know. You say you care about art, but you don't. If you did care about it, you'd be doing it. But all you care about is the idea that you care about art, because the idea makes you seem like a neat person, not just a rich girl who doesn't try to do anything because everything's already taken care of for her."

Marinda stared furiously at him, then her stare collapsed. She picked up an empty wine bottle from the table as if using it to say something, squeezed it in her hand, put it down. "And the reason you think I need to know this today?"

"So you don't run around trying to destroy your life, hooking up with losers who won't shut up and thinking that makes you an artist."

"According to you, I should be doing what instead?"

"Spending your time with people who understand you, who aren't going to mess you up."

"Who is that exactly?"

"I've been thinking about it awhile," Jerry said. "I don't see any reason why we shouldn't get married."

Marinda sat back in her chair, stunned. Then she laughed. At first it was a small laugh, coming from back in her throat, then it came from farther inside her, all the way in her stomach. It kept getting louder. It came from her in waves, shaking her whole body like crying but it was laughing. She couldn't stop, until finally it burned itself out into silence. She started laughing again, stopped, started, stopped.

Jerry was staring at her. "Are you okay?"

"We really should," Marinda said, gasping. "It would be too perfect. I can just imagine what Herbert would say."

"It's that funny, is it?"

"Funny?" she said. "No. It's the least funny thing I've ever heard. It's a tragedy. A hilarious pointless tragedy."

"Screw you," Jerry said.

"What do you want me to say, Jerry? If I thought you were serious, I don't know what I'd do."

"Maybe I *am* serious."

"Come on. What on earth would give you an idea like that? I mean, I know we joke sometimes… but really?"

Pouting shyly, Jerry picked up a cork and fiddled with it. "When I got home last night, I started thinking." He fiddled more with the cork. "I've been getting these weird phone calls lately. Some kind of odd mistake I'm going to have to call the phone company about. I pick up, and all I get is this strange pattern of beeps. I was about to fall asleep, and the phone rang. Only no one was there except the beeps, and I listened to it and was thinking. We understand each other, Marinda. We're from the same kind of people and world. But we don't do it their way; we do it ours. And between the two of us, we have access to a fortune. I mean, I know, there are all sorts of reasons to be skeptical, but why more about this than anything else?"

"But Jerry." Marinda rested her chin on her hands and looked at him. "I don't love you, not romantically. And even if I did, you don't love me."

"Why do you think you can tell me what I'm feeling?"

"And you don't do the same to me? Please. What makes you think even for a minute you want to marry me?"

"All the reasons I just said."

"You maybe just gave me reasons to open a business with you, although I'm not even sure about that. But there's this whole issue of being, you know, in love. That's a big missing piece." Marinda straightened her back against the chair, distancing herself.

"Maybe not as big as you think. A lot of people in love get married and it ends up a disaster."

"Sure. But that doesn't mean the solution is to marry someone you don't love."

"Okay. But that's the thing." Jerry balled his hands into fists. "Maybe we do love each other. Maybe we're just looking past the obvious." He opened his hands out towards her, as if hoping she'd understand.

"Jerry, you don't love me."

"Why? What makes you so sure?"

"Are you really going to make me say it?"

"Say what? Damn it, Marinda, stop being so cryptic."

Marinda sighed. "Jerry, I know you like to look out for me, and that I'm important to you. Being around me and knowing what I'm doing makes you feel safe, and sometimes makes us both feel safe. You love me like I'm your sister. But you don't love me the other way. I don't think you understand yourself, or are even trying to, despite what you say. I know I've joked about it before, but I have to admit: I'm not even sure you're straight."

Jerry stood. "You have no right to say that to me."

"All I'm saying is, people should think carefully about who they are before they rush into anything. I don't think you've done that. Maybe if you start to acknowledge the truth about yourself, you won't have to be alone your whole life. Maybe you're not gay; how can I say? But what I do know is this: your behavior around women is strange, Jerry. I know, sometimes, that there's been evidence to the contrary, but I've never been convinced—never—that you're interested in women sexually at all."

Jerry put his hand down hard on the edge of the couch. "Stop it now," he said. "I mean it."

"Why?" Marinda looked at him closely, trying to pull a hidden answer out of him. "What would be so terrible about being gay? I'm not saying you are. But if you were, wouldn't it be better to recognize it and go on and be happy?"

"You're just jealous about that blonde, aren't you? Can't stand that other women find me attractive."

"Jerry, I don't care what other women think about you. Usually, *you* don't care what they think about you."

"You better not say that again." Jerry's face was red. His hands were shaking.

"I can't help it," Marinda said. "I think there's something very confused about both of us. We're lost, and we don't understand enough about ourselves or anything else not to keep being lost, unless we do something about it. It's like we're stuck doing some freaky dance while the song plays over and over and we don't have the sense to stop it."

"I can stop it," Jerry said. "Now." He moved towards the door.

"Oh come on," she said. "Where are you going?"

He spun around to face her, clenched and unclenched his hands. "No one, no one, talks to me that way. You just have no right, Marinda. At all."

"Jerry…"

"Fuck you, Marinda," he said. He slammed the door.

Marinda sighed, in exasperation or fury she didn't know which, and rubbed her eyes to push out the pressure she felt. She looked around at the disheveled room, at the clock. One-fifteen. And nothing, just nothing, to do or think or care about. She stood, grabbed the empty wine bottle from the table as if to throw it away, then set it back. She stayed standing in the middle of the room, as if hoping to bring time to a stop.

*

"I don't know if I can explain," he said. "It's like a darkness that's totally empty, abandoned. I know something should be there. But it's gone, so far away it's probably never coming back."

"You have a wallet?" Sarah asked.

"What? I don't know."

"Find out."

Across the kitchen table from her, he squirmed in his chair, reached for the back pocket of his jeans. Sarah could look at him now. The fire in his eyes had cooled to a dull reddish glow, although it was still simmering, waiting for its chance. Her kitchen was cool with the early morning breeze coming through the open window. Enough light came in that she didn't turn on the overhead.

"Yes, here." He pulled it out of his pocket and tossed it on the table.

"At least you don't have any problem knowing what a wallet is."

"What?" he said. "I...no, you're right. I know what a wallet is."

"That's one of the things we'll have to figure out," Sarah said. "How do you know the things you know?"

"I'm not even sure *what* I know, much less how I know it."

She started pulling cards out of the wallet. "You're David Carroll, forty-eight years old, 195 pounds, brown hair, brown eyes, New Jersey driver's license. Here's an ID card: you're a faculty member at Rutgers University. Health Club Membership—although frankly, David, if I can call you David, I'm not sure you use it much. Two credit cards, then insurance cards. Nice coverage—you must be thorough. No pictures though. Do you have a family? And what are you doing in the city? I mean, it's pretty far, and you don't work here. You're wearing jeans, a button-down shirt, New York Yankees sweat shirt over it. Maybe you came up for a game last night? I don't see a ticket stub or any stray bits of popcorn, and you don't smell of beer. It's all pretty stripped down. You have the essentials but not much else. Pretty bland, not sentimental or flamboyant. If you care deeply about something, nothing here suggests what it is. I can't read your language because, you know, it isn't there. That is, David Carroll's language isn't there. I get no words off you at all. Then again, you pretty much sent me up in smoke before, didn't you?"

"You're going awfully fast."

"You don't remember anything?"

"I feel like I should, like it's there. But I can't get at it."

"Maybe you will later," Sarah said, inwardly marveling. "I'm still surprised it's such an inexact process. I'm not sure why I'm surprised though. Every part of it I've seen is about as haphazard as can be."

"I'm not really David Carroll, that's it, right? I understand that much." His eyes went pained and distant.

"No, you're not David Carroll." She put a hand over his hand, tried to be comforting. "But while I may be able to figure out who David is, there's no way I'll be able to figure out who *you* are, unless you remember something about it."

"Think I will?"

"Who knows?" Sarah looked at him uncertainly. "I expected you to be telling *me* things. I guess that's not the way it's going to work, at least for now. We'll just have to start with what we know."

"How do we do that?"

"We have your address on your driver's license, unless you've moved in the meantime. Could you go home? Do you by any chance remember who if anyone you live with?"

"I have no idea."

"So that's no good." Sarah paused, considered the situation. "Anyone living with you would see there's a problem right away. They also might be upset that you're missing, which is something we need to know because someone might come looking for you. But I'm not sure that David—the original David—is ultimately the point, unless you go back to being him. Still, we need him, because you're going to have to be him for a while, maybe for good. We also need to know how it managed to be him that you, I don't know, got into, or whatever it should be called."

"You'll have to explain that again."

"I'll try," Sarah said. She sat back in her chair and talked more slowly. "Wherever you come from, it hasn't been easy getting here. I can tell that by all the missed connections I've seen. So you came here one of two ways, or by some combination of both."

"And those are?"

"The first is pure chance. You were sent from wherever it was in some kind of random or controlled random pattern, and David just happened to be the person you found. That could be, but it's not persuasive. The other is this: there was something particular about David that made his mind available for taking."

"Such as?"

"Who knows?" Sarah shook her head. "There are too many possibilities. Are some people's minds taken more easily than others? The answer's probably yes. It would certainly be yes if we weren't talking about something so extreme. People get their minds taken all the time. But this is different. That is, I think it's different." She paused. "Maybe it isn't though. Maybe it's the same." She looked at the kitchen wall as if the wall made no sense. "Wouldn't that be odd?"

"What?"

"If the same thing that made people malleable to the mind-set of others was the thing that made it easier for this process, however it works, to take their minds. It's a neat idea, but if it's true, it's not good."

"You seem to know a lot about what's going on." He looked at Sarah searchingly, as if only now recognizing that there was something as strange about her as about him. "Why you more than anybody else? No one else could see."

Sarah ran a hand through her hair and looked over at the kitchen cupboards. "It's difficult to explain. Let's just say I notice things, words especially. It's not a skill that's really admired, I hate to tell you. I think most people would call it a curse."

"What do you call it?"

She smiled ironically. "A lot of things. But that's not important right now. We need to get at what *you* are, as much as we can. There's too much about it that confuses me."

He sagged, his expression both depressed and confused. "Me too. What in particular?"

"Well, you can't remember much, but it's not like you know nothing. You know what a wallet is. You know how to buy a cup of coffee and sit at a table. You even know how to speak English. Nor are you really surprised that you're not from this world. You looked frightened when I told you, but you didn't resist. You seemed to be waiting for the news—like a patient waiting for a diagnosis. You were expecting me to tell you something, and when you heard it, it didn't surprise you."

"I don't know why it didn't."

"It didn't because part of you knew already, or was prepared to hear it."

"I don't know why that is either." His shoulders tensed with frustration. He looked away, staring uncertainly at the wall.

"It's odd, isn't it? Let's say, for a minute, that what we think we know about you is true. That you're some combination of David Carroll, faculty member at Rutgers University, and someone who's been sent here from another world, probably for some important reason, unless it was just a mistake. So you're a combination of two people. But for some reason, you're not both of them, which you could be. You could remember all of what it was to be David Carroll and all of who you were in that other world. Instead, you remember neither. You have small bits of both, but they're not integrated. You could change, I guess, if you start to remember. The fact is, the combination isn't really a combination. It's not about multiple identities. It's almost about having no identity at all."

He rubbed his forehead with his hands. "That doesn't sound good. But it sounds, uh, right. I don't know who I am. I don't feel much like I have any characteristics."

"Yes." Sarah stared at him. "But you're prepared to know that you don't know who you are. That's interesting."

"Why?"

"People who don't know who they are often assert very aggressively that they do. It's a defense mechanism. But you're not asserting anything. You're all these absences and you don't like it, but you're not denying it either. You might be running around in some sort of frenzy, pretending you know what's going on. It's not like people who have an identity crisis are eager to admit it. Reveal it, yes, but admit it? And that means you know something, and something pretty sophisticated, because it's something many people *don't* know."

"I almost feel flattered."

Sarah looked at the sun streaking across the floor, then up again. "We need to be more exact about this. We need to know what you remember. What's the first thing?"

He squinted, reaching for it. "I guess the darkness. It's not an experience, though, like one remembers an event. A lot of things aren't there, in my mind, but my sense that they're not there, that's there. So that's what I have. A sense, I guess, of what you're calling "absence." I don't like it. I'm aware of how much I don't know."

"You don't like it. What *do* you feel about it?"

"It makes me ill. If I thought about it too much, I'd probably get sick."

"So it's traumatic?"

"I guess so, yes. Not just traumatic. More like deadly."

"Oh," Sarah said. "Okay. There's this deadly absence that makes you ill. Then what?"

"Then… I'm on the street. Just sitting there."

"How'd you get there? What are you doing there?"

"I don't know how I got there. Then, oh…" He trailed off. His face flushed.

"What?"

"It's embarrassing, but I'll tell you, okay?"

"It's embarrassing?" She looked at him curiously.

"I was holding my crotch. I felt it and wanted to know it was there."

Sarah suppressed a laugh and kept her expression serious. "No need to be embarrassed. It's funny, but not surprising. I already know the dreams are sexual. That's not all they are, but it's a lot of what they are. What happened then?"

"I stood up. Looked around."

"What did you see?"

"Not much. People, cars, the street, the sidewalk, buildings, different kinds of stores."

"You knew what those things were?"

"I don't understand."

"You knew what people, cars, buildings, stores and things like that were?"

"I did. Oh…"

"Right," Sarah said. "What we need to figure out is *why* you knew that. Did you know it because part of you is David and it was familiar to you? Or for some other reason?"

"I'm not sure."

"Was the place familiar to you? Do you know New York City, for instance?"

"No. And I didn't know where I was."

"But you know what a city is."

"Yes."

"So you had the concept of what you were looking at, but not the specifics."

"I guess so, yes."

"None of the specifics?"

"I don't think so."

"You didn't know whether you had a car, for instance?"

"No."

"You didn't think about family, a past, some other person?"

"No."

"So you're standing and looking around. What did you think?"

"That I needed coffee and something to eat."

Sarah laughed.

"What?"

"You wake up in a new world, and the first thing you think is you need coffee?"

He blushed. "It's ludicrous, isn't it?"

"There it is again," Sarah said. "You know to be embarrassed. Why do you know when to be embarrassed?"

"I don't understand."

"You learned it somewhere. Where did you learn to be embarrassed?"

He thought a moment. "I don't know. But I know it's back there, in the darkness."

"So you went to get coffee. Just walked down the street, hoping to find a place?"

"Yes."

"Did you realize you didn't know who you were?"

"Not at first. I wasn't thinking about it."

"You were thinking about food and coffee. And you recognized the coffee shop? Was it a place you knew?"

"No. It was easy enough to see I could get coffee there."

"So you ordered coffee, and what else?"

"I asked for donuts. They didn't have them, so I got a muffin instead."

Sarah shook her head. "I bet I'm right about you not using that health club membership. A forty-eight-year-old man breakfasting on donuts and coffee. I wonder what other bad habits you have. You had no trouble paying for your food?"

"There was money in my wallet."

"You knew how to count it?"

"Yes."

"That's got to be David Carroll," she said. "Just like the English is."

"Why?"

"I suppose it's possible they have cars and streets and stores where you come from. I find it hard to believe they have quarters and similar verb structures."

"Oh." He nodded.

"While you were paying, it still hadn't crossed your mind that you didn't know who you were?"

"No."

"You were focused on the task at hand?"

"Yes."

"I wonder whether that's you or David."

"I don't know."

"I wonder if that's even the right thing to focus on though," Sarah said. "Whether there's a way to separate you into David and not-David. When did you first realize that you didn't know who you were?"

"When I was drinking my coffee. It was only then I started to think."

Sarah resisted an amused smile. "That happens for a lot of us. And you thought what?"

"That I didn't know who I was or what I was doing here."

"When you say 'here,' what do you mean?" Sarah leaned in closer. "That is, did you mean by 'here" just the coffee shop, or did you mean you didn't know what you were doing in this world at all?"

"I thought at first I just meant the coffee shop. Then I realized that something more disturbing was happening."

"How did you realize it?"

"I'm not sure I can explain." He glanced around silently a moment. "I didn't believe I belonged where I was. I felt like something profound was happening. Like my sense of time was wrong, or that space was distorted. I can't be more exact." He shook his head, frustrated again. "It wasn't a perception, just a sensation."

"Then I was there, and you noticed something about me."

"Yes. At first I only noticed you noticing me. Then…it was like you knew I didn't know who I was, and it scared you. More than scared you, it was physically affecting you. It wasn't affecting you like it was affecting me, but the sensation was nearly as powerful. So I followed you outside and you were sitting there on the sidewalk, obviously shocked, and holding onto yourself like you were in pain."

"Okay," she leaned back. "So that's what we know."

"What happens next?"

"We find out more about David Carroll. It can't hurt to know more about who you're supposed to be. And we see if there's some way to help you remember who else you are."

"All right." He looked at her uncertainly. "You have to understand. I'm not sure I want to remember who else I was. I mean I do, but I'm afraid. It's hard to believe that the reasons are anything but trouble."

"I'm sure they *are* trouble," Sarah said. "We just don't know what kind yet. Come on."

"Where are we going?"

"For a walk, I guess. What does anybody do on a Sunday?"

*

In small groups, the members of the Church of Good Dreams took elevators in the conference building up to the fourth floor and came out on a darkened hallway. An usher stood by the entrance to the Dreamatarium, as the round, planetarium-theater was called. Another usher stood inside the entrance and helped the members to their seats. The Dreamatarium was the crowning achievement of the Church of Good Dreams, a multimillion dollar theater with state of the art laser and sound equipment, a technological wonderland far beyond other constructions of its kind. The seats were gently reclined, ultra-plush, with wide soft armrests. The air was carefully controlled, fresh and cool, never stuffy or cold. Nearly every member of the Church bulged with pride upon entering the Dreamatarium. It was built with their donations, from some as much as a million dollars.

When everyone was seated, the ushers closed the door to the hallway behind them as they exited. The low lights dimmed to blackness.

"I want to welcome all my fellow travelers on the Way." The Reverend's voice, in the blackness, surrounded them from multiple speakers. It was impossible to tell whether the voice was prerecorded or live. "We are gathered here today for the Story of the Mysteries. Think of what you are about to hear as our great communion, a chance to tell ourselves what it means to be on our own spiritual journey, and to acknowledge, without interfering in, the spiritual journeys of others on the Way.

"Once upon a time, before the universe existed, God lay in a dreamless sleep." Near one of the lower edges of the round ceiling screen, a creature was projected, many arms and legs in frenetic motion beneath a great gold crown. The creature's face, florid and large, vaguely resembled the Reverend's. "In that sleep, he knew that all he had to do was dream a universe and the universe would be. Then lo, there it was, the universe." The projection of the God-figure vanished. Slowly, the round ceiling of the Dreamatarium turned into a pattern of pinpoint lights. "And God saw that it was good. And he dreamed again, and again, and for each dream God dreamed, another galaxy, another star, or another planet was born.

"At first, all dreams were good, because God can dream no dream that is not good. But a dream, once God dreams it into the universe, has the ability to become what it wishes, without necessarily seeking the guidance of God.

"Many dreams, certainly, chose to stay good dreams, and continued to look to God." The ceiling glowed with light. On it appeared a collage of images: well-drawn cartoons of churches or temples; a golden-haired man and woman walking forward together, hands held up towards the sky; a high pile of jewels and gold that glinted like small stars. "These dreams remembered God and followed God's Way, even as they sought their own independent paths.

"But in giving his dreams freedom, God understood that some dreams might turn from him." Here another figure of God was projected, eyes half closed as if in pain, one of many pairs of hands held against his ears, many arms floating about his head as if to protect it. "Yet God knew his anguish was necessary. For the universe of free dreams he envisioned was not a universe without conflict, but one in which conflict would strengthen the resolve of good free dreams. The value of a dream is never clear until it is tested.

"Soon, then, the universe was alive with the conflict of dreams." Lasers of different colors flashed off the ceiling, in many degrees of brightness, some lasting longer than others, a great blinking and crashing and melding of laser color. "And God sat back to watch his dreams, to see what they would do." The laser color reached a crescendo, then faded.

"The universe is a vast battlefield of dreams, where good and evil test themselves endlessly. Only God can know all that these dreams are and all they might become. But on one small planet in one small galaxy, one small dream dreamed of people, and so people came to be." There was a picture of Earth seen from a telescopic distance, then a series of images of people from all over the world, young and old, men and women, rich and poor, European, African, Asian, North and South American. "People are the products of a dream, and they are dreams themselves. And like all dreams in God's universe, they are free. They can become good dreams and walk in the ways of God, or become bad dreams and reject God. And though God finds this rejection painful, he knows it must be.

"People on this small planet dreamed as many dreams as they could imagine, and many they never intended to imagine. And even though people dreamed freely and independently, some, in their freedom, loathed independence. They did not wish to be responsible for themselves, to be accountable for their actions, and longed for something to take responsibility for them. So the irresponsible dreams were born." Again, a series of images appeared on the ceiling, this time of robbery, murder, war, poverty. "It seemed, at times, as if the world might succumb to them.

"In a world confused by such dreams, even people who wished to dream good, responsible dreams sometimes faced great difficulty. How to know which dreams were good? How to find the proper path of the Way?" The screen now showed people walking over distances or looking up at the sky for guidance. "And there did arise, among the people, wise men who understood the Way, but also men of false wisdom who obscured the Way they claimed to know. So the people were faced with a further dilemma: how to know wisdom from falseness.

"Yet there is a sign for each of us, if only we look carefully." God again appeared on the screen, hands reaching outward. "For God has always wished his dreams to be independent and responsible. All those who live independently—emotionally, financially, and spiritually—show us, by their example, how to pursue the dreams that are proper for each of us."

"It is a great and endless universe." The pictures disappeared, and the ceiling was lighted again with stars. "One can never know from where we will next be confronted by new dreams, new possibilities, responsible or irresponsible, beautiful or deadly. Picture, for instance, this possibility—in a city on another planet, who knows where in the galaxy, the war over dreams has reached a crisis, and all is on the verge of destruction." In the sky of stars, more film of warfare appeared. "What if this city, crumbling in the face of its own anguish, should attempt to send its dreams into the universe? Would you be prepared not only to fight off your own capacity to dream evil dreams, but to fight off the dreams of some other planet whose existence you never imagined? Only great vigilance, a constant and determined focus on the good dreams of the Way, could keep you from being a casualty in that war.

"Here at the Church of Good Dreams, that constant and determined focus is our main goal. We do it for ourselves, for our belief in the value of good responsible dreams." Pictures showed the outside of the conference building, many stories high and crowned by the Dreamatarium; smiling members walked the lush grounds that surrounded the building and wandered in and out of its sleek, glistening central chapel. "The Church of Good Dreams, located in the hills near the city of Los Angeles, is officially licensed by the state of California Registry of Independent Churches, with a congregation of several thousand, and more joining all the time. We welcome you to our facilities: our meeting rooms, our spiritual and physical health centers, our array of programs encouraging emotional, financial, and spiritual independence. We welcome you to good fellowship and good friends. We welcome you to the magnificent Dreamatarium, a combination planetarium and circular dream screen, three hundred feet in diameter, with state of the art laser, film, and planetarium technology. We welcome you to the teachings of Reverend Roderick Domville, licensed pastor, who spent years roaming the world, exploring its mysteries, and who brings his unique and vast wisdom to you via weekly discussion and reflection. He can be heard Tuesdays and Thursdays at noon on WFAR FM, 93.7, for his half-hour program, Reflections on the Way. Most of all, we welcome you to yourself, to your own discovery of your own independent way. You have found, here, the home in which to discover your path to freedom. In a vast universe of possibility, we welcome you to your own good dreams."

The Reverend's voice stopped. The ceiling was covered with stars for some moments more before they faded and lights came up in the Dreamatarium. The doors opened, the ushers entered again, and the members left, slowly and thoughtfully.

*

Steve had a headache, common for him Monday mornings. It had been a boring weekend, though that didn't mean he wanted to go to work. He was going to have to call somebody about his phone problem too. The beeping had continued on and off all weekend. The rhythm played in his head even now. He walked down the Williamsburg streets and into the subway, feeling rather than looking at the people around him. No one touched him, but they pressed near him almost unbearably. Too many hands and faces, too much confused grasping, not enough values or principles. The world didn't need so many people. They're like cockroaches, Steve thought. The world is a battle between people and cockroaches, yet maybe the people are cockroaches and the cockroaches people. He reached into his pocket, imagining the gun was there. So far he'd never carried it around, though at times like this he wished he had.

The train finally arrived at his stop. He walked up onto the street. He straightened his jacket and tie. Just another asshole in a monkey suit, he thought, that's all I am. He looked around at the people in their business clothes, heads down, briefcases at their sides, hurrying forward to make a buck. I'm no better than you, he thought. Sure, I have ideas and you don't, but what the hell am I doing about my ideas? Taking them to an office where I can forget they ever existed.

He walked into his building, pressed the elevator button for the ninth floor like he always did. I just press that button automatically, he thought; I don't even notice anything else. If something interesting was happening, would I even see it? Well, that was life these days, he told himself. No one noticed anything because no one had to notice anything. And if you did notice something, that only got in the way of doing your job, which required the same thing over and over. It was no wonder the world was getting more disgusting. Who was paying attention?

When he was with Marinda, life had been hard but there was hope. There were days they'd spent together when he'd felt wildly alive; everything he saw mattered. Thinking on it now, he realized it was that feeling, both in him and in her, that Marinda couldn't stand. She loved it, but she was too screwed up to stay involved with anything (or anyone; he winced) that made her feel alive. Marinda wanted to be dead. She wanted her father, that rich, religious, mindless idiot, to be right, and she wanted to be wrong. She had potential, and Steve had showed her all she could be. That's why she'd left him. She was hiding from him because she knew he could change her mind.

Then he was at his desk. People in the office were quiet this morning, more than usual. Or maybe it was typical Monday morning deadness. He certainly didn't feel like talking. Some new work had been dropped into his In Box. He looked it over cursorily. Nothing he couldn't handle. There was never anything he couldn't handle.

He made a few phone calls, started to gather the necessary information. A shadow hovered behind him. He turned around. In a tight fitting work suit that highlighted her figure well, her expression much more energetic than his, Cynthia leaned towards him. "Did you hear?" Her eyes narrowed in a way both pained and conspiratorial.

"About what happened to Joseph?"

"I don't listen to office gossip," Steve said.

"He was mugged on the way home that night."

"Oh." Steve looked at his work, as if he'd rather get back to it.

Cynthia didn't seem to notice his lack of interest. "I guess he went home really late and really drunk."

"That's not surprising, is it?"

"No," she said. "But this time he got jumped."

"Oh yeah? By who?"

"He doesn't know," Cynthia said. Her excited voice startled Steve. "They came out of the darkness, at least that's what Renee said he told her. They beat him up pretty badly. Broke his ankle, tripped him with some kind of stick or board or something."

"His ankle?" Steve's headache rushed forward again, along with that idiot pattern of the beeping phone. Something seemed familiar.

"He was in the hospital all weekend. Can you believe it? It's terrible."

"That's too bad," Steve said. "I wouldn't wish it on anybody, even if he is a jerk." Maybe you *would* wish it on someone, a voice in his head suggested. "It's a weird coincidence though. He argues with me and a few hours later somebody beats him up."

"I guess." Cynthia stared at him curiously.

"I don't believe in superstitious stuff, myself," Steve said. "But it's the kind of thing my last girlfriend would have been all on about."

"How so?"

"I can just hear her saying, well, if you want to hurt somebody and that person gets hurt, then maybe you wanting it made it happen."

'That's ridiculous. Besides, you didn't really want to hurt him. He was acting like a jerk and you let him know it."

"Yeah. Still, it's an odd coincidence."

"It *is* odd. But not the oddest thing I've ever heard." Cynthia smiled. "I had a lot of fun with you Friday. I hope you did too."

"I did," Steve said, forcing himself to smile back.

"Busy week?"

"The usual, you know. I've got a headache this morning though, I'll tell you. It's the city air."

"That's too bad," Cynthia said. "I feel really good myself."

"Why's that?"

"I don't know." She smiled. If Steve was supposed to read something in her smile, he didn't know what. "Are your evenings filled up this week?"

"Mine?" Steve said. "No."

"Let's do something then," she said. "Like tomorrow or Wednesday? A nice midweek break, you know."

"Okay," Steve said. "Assuming I get rid of this stupid headache."

"I hope you'll be rid of it soon." Cynthia smiled again.

"Who knows?" he said. "Sometimes I think I'm going to have it forever." He paused, looked at Cynthia, felt a twitch along his forehead. "His ankle?"

"What?"

"They broke his ankle?"

"Yeah. Scary."

"Yeah," Steve said. "Well, I better get back to changing the universe here."

"Okay. So tomorrow, Wednesday?"

"Either one," Steve said. "I'll be around."

Cynthia floated away. Steve gave in momentarily to the pain against the back of his eyes. It still seemed mixed up with that beeping phone. Why was there something so familiar about the ankle…oh. His dream from several days ago. He remembered it. He had dreamed that he had taken what? A table leg? His parents' kitchen table leg? And broken it over Joseph's ankle?

Hold it together, Steve, he said to himself. The whole thing's ridiculous, just like Cynthia said.

He turned to his computer, wrote a few opening sentences for his article. His head pounded. He'd heard that beeping over and over all weekend. Say for a second he could dream something and it would happen. What would he do then? Other people couldn't get away with what they got away with now. They couldn't talk to him the way they did, ignore him the way they did. Marinda couldn't run from him. He'd know where to find her and bring her back.

Stop fantasizing, Steve told himself. The world doesn't work that way.

But the beeping headache, didn't it tell him something different? Maybe Marinda couldn't just disappear, not if he didn't want her to. Maybe if he wanted something badly enough and dreamed about it seriously enough and made his best effort to make it happen, it would. Did he know for sure it wouldn't? Imagine if that asshole Joseph got what was coming to him because he'd dared to mouth off to someone better than he was.

Yes, that would be amazing, to make things happen because you dreamed them.

All right, Steve told himself. Let's see what I'm capable of and what I'm not. Let's see if Marinda can get away from me so easily. He turned back to his computer and felt the words for the article flow magically from his fingers.

FIVE

On Monday they tried to find out about David Carroll.

"I don't know whether you'll have to be him at some point," Sarah said. "I hope not. Still, we need to see what we can help you fake."

The new David—that's what she called him in her head, to keep things straight—nodded, his shoulders narrowing. "I don't know how much I can do." The day before, they bought him, with his credit cards, some extra clothes—most of them more urban and up-to-date than the old David would have worn—and a few, like a Yankees sweatshirt, that seemed in keeping with the old David's style. In his new clothes he could have passed for any New York City professional with a slouch who needed to take better care of himself. He still looked lost, although his eyes seemed less wild.

Rutgers University information gave them David Carroll's office number. Sarah dialed. After four rings, the answering machine picked up.

"You've reached the office of David Carroll in the History Department at Rutgers University," the message said. "I can't take your call now, but if you'll leave a message, I'll get back to you as soon as I can. If you need help right away, please call the History Department main office at 234-5620."

"Well?" the new David asked as she hung up.

"A generic message," she said. "It's your voice though. You're a historian, by the way. I wonder of what. Suppose you could teach history, if you had to?"

"I can't remember anything."

"You'll be perfect then."

She dialed the History Department and a woman answered.

"I'm trying to reach Professor David Carroll. When will he be in?"

"Let me check," the woman said. "His spring office hours were Monday and Wednesday three to four. Finals are over, so I don't know how often he'll be around."

"Can you tell me something about the courses he teaches? He was recommended to me by a friend."

"No kidding," the woman said.

"Is that surprising?"

"I wouldn't claim to know," the woman said cheerfully, if evasively. "Let me get the schedule…okay, here it is. This fall he'll be doing two sections of Intro to American History, plus his usual upper level course on the Civil War."

"The Civil War? I didn't know history departments still taught classes like that. Isn't the emphasis more on social history?"

"A lot of what we do is. But David's been here awhile, and he likes to stick to what's tried and true."

"He teaches the same classes a lot?"

"Always," the woman said.

"Does everybody in the department do that? Or just Professor Carroll?"

The woman paused, as if considering how to answer. "You

might say some people try more new things. A student of ours recommended him?"

"Yes. She was very enthusiastic."

"No kidding," the woman said again.

"Is it possible to reach him at home, if you don't know when he'll be back in the office?"

"I can give you a home number," the woman said. "Hold on, here it is."

Sarah wrote it down. "It's okay to call him there?"

"I don't see why not."

Sarah hung up and turned to the new David. "Seems you're not a risk taker, at least as a teacher. The woman was surprised someone would like your courses. Maybe at some point we should look at your office. You probably have the keys on your ring."

"What if somebody recognizes me?"

"We'll figure it out. So…I've got your home number. What do you think?"

"I guess you better call. But it makes me queasy."

"What does?"

"That I have a house and a life I don't remember. I mean, to the extent that I *am* him. I keep hoping I'm not."

"That's interesting." Sarah stared at his worried grimace. "Why?"

"It's hard to explain. It's not as though I enjoy not having a past. Still, I keep thinking I couldn't possibly have a past *here*. I don't want to."

"But the idea of being from elsewhere?"

"I don't know. It's blank. But I'm afraid to find out about my life here."

She nodded. "Do you suppose that's David, or not-David, who feels that way?"

"How can I tell?"

"Is it malaise or anxiety?"

"Anxiety. I don't want to have a life here."

"Okay." Sarah dialed. "I'm going to make this call."

"Yes?" a woman answered after a few rings, voice harsh with annoyance.

"I'm trying to reach Professor David Carroll. The Rutgers History Department gave me this number."

"He's not here. Can I take a message?" The woman's tone was still annoyed.

"Do you know when he'll be back? It's kind of important I talk to him."

"I actually don't. I'll have to take a message."

"It's just that I'm taking some history classes at Rutgers in the fall. A friend of mine recommended his courses, and I want to make sure to get into them and talk to him and all that. I haven't been in school for more than ten years. I'm a little nervous about it."

"Someone recommended David's classes to you?"

"Yes, a friend of mine…"

"What do you want?" the woman said. "Why are you calling here? Have you seen David?"

"What? No, I'm a…"

"No one likes David's classes. *He* doesn't like them. He doesn't like to teach, he doesn't like his subject, and he doesn't like students. So why are you calling? Do you know where he is?"

"I'm sorry?"

"Have you seen David? He hasn't been here for three days. Is he with you?"

"As I said, I'm a student…"

"Has he run off with you?" the woman said. "If he has, you can tell him I don't care. I'm happy without him. I'm goddamned ecstatic."

"I'm sorry, you must be confusing me with someone else. Perhaps I'd better call another time."

"I hope you know what you're getting into," the woman said. "My God, I bet you think he's charming and intelligent. You probably *are* a student, aren't you? You do sound older though. That's something, I guess. I can't imagine David having the guts to run away with a twenty-year-old. Not that he hasn't gone off who knows where before. You want him, you can have him. I've had years of it, you know? Maybe you don't. You'll find out—the grumpiness, drunkenness, selfishness. The constant grinding boredom of the man. You know, I was about to say I hope he ruins your life like he's ruined mine, but he hasn't ruined mine, he was just an eighteen-year minor mistake. You can tell him I'm going to sue him though. I'm going to make sure he takes care of his daughter."

"I'm not who you think…"

"Yes you are," the woman said. "You're still listening to this. You wouldn't be, if you were who you said you were."

"I'm sorry, I just wanted to find out…"

"You'll find out plenty," the woman said. "Is he there? I want to talk to him. He doesn't need to worry. I have no intention of asking him to come back. Put him on."

"I don't know Professor Carroll. I'm just trying to make sense of what you're saying, and why you're saying it to me."

"If you're not going to put him on, you're wasting my time. He's wasted enough of it already."

"Will you just tell him I called?"

"As you may have noticed, dear, my chances of telling him anything anytime soon aren't good. Why don't *you* tell him *I* called?" The woman hung up.

Sarah looked at the new David, who was watching her intently.

"What's going on?" he said.

"She's pretty upset."

"That I left her?"

Sarah sighed. "That you ever existed in the first place."

*

Subject: Oliver Lowell
Second Psychiatric Interview
Lorton Prison
March 27, 1999

Dr. Rudolph Stein and Dr. Henry Whitlow

Q: We'd like to hear more about this other world that sends you messages. We've talked to some scientists and they don't know anything about it.

A: I'm not surprised. None of you guys know much.

Q: You said there was a crisis in that world, and that's why you were contacted?

A: There was a lot of pressure there, yes. Things were worst in the main city.

Q: What city is that?

A: I don't know its name, not completely. "My" something. I can never quite work out the rest.

Q: I see. What caused the pressure and the crisis?

A: A larger and larger number of people were thinking all sorts of crazy things. If you let people's dreams go unchecked, who has any idea what they'll come up with? A lot of weird stuff was happening. At a certain point the people in charge realized they had to do something or else everything was going to be destroyed.

Q: What sort of weird stuff?

A: Just outright moral decay.

Q: Could you be more specific?

A: People were inventing all sorts of weird new religions and
      philosophies, in which they worshiped all sorts of things
      and believed whatever they wanted. Everybody forgot their
      place, didn't know who was in charge anymore.

Q: What do you mean, forgotten their place?

A: There was a lot of intermarriage. Different races getting
      married, different religions getting married, people of the
      same sex getting married. There was just a whole lot of
      sinfulness.

Q: So forgetting their place was about marriage?

A: No (angrily). That's just part of it. Some people weren't even
      married and had sex anyway. Nobody wanted to work.
      A lot of people weren't polite or didn't take showers. Do
      you know how bad it can get, when people start to stink?
      Homosexuality, rudeness, murder. It got to the point that
      things couldn't get any worse. The city was going to collapse
      if the right people didn't take charge.

Q: So the right people had to take charge. How did they do
      that?

A: They developed a plan to help people think right again. It
      involved a little operation, a chip inserted in the brain.

Q: What was this chip supposed to do?

A: It helped people dream the right dreams. It should have
      been a minor adjustment, a good health thing. Like taking
      your vitamins.

Q: But it didn't work?

A: Hey—who knew that people could get so depraved? It wasn't the fault of their leaders, who just assumed that all people had good dreams somewhere, if they could remember them. I mean, everybody knew some people would be a problem, but those people should have been a small minority and that didn't turn out to be true.

Q: What went wrong?

A: The operation stopped too many people from dreaming at all.

Q: How did that happen?

A: A lot of people turned out to have no good dreams. So when the people who ran the city tried to help those people have better dreams, what happened instead is that they couldn't dream at all. And they went crazy, did things a hundred times worse than they'd done before and didn't even know because they couldn't tell right from wrong. They never had been able to tell, of course, but now they couldn't think because when their bad dreams were taken away, nothing was left.

Q: Was there anything the people in charge could do?

A: Sure. They were even succeeding, to some extent. It was just a matter of cleaning up the contamination, getting the animals off the streets. It was working. That's the point.

Q: But something kept it from working?

A: There were some people who didn't *want* it to work. A level of sinfulness you can't imagine. There were actually a few rebels who managed to avoid getting the chip, not many, but enough. They tried to counteract the activity of the chip. To some extent and in some cases, they did. Then they started sending their dreams through to *this* world, and obviously the people in charge couldn't let that happen.

Q: Could you explain why not? What were they were afraid of?

A: That the escaped dreams would contaminate the universe. They knew it could turn back on them anytime.

Q: Do you think they're going to succeed?

A: I don't know. They can, if you'll let me help them.

Q: Tell us more about these people who managed to resist getting the chip. What kind of people are they?

A: Oh who knows? Transvestites, mixed-race mongrels, cripples, retards, fags, that must be most of them.

Q: The way you say that, though, doesn't make it sound like they're people who could mount much effective resistance.

A: They don't have any wisdom, but they're clever. They've got all the evil dreams on their side. They cultivate them.

Q: How do they do that?

A: They have an underground network and are able to communicate with each other. They're freaks, you know. If there's one thing that's true about freaks, it's that they recognize other freaks. It's a thing they have.

Q: So if you were going to describe conditions in that city right now, what would you say?

A: There's a lot of chaos. Some of it is being brought under control. But the resistance is determined to extend the chaos everywhere.

Q: Chaos? How bad is it?

A: People live in the streets, many buildings have been destroyed. There's a lot of copulation going on, God knows between who. People run around and steal and they don't work and they don't speak nicely. The city is polluted from destruction and overcrowding. The countryside's so devastated nobody can stay there and survive.

Q: We just have one more question today. Why do you care so much about this other world? It's not your world. You're not responsible for it.

A: Who says it's not my world? If you let contamination grow, wherever it is, sooner or later it may grow in your own backyard. Sometimes I forget it's another world I'm talking about. Sometimes I think the problem began with the Liberal Jews, or whoever. The difference doesn't matter. You've got to get rid of evil wherever you find it, and whatever way you can. If the laws have become so corrupt that they end up protecting evil, then you've got to go outside the law. Have you seen what happens when you let corruption fester? You haven't, I know. You don't see anything. You can't imagine the way they touch each other. You can't imagine the sores on their bodies and the lewd expressions on their faces. They're amazingly dumb and uninformed. They'll steal what they can, hurt who they can, they take nice sweet girls and turn them into prostitutes. They shut off the water, heat, and electricity in your apartment. They worship all sorts of odd gods and spirits and devils, and they laugh at everything good and decent and hardworking. Sometimes, if you're not careful, they'll even get in your head, and you'll start feeling like maybe it's you who's to blame. Maybe the problems have been yours all along and you're going crazy. If you're not careful, they'll start saying things inside your head.

That's the worst thing—if you see too many of them, you start believing everything's your fault. If they have their way, madness will seem like sanity, and sanity will seem mad. They'll make you believe in rape, murder, homosexuality, child molestation, atheism, and Negroes. And maybe one day you'll wake up and say to yourself I want to be a Negro atheist child-molesting homosexual, and I should rule the world.

Q: Are you saying that you yourself have these feelings sometimes?

A: These feelings wouldn't be dangerous if we didn't all of us have them sometimes. Don't we all sometimes hear voices in our heads? Don't we all doubt God? Don't we all sometimes think we're homosexual, or that we want to touch children?

Q: It seems like it would be hard to generalize.

A: You're politicians, I can see that. I don't expect you to say anything true. The world could be falling apart and you'd still be worried about you who offend.

Q: You've been very helpful today. We appreciate that, and we'll take it into account.

A: You'll need my help more later. Maybe when it's too late.

*

Cynthia had spent much of the previous Saturday and Sunday with Steve. Just the night before they had gone, after work, for dinner and a nice walk around the city. She was feeling buoyant and light when, that morning at the office, she received an email that had been going around in New York and apparently also in Boston, Philadelphia, and D.C. It began with a note, added to the original text, by the woman who had sent it around:

9:50 a.m. June 2, 1999
From: Miriam Raworth
To: Multiple Recipients
Subject: Pass It On: "re: Let's Meet Again?"

This is an email a friend of mine received from a man she doesn't even know. She met him at a dance club and gave him her email address. When he messaged her, she wrote him back with a few get-to-know-you questions, like "What's your last name?" This is how he responded:

7:45 p.m. May 27, 1999
From: Bill Webster
To: SusanStanton@aol.com
Subject: re: Let's Meet Again?

My life is at a point when I'm looking seriously and systematically for a woman to share my life with. You seem nice, and I don't mean this as badly as it might sound, but I don't have time for twenty questions by email. I met five girls Saturday night, have already booked a first coffee with three of them, and meet more every time I go dancing…and I go dancing at least three times a week.

I automatically rule out women who make dating too complicated. I don't do this because I think there's anything wrong with them, or because I'm arrogant. I do it to economize on time.

I know that dating in this city is difficult and scary for women. But keep in mind it's that way for guys too. Most of all, remember that you're competing with thousands of other women who don't insist that the man do all the work establishing a connection.

Now, maybe you'll find someone who's so taken by a single

dance with you that he's willing to negotiate by email for a chance to trek all the way up to your part of town. But you might not. And if such a guy did exist, and you happen to cross paths with him—what do you imagine a guy that desperate would have to offer?

In the hopes that this email might get back to him after being seen by thousands of women along the way… please send this on to a friend. Thanks!

Miriam

Soon after receiving it, Cynthia began getting messages from her friends, with various degrees of baffled outrage or sarcastic cynicism. Apparently the letter was being forwarded by young professional women all over the east coast. One of Cynthia's friends said she'd received the letter nearly a dozen times since the day before.

Cynthia had work to do, but it was hard to concentrate with all the commentary flying around. She had just settled down to getting something significant done when her phone rang.

"Oh my God can you believe it?" her friend Alicia said. "Just when you start to think that maybe men are the slightest bit civilized…How much of a jerk must that guy be?"

"I'm afraid I *can* believe it." Cynthia laughed. "I probably know twenty different guys who could have written it."

"Twenty? Twenty thousand is more like it. Everybody I know is talking about it. How about over there?"

"Same. I've been getting messages all morning. I've been trying to work but it's not happening."

"It's not happening here either. Really, this is ridiculous. It's never going to get any better. We're all going to die old and alone."

"It's not that bad," Cynthia said.

"Not that bad? Listen to you. Last month you would have been ranting."

"Yeah, but last month I was still looking and had been for a while. Things are different now."

"Steve, huh? You like him that much?"

"We're having fun," Cynthia said. "I don't know if it's anything more than that—yet."

"You've been going out with him a lot, haven't you?"

"I guess I have," Cynthia said, smiling to herself. "One of the things I like about Steve is he doesn't leap right into things without knowing what he's doing. He seems, I don't know, thoughtful. But not weird, just straightforward and honest. I've never met a man with his sort of inner, quiet confidence. He doesn't brag, but you can tell he's sure of himself."

"How far have things gone?"

"That's for me to know and you to find out. How are things on your end?"

"The same. I meet arrogant guys, dumb guys, inconsiderate guys, even smelly guys, sometimes guys who are all at once. But interesting or fun guys? No."

"I'm sorry," Cynthia said. "I know how tough it is out there."

"Is the one who broke his ankle back in the office?"

"Joseph? Yes. He's getting better. I haven't talked to him much though. Steve doesn't like him."

"Is Steve one of those guys who doesn't like other guys?"

"Maybe a little," Cynthia said. "He's so cute, especially when he's annoyed."

"He's cute when he's annoyed? Oh no. You better watch out, Cynthia."

"How so?"

"If he's cute when he's annoyed, the next thing you know, he's cute when he leaves his dirty clothes on the floor of your bedroom and forgets to put down the toilet seat."

"Maybe he is."

"Listen to the lovebird."

"Oh cut it out," Cynthia said.

"I'm just kidding," Alicia said. "Seriously, I'm happy for you. I know things hadn't been working out well for you lately."

"They hadn't," Cynthia said. "That's why, when I meet a guy like Steve, I want to make sure to do things right."

"You go, girl. Sounds serious."

"It's too early to tell. It could be. He likes the idea of being married, and I think he wants kids."

"You know a guy in the city who wants to get married and have kids? I didn't know there were any of those. How did you find him?"

"There's no formula," Cynthia said. "Meeting Steve was just luck. I can't account for it."

"I've always been wary of luck," Alicia said. "Maybe it's time to start looking for it."

"Maybe it is," Cynthia said. "If you don't go looking, you can't complain."

"Oh I'm looking," Alicia said. "It's just a matter of who I keep finding."

"You'll find someone," Cynthia said, "who'll love you like you deserve."

"Maybe you already have."

"Maybe I have," Cynthia said. "It's funny how things work out sometimes, isn't it?"

*

After the phone call with her father was over, Marinda decided she was going to see Herbert, not Jerry. It wasn't that she expected

Herbert could help in any practical way. Instead, unlike Jerry, who she hadn't talked to since their fight the previous week, he'd make no attempt to offer help that was really designed to control her. She hadn't been to Herbert's apartment yet, but knew where it was. She couldn't call; Herbert didn't have a phone. "If I had a phone, I'd be obsessed with everybody who wasn't calling me," Herbert said when she'd asked him why. "Not having a phone makes me mysterious and inaccessible, so everybody's always desperate to find me." Besides, he said, making phone calls from his apartment depressed him, made him feel lonely and trapped in his own privacy. He preferred public phone booths or borrowing somebody's cell phone, so people could overhear his conversations. Good as his word, he'd called her several times from phones with a lot of background noise. At least he'd called her, also unlike Jerry.

She took the subway to Brooklyn, then walked to the address Herbert had given her. Spring seemed suddenly over. It was hot out, and hotter in the subway, in a way it never got in California. Hazy, sweaty, dirty, and close. Other than the weather though, she had no desire to go back to California. Right now, she might be happy never to see California again.

She couldn't be sure that Herbert was home, though he'd said he almost always was during the day. He was secretive about his work. She had the sense that he did things with computers, often from home, sometimes late at night. But he hadn't given her an email address either. Could someone without a phone really work on computers?

It was early afternoon and he was probably just getting up. It was strange that she still couldn't tell how much money he had or whether it came from him or somebody else, although whenever someone's money sources were unknown, that usually meant a fair amount of it was floating around. Still, for someone who talked relentlessly about what he was thinking and feeling, Herbert rarely said anything about the specifics of his life. Considering that as she came out of the subway, Marinda smiled. Even thinking about Herbert, she started to sound like him.

She found the rowhouse where his apartment was. The front steps were dusty. Signs of repair work littered the front steps—piles of cloth, pieces of metal, even a ladder. No one seemed to be working there today. There were six doorbells and she rang his. Herbert's voice came over the intercom in a metallic rumble. She felt a little surprised that finding him had been so easy.

When he opened the door to his apartment and smiled, a blast of cold air hit Marinda. She felt like she was walking into his refrigerator.

"You've got the air conditioning on," she said.

"I can't stand natural air." In his awkward, loose-jointed gait, he led her into the living room, which was sparse. A couch and a chair. A coffee table. Two bookcases with a few books. A stereo. No TV. A few framed abstract designs hung on the walls. A mild bit of incense floated through the chilly stuffiness. Herbert motioned Marinda towards the couch and offered her hot tea. When he'd brought back cups for both of them, he sat in the chair and pulled a blanket over his knees. "Should I be surprised to see you during the day?" he asked. "I'm a little surprised to be up myself."

"I don't know," Marinda said from the couch. "I'm thinking I need to change the way I live."

"It's dull to do the same things all the time," Herbert said, "so of course it's irresistible. But if you've come all the way out here to find me, something serious must be happening. I have to say, though, I don't like revelations, unless they're painful."

"My father cut me off," Marinda said. "He does it every so often. I think this time he means it."

Herbert shook his head, simultaneously understanding and ironic. "It's always a bad sign when somebody thinks they mean something. These days it's not possible to mean what you say. If somebody thinks that's what they're doing, you can be sure the lie is going to be dangerous."

"Herbert," Marinda said, "shut up."

"I'd love to."

There was a blanket on the couch too; Marinda unfolded it and pulled it over her knees like Herbert had. "He says I can't be who I want as long as he's selfish and tries to control me. He said he hoped I could forgive him for trying to force me to follow his path, and that from now on I'm free to follow the path I choose. He apologized for supporting me all these years. I didn't know what to say. I swear there were a couple moments when I thought he was you. Only you're conscious that you've turned things upside down. With him, the more upside down things are, the more he thinks they're right side up."

"Compared to him," Herbert sipped his tea, "I'm a sloppy poseur. What are you going to do?"

"Get a job, I guess. I do pretty well at jobs when I have them. The thing about my father, he always talks to me about needing to get a job, then makes sure I don't get one. Or if I do, he makes sure I don't keep it."

"I'm almost finding this difficult to follow."

Marinda stuffed her hands under the blanket. "How can I explain? My father talks endlessly about the importance of being independent because he wants me to be *dependent*. He doesn't like the idea that anybody has any success separate from his. He's actively prevented me from doing things I was interested in doing, even things I was only barely interested in doing. Right out of college, I had a job working for some friends of his who were in the film industry. I can't say I loved it. They were Hollywood people: talk about seeing everything upside down. But I did well. He came to visit me and saw that. Next thing you know, he said we had to go on a trip to Europe, three or four months at least, long enough that I wouldn't have the job when I came back. I told him I didn't want to go, but he pouted, said it was important, that a woman of my background needed the refinement that only long trips to Europe could bring, and he had the money and time right then and we needed to go. So I went. He got bored, of course, as soon as we were there and he could see that the only way I was going to get along was with his money. He left me in Greece with some friends I'd made and went home again. I had a great time, by the way, it's not that. But I didn't have the job anymore when I came back, and what's more, I didn't want it. I'd been away from it just long enough to recognize it for the big time con it was."

"Sounds like being left penniless might be the best thing that's ever happened to you."

"Maybe," Marinda said. "It's not that I hate being on my own. But it's on his terms again. It's about him wanting me to be dependent on his idea of my being independent. I don't know if I can explain."

"I think you have. I take it you've got a therapist who makes sure none of these problems get solved?"

Marinda sighed. "You know, Herbert, the only thing I've ever wanted to do is paint. And it's crazy that I can't make myself do it, lately. When I was talking to my father on the phone, I realized that maybe I can't paint because the only reason I ever did was because I wanted him to approve of it, while I also know that it's the thing about me he's least likely ever to approve of. He knows that painting is mine, not his. That's why he never wanted me to do it. Still, if I need his disapproval to paint, then my painting *is* his."

"That's what makes art so central and irrelevant," Herbert said.

"What?"

"That all the difficulties and confusions we have show up there, especially when we don't know it."

"It was the only thing that ever seemed like *me*," Marinda said. Under the blanket, her body felt like it might disappear. "It's never been easy to paint. But there have been times when I'm doing it that something comes clear. I have this sense of having some level of, I don't know, power, to respond to the world and make it something I want it to be. It's not power *over* life. It's the power to be *part* of it, on terms I can create, at least a little—to be *with* things, not just under them. The feeling doesn't last. Sooner or later, I'm hanging out with Jerry again, drunk somewhere and saying something stupid and being afraid and feeling lonely and not wanting anyone to get near me because if they do, they'll know exactly how stupid and afraid and lonely I am. So painting doesn't make me any wiser. It's about being in touch, literally, the way I can touch the paint and the canvas and it's real, I know it's real and I am too because I'm touching it. It means more to me than anything else, and I can't do it at all."

"Maybe you have to stop caring about it so much," Herbert said.

Marinda stared at him. "That's the first time you've sounded like Jerry. I don't like it."

Herbert put up his hands. "No, listen. What I mean is, have you ever noticed that when we decide something is the most important thing we have to do, maybe we've decided that because we don't want to ever actually do it?"

"What do you mean?"

"I have a friend who's a novelist," Herbert said. "He's published seven or eight books. He's quite successful in a way I myself couldn't stand. If you ask him, he'll tell you the reason he's so successful is that he's never been able to write the one book that matters to him. It sits in a box above his desk. He's never going to finish, but he says it's what makes him successful. Because all these other books he's written, they're never *the* crucial book for him. He can write them because he's worrying all the time that he's not writing his great book."

"Is the great book any good?"

"I don't know," Herbert said, "and I'm sure he doesn't. He doesn't *want* to know, although he says he does. It's too important to understand. He's able to put what's important aside and get on with the business of doing what's possible."

"You're telling me I should stop thinking painting is so important, and just paint?"

"I'm saying maybe you've made painting so important so it *can* be impossible. You don't want to paint, or part of you doesn't anyway."

Marinda looked away from him, towards the window. She drank her hot tea and shivered. "Do you have another blanket? I wonder if it's too early for a real drink."

Herbert went over to a closet, brought back a blanket for her. "Can you imagine what would happen," he said, "if we ever did the thing in the world we most wanted to do? Who could stand it, to know that they'd already done the thing that matters most? Of course, it happens. And sometimes it really hurts the person who recognizes that it's happened."

"So if we do something great and recognize it, it will destroy us?"

"Not undoubtedly, but it could. Besides, great things may be less interesting to me than any other possibility in life. It's what happens after a great thing, or instead of a great thing, that seems interesting to me."

"So maybe I should get a job and forget about painting, or let it take care of itself?"

"I have no idea what you should do." Herbert smiled, wanly as usual. "I hope you don't think I'm giving advice. I never do, except by accident. I'm not interested in what people should do. What they actually do is much more fascinating."

Marinda pulled the second blanket closely over her. "It's cold in here," she said.

Herbert said, "Isn't it fabulous?"

*

In the days after hearing about Joseph's ankle, Steve found signs of his new power everywhere. On the street one afternoon, he watched a man in a new suit who had obnoxiously slick, stiff hair. Just as Steve was thinking how guys like that were responsible for the kind of world everybody had to live in, the man reached a corner and tripped, falling to his knees. His briefcase crashed open on the ground, papers scattering across the sidewalk. After a moment, the man stood, cursing, and started to pick up the papers. He and Steve both looked down to see a hole torn in the knee of his pants. Steve grinned and the man's eyes flashed fury at him, but something the man saw in Steve's stare made him look away. Steve walked off triumphant.

Another time, a couple of teenagers began a loud, inept attempt at a rap song in the subway car where Steve sat one morning. Their shrieks made his head hurt. He imagined himself walking up and grabbing one—the ringleader, a tall, muscled, if skinny, kid—by the neck and saying something vicious that would frighten them all into muttering silence. Just then, the door between cars opened and a cop stood there. The kids went silent, looking at the cop with sullen resentment in the same way Steve imagined them looking at him. They were silent for the three more stops it took Steve to get where he was going.

There were other, smaller moments like these. Then again, there were just as many when he wished something would happen but it didn't. If he had the power to make his dreams a reality, he soon realized it couldn't be forced. Maybe there was some pattern to the ability, if he had it. The weird beeping on the phone seemed to have something to do with it. He hadn't called the phone company about getting the problem fixed.

Joseph came back to the office after several days off. Steve hadn't noticed him much before their fight; now, of course, he ran into him all the time. Steve half-expected that Joseph would treat him defiantly, but in his cast Joseph seemed oddly restrained. His expression, not just to Steve but to the whole office, looked almost apologetic, as if he realized something about himself he didn't like. Rightly so, Steve thought. In any case Joseph didn't continue the fight. He wasn't friendly, obviously, nor would Steve have wanted him to be. Whenever he saw Steve coming, he turned away as if embarrassed. "Good for you," Steve told him silently. "You've gotten smart and don't want to risk it."

Steve had been spending a lot of time with Cynthia, although he wasn't sure he should. She was nice enough, and attractive, although ultimately, despite her more openly flowing hair, she had that well-put-together professional look common among women who cared mainly about trying to be part of a corrupt, mindless system. Worse, she had no thoughts that weren't mind-numbingly conventional. Marinda, for all her insanity, at least was original.

He had given up thinking that Cynthia had any connection to Marinda. Cynthia's initial interest in talking about her had faded. Now, when he mentioned Marinda's name, Cynthia often frowned. Maybe Cynthia expected she was going to replace Marinda, as if such a thing was possible. In any case she kept calling him and wanting to do things together. That was fine, kept him from getting too bored while he figured out the extent of his powers. In fact, maybe Cynthia was an example of those powers. She seemed drawn to him in a way that hadn't happened with women much before, although he'd had a few girlfriends before Marinda.

"Hey cutie," she leaned over his cubicle and kissed him on the head. "What's my big guy doing this morning?"

"The usual junk," he said. "Always more of it."

"Early morning grumbly," she said. "Things pretty much as usual, huh? Still thinking you might quit?"

"Soon as I find the right thing. I need to be sure of some things, then I'll be set."

"Sounds like you're hatching big plans. I hope you'll let me in on them."

"When it's time, I will."

"Do you suppose they're plans I could be part of?" She smiled enigmatically. He wondered if she knew something he didn't.

"We'll see," he said. "Anything's possible."

Cynthia tightened up slightly. "You're very open-ended, aren't you?"

Not understanding, Steve looked at her. "I haven't got it all figured out yet. You'll know right away when I do."

Cynthia relaxed, a little. "Want to go somewhere tonight, or will that interfere with your scheme?"

"It'll help," he said. "What did you have in mind?"

"Dinner, a movie, then… the possibilities are endless, aren't they?"

"They could be," Steve said. "They very well could be."

Cynthia beamed. "By the way, I talked to Joseph yesterday."

"And I'm supposed to care about that because…?"

"You're not still angry at him, are you?" Cynthia looked at him curiously.

"No. I don't care one way or the other."

"He told me more about what happened. He didn't want to at first. He knows you and I are going out. But he did get really drunk after we'd left, like I heard. Apparently he was still pretty pissed about you. He didn't say that exactly, but I could tell. So he was in a belligerent mood and went this short cut way home that he doesn't usually go. Apparently this thing about them coming out of nowhere is true. He said it was almost like magic, like he got jumped by some weird shadow. He only caught a glimpse of a face for a minute. He even told me—get this—that the face reminded him of yours. In any case he was lying there screaming with pain until somebody came along and helped him get a cab to the hospital."

"He says the guy's face looked like mine?"

"He didn't mean literally, I don't think. Just that everything was jumbled together. He says he's been trying to cut back on his drinking since, and of course it's hard to go out in that cast. It's clear he's been thinking about the way he lives. He's depressed."

"Serves him right," Steve said.

"You can't really be that harsh?"

"I don't know." Steve shrugged. "If he changes his ways, okay. If not, I think I'm just being fair."

"Guys are so funny," Cynthia said. "You never have any sympathy for each other."

"I have sympathy for people who deserve sympathy," Steve said.

"Okay, hard guy. I'll be done about six-thirty tonight. Is that good for you?"

"Sure," Steve said.

"I'm looking forward to it." She floated away.

So Joseph had said that whoever attacked him looked like Steve. Fascinating, but not surprising. It fit with the other signs. Like some kind of weird shadow, Joseph had said. If he had to be a shadow for now, he would, until he figured out what this power was. Then he'd be something far more serious.

He had to be sure though. There was only one way. If he had the ability, it would help him find Marinda and get her back. If that happened, he would know. And if it did, Joseph and all the other asshole suits would have watch the fuck out.

*

After a week with David, Sarah was beginning to see words again. Finding him in the coffee shop burned her out longer than had ever happened in her adult years. As a teenager, she had been through more extreme fluctuations. The first few days of letting David stay at her apartment had gone forward in a gray quiet. Was this flatness, this lack of texture—she kept describing it differently—the way other people experienced the world all the time? What was amazing was how easy it became to walk right past people and not think about them. The cocoon-like obliviousness was almost comfortable. She had often wondered about the unaware selfishness, frequently enough pained, that many people gave off as their strongest aura. This was what it must feel like—experiencing others almost as a dream, one that could vanish with a blink.

Of course, she wondered what she had missed. The energy that had taken over the ex-David Carroll could have found many people by now. Nothing in the immediate neighborhood seemed different, although the early summer outpouring of excitement, with sinister and angry edges now that the weather was hot, seemed powerful, even in her deadened state. But that excitement was nothing more than teenagers on the street or the normally hidden domestic conflicts of adults taken out into more public spaces. And of course the omnipresence of sexuality, which even in her temporary flatness was overwhelming.

David himself wasn't much help, though she hadn't expected he would be. The fact that he could function at all without knowing who he was or why things had happened was already a testament to his strength. He could have been hysterical, terrified. Instead he had a steady, calm curiosity that she found admirable under the circumstances. At worst, he lapsed into moments of depression. She kept asking if he had any clues to the source of the personality he had taken on. No, he said repeatedly. It just seemed right to figure out, carefully, as much as he could about who he was, and not expect everything to be resolved immediately.

Then, after a slow weekend when they walked around the city in the morning before being driven indoors by the afternoon heat,

Sarah felt the words returning, not completely, but undeniably there. It wouldn't be much longer before she felt her full range of always-fluctuating perception again. "We need to go to Rutgers and see if we can find out anything about you from your office," she said to him one morning as he sat in a chair reading a Don DeLillo novel. They rented a car. David Carroll's credit cards were in good standing. But he had no checkbook, no information about potential bank accounts. His office might give him access to funds they could use.

"If we can figure out more about why this happened to you, maybe we can figure out how it's going to work with others," she said, as she already had a number of times, when they were finally in the car and headed out of the city. At first she thought she was going to have to drive, something she didn't look forward to because, living in the city, she didn't do it often. David insisted he knew how, although when pressed, he didn't know why he knew. He was right though. He handled the car deftly even in heavy city traffic.

"What do you think we might find?" he asked. His shirt, a pink button-down, which she uggested he should wear, was almost certainly the kind of shirt the old David would have been seen in. In the shirt and a new pair of tan slacks, he probably looked less frumpy and slouched than usual.

"I don't know. There will be a fair amount of work information, and we can get a sense of how the original David occupied space. But I don't think we're going to your house any time soon." She laughed.

David smiled ruefully. "I still feel pretty bad about my, uh, wife. No further ideas about that?"

"I'm not sure there's much we can do. Unless you're thinking about trying to patch things up."

"I guess not," he said. "But I don't like the idea that I'm putting some woman I don't know through this kind of pain and annoyance. I realize, by the way, that in saying that I could be talking equally about you."

Sarah looked at him, impressed. "That must be the not-David part of you speaking. I get the sense that the old David didn't care how much pain and annoyance he caused. He might very well have liked it."

David winced. "If he did, it doesn't appeal to me now."

"That's good," Sarah said. "Maybe we need more people to land here from other worlds."

"So we're just going to walk into the building and go to my office like nothing's the matter? What if somebody who knows me is around, wants to talk department politics?"

"Not that many people will be around. It's summer. Besides, I don't get the impression that the original David was a chatty man. If anybody tries to talk to you, just be gruff, abrupt, and uninterested. If someone presses you, say something pessimistic. Even if it's not exactly like the original David, my guess is it'll be close enough for a short conversation. Besides, what's the worst that can happen if somebody thinks you seem different? They'll probably like the new you better."

"I suppose that's comforting."

"Wait," Sarah startled. "How do you know about department politics?"

"I don't know anything specifically. I just thought all academic departments were eaten up with petty infighting."

"But why do you think that? I mean, where do you get that idea from?"

"I don't know," he said.

"I wish you'd stop doing that," she said.

"What?"

"Knowing things, then not knowing how you know them. Nothing personal, but it drives me crazy."

"I'll try to stop."

"No," she said, "don't do that either. It's information we need. It's just frustrating, that's all."

"I'm getting used to being frustrated," he said.

"Now you do sound like the original David."

"I'm practicing." He smiled.

Eventually they arrived at Rutgers. There was a big campus map near the main entrance. Sarah managed to find the building that housed the History Department. There were only a few students and what seemed an occasional office worker outside on the campus, which stood near a decaying urban wasteland of the kind common enough in New Jersey. They found a practically empty visitor's parking lot, left the car there, headed to the History Department building and went inside. Posters in the hallways leapt out at her with a combination of officious and haphazard insistence, program opportunities alternating with advertisements for restaurants, summer jobs, or editorial services. The building seemed more like a high school than a college building, generic and dusty and bureaucratic rather than seriously intellectual.

Since they didn't want to call attention to themselves by speaking to anybody, it took them awhile to find David's office. Eventually they saw his nameplate on a brown wooden door. David had a number of keys. They tried several before finding the right one.

Bookshelves ringed the room, filled, obviously enough, with books, although there weren't as many as Sarah might have thought. The shelves seemed less used, more tidy, than they ought to have been. There were no loose stacks of books anywhere in the room. A slightly outdated computer stood on the desk next to an even more outdated printer. Several small stacks of paper also sat on the desk. She began going through them: a few ungraded student essays, some official memos, other miscellaneous bits of minor workplace correspondence. On the wall hung a Ph.D. diploma from Princeton, an advertisement for the Ken Burns public television series on the Civil War, a 1996 Yankees World Series pennant, and a large map of the United States with pins stuck in it. A closer look showed that the pins marked Civil War battlefields.

David was standing uncomfortably in a corner, as if afraid to move. Sarah began going through the desk drawers, finding one full of office supplies and others stuffed with bureaucratic documents: book order forms, class lists, and old grade books, which she went through closely. There were quite a few C's and D's on the books, as well as the occasional F. Not an easy grader. She stepped into a small walk-in closet at the back corner of the room; in it were an old raincoat, a decaying winter coat, two umbrellas, a sweater and a couple of empty boxes.

She came back out. David was sitting on one of three small wooden chairs facing the professor's desk. Sarah flipped the switch that turned on the computer.

"Well?" David shifted nervously in the chair. "What do we know?"

"Let's just say it's an office not quite bursting with personality." She rested a hand on the bookshelf beside her. "I'm picking up as much from the absences as I am from what's here. Two things immediately stand out. No pictures of people, and not a single thing that looks like your own writing, except for a few short scrawls—and I do mean scrawls—on some student papers. There's not even a book review, much less a chapter of a book or whatever else, not even jottings. If you've published a book in the past, which you probably must have to keep this job, you don't even have a copy of *that*. Hardly a sign of scholarly self-confidence." She took a random book off the shelf. "You don't write notes in the margins either," she held the spine open towards him. "I could pull out fifty more books and find not a single note written in the books or even stuffed in on a piece of paper. If you're reading anything new or even thinking about it, there's no indication. I found your computer passwords taped inside the office supplies drawer, by the way, so we won't have any problem accessing what's on your computer."

She logged on and a moment later was cruising through his files, which hadn't been arranged into subdirectories but were just listed haphazardly: syllabi, business letters, memos, etc., all tossed together without any identifiable filename system, so that she didn't know what she was opening until she was looking at it. Eventually she turned away from the computer and sat back.

Fidgeting, David hunched further into the chair. "I feel like I'm on trial."

"Unhappy being evaluated this way, are you?"

"I guess so. What's the diagnosis, doc?"

"You're the doc, not me." Sarah laughed gently. "For the most part I'm not thinking any more than what anybody else could, although I get a lot from your handwriting in the gradebooks. David Carroll is not an intellectually involved man. He's going through the motions of being a professor, maybe because he gets a small thrill out of the appearance of authority, although maybe not; I get very little sense that he makes an attempt to keep up in his field. It's amazing, in fact, how little personality he's imprinted on the office. His interest in baseball is about as intimate as it gets."

She came around the desk and stood closer to David. "There *is* a fair amount of resentment though. It's not easy to decipher the crabby little bits of handwriting, but the short notes to students, and I do mean short, are pretty snotty. Even the A-minuses are grudging. He resents and dislikes his students. He resents bureaucratic details; documents of some importance are lying around haphazardly, and he throws files onto the computer like he'd rather not know where they are. He's not disastrously disorganized, although he's not hugely organized either. In fact there's more organization of things that other people will see, like the bookshelves, than there is of things like his computer files. So he does care about appearances, to some extent. I would say he creates an image of himself, but what lies behind the image? I suppose his attachment to the Yankees could be passionate, but that would be a small, out-of-character wrinkle. There's no passion here."

"I appreciate you calling him 'he,'" David said.

Sarah nodded. "He doesn't seem much like you. Although I suppose there's some link in the calmness. David Carroll is uptight but not excitable. He probably feels stress but clamps down on it. I wish I could say I detected some undercurrent of a strong death drive, because it might seem that a man like this could be secretly suicidal, although he'd be inclined to kill himself slowly. But I don't see that. Smug, occasionally resentful, not up-to-date, not passionate, not comfortable, but not uncomfortable enough to care—that would seem the heart of the matter. Hard to guess what made him this way. There's no story of a past here, except he's Ivy League."

"So has this been any help at all?"

"A lot." Sarah looked around the room. "What we want to know is whether what happened to you happened randomly, or on purpose in some degree. People who lack involvement with things or who need direction from others might be easier targets. People who don't know their own minds, who don't know why they dream what they dream, and are secretly waiting to be told."

"You think David Carroll fits that profile?"

"In part. It seems likely that David Carroll lacks a strong sense of self and keeps others at a distance because of it. On the other hand I don't see him as seeking direction. He may feel like there's nothing he needs to know."

"Okay, I follow all that," David said, "although it's hardly pleasant." He smiled weakly. "He doesn't exactly fit the profile of a person who wants to be rid of responsibility for his own mind, but he's close enough to confirm that the profile may well be right. Still, one person can hardly be enough basis to be sure."

"Absolutely not. We'll just have to see what happens next."

Still clearly uncomfortable, David fidgeted again in the chair.

"Let me know when we can leave."

"You really don't like being here, do you?"

"No."

"Do you remember anything about this place?"

"I don't think so. I could be wanting not to know. I think I hate David Carroll."

"I don't like him much either," Sarah said. "We can go. Let's take a few things, just so we have access to a little evidence."

After she filled a few envelopes with bits of paper and the Yankees pennant, they left the office. Just as they locked the door behind them, a man turned the corner of the hallway. He had gray hair, a slight stoop, and thick glasses behind which his eyes moved unfocused. He was wearing a striped short-sleeve shirt and slacks similar to David's.

"Well, Professor Carroll," the man said from down the hall with a consciously ironic formality. "Who would have thought I'd see you here this time of year?"

"Hello," David said tensely.

The man was still walking towards them. "What brings you in?"

"Just picking up a few things. Headed out now."

For a moment it seemed the man was going to stop and talk, then he kept walking. "All right, see you in the fall," he said, and went past them down the hallway.

SIX

"Imagine running into you this early in the day," a woman's voice said behind Marinda on the sidewalk. "Thought you avoided the light."

Marinda turned. It was Geena, whom she hadn't seen since that night at the bar some weeks back, so indistinguishable from so many nights at so many bars. Geena's blond hair shone in the rapidly warming morning sun. She was frowning rather than smiling and bristled with what almost seemed hostility. Still, she looked plump and glowing in her loose, light-colored dress.

"I've been doing some temp work," Marinda said. Her large sunglasses shielded her from too much morning brightness. Other people moved around them on the sidewalk, some sluggishly, others ducking for shade, all protecting themselves from the muggy air soon to turn stifling. "Keeps the mind active. I was about to get a quick coffee. Join me? I was going to take it to the office but I'm early, if you can believe it."

"You're actually working?" Geena looked like she was trying to scowl. "That's good-hearted of you. Who are you temping for?"

"A dog magazine, if you can believe it. They deal with dog shows, trends in dog care, the breeding industry, things like that."

"What made you enter the world of those who actually support themselves?" This time, Geena's hostility was unmistakable.

"A lot of things," Marinda shrugged. "What's up with you, Geena?"

"He's not gay, you know. You shouldn't have said he was."

"What?"

"Jerry's not gay." Geena tossed her hair indignantly. "I know you always need to be the center of attention, but don't you think that's going too far?"

Marinda looked at her, tried to understand. "How do you know about that? Have you been spending time with Jerry?"

Geena raised her chin proudly. "More than you have. We've been dating. You shouldn't say people are gay just because they're not interested in *you*."

"You and Jerry have been *dating*?" Marinda tried to focus her morning mind.

"Yes we have, thank you very much."

"Since when?"

"Since he realized that all you ever do is tear him down."

"There's no need to be obnoxious, Geena."

"Isn't there?" Geena put her hands on her hips defensively and added a bit of aggressive sway. "He was your friend, Marinda. And all you do is criticize and tear him down and tell him he's not a man."

"I never said he wasn't a man." Marinda tried to keep her face from showing her astonishment. "I didn't even say he was gay, if you're interested in facts. I just said maybe he didn't understand himself, and he should realize it and do something about it if he wants to be happy. Being gay has nothing to do with not being a man—whatever 'being a man' is supposed to mean."

"He's happy enough now, thank you. He just needs the kind

of woman who can understand him and who's willing to take care of him."

"Who's willing…? How often have you been seeing him?"

"A couple nights a week." Geena drew herself up haughtily.

"Really? And doing what? Does he kiss you? Go home with you?"

Geena's eyes flashed. "That's just like you. Reduce a sensitive and kind man to some crude sexual fantasy."

Marinda blinked behind her sunglasses. "Geena, what are you talking about? Look, I know Jerry. I wouldn't want you to get hurt because he's playing some game. Although the way you're talking right now, I don't know why I care."

"He's not playing a game." Geena smiled scornfully. "He's just not interested in *you*. I'm sorry you can't accept that."

"Can't accept that?" Marinda looked closely at Gina's mouth. "Why do you keep on saying… oh. Did Jerry tell you I can't accept that?"

"Jerry's told me a lot of things," Geena said.

"I can imagine."

"I don't think there's any excuse for the way you've treated him," Geena went on, apparently oblivious to anything Marinda had said. "All he's been doing is trying to be nice to you while you get your life figured out. What do you do in return? Try to make him feel like he's not a man. What gives you the right, Marinda? Just because your father's rich and you don't have to take care of yourself like the rest of us."

"I'm sorry," Marinda shook her head, amazed, "but that's not fair. You don't know what you're talking about, and I don't think I'm going to discuss it with you. You want to find out about Jerry, go ahead. He doesn't purposely play with people—not usually. But whatever his problem is—and for the record, I don't claim to know—he's determined not to figure it out. Anybody who gets involved with him is going to pay."

"I'll tell him you said so. He's taking me to a lovely restaurant tonight. He's very romantic, you know."

"Good," Marinda said. "I hope it works out. Really. Take care of yourself, Geena."

"I wish I could say see you later, Marinda, but I don't think we will be seeing you later." Geena turned and walked away, her dress swishing down the sidewalk.

Marinda stared after her. "I don't know what you're doing, Jerry," she said as Geena crossed the street a block ahead, "but sooner or later, if you're not careful, you're really going to hurt somebody." Her mouth grew grim. "And if you do that, I'll never speak to you again."

*

Now that her ability had come back fully, Sarah realized over the next few weeks how much she had missed. Most times she went out, she ran into people who were no longer what they had been. As the weeks passed, more and more people on the streets of New York were being invaded by dream language from far away.

It wasn't always easy to tell the difference between people who had been invaded and people who hadn't. She'd come across no one with eyes on fire like David's. Instead, by the phrases they gave off, or the strange blanks in the phrases, she could sometimes identify people who didn't know who they were. There were others who had not forgotten themselves but had become themselves more wildly, become more determined to cause trouble or fall apart—people whose thoughts and feelings projected more overtly into the world.

She'd followed quite a few people. So far, she hadn't managed to establish any trust, or even hold an extended conversation, with anyone besides the new David. For some reason, he was conscious of his situation and they weren't. There was a young woman, for instance, early twenties, tasteful summer dress, fashionably short blond hair, who gave off fairly intense blanks followed by equally intense surges of confused pain, her awareness of her own identity nearly erased. Reading the forcefulness of the woman's aura, Sarah followed her on some errands along Fifth Avenue. The woman was managing to function although it was all rote. She did what she did because of some vague memory of doing it, similar to the way David knew things without knowing how he knew them.

After following her for a while, Sarah approached the woman just after she bought a small vanilla frozen-yogurt cup in an ice cream shop. "You don't know why you're doing that, do you?" Sarah said.

The woman stared defensively, as she might have at any stranger speaking to her. She began eating her yogurt.

"I can help you," Sarah said. "I know what's wrong with you."

"There's no help for me," the woman said.

"You don't understand. I know who you are."

"I'm not anybody," the woman said.

"Yes you are. Something has happened to you, and you don't know what it is. I do, and I can help."

"I don't want help," the woman said, clutching her yogurt tightly. "Why are you talking to me? I don't even know how you *can* talk to me. I'm invisible."

"You're not invisible. You just feel invisible. Come sit with me in the park and talk? What can it hurt?"

"Talking always hurts," the woman said.

"Just give me a couple minutes of your time. Please."

The woman backed away. "I don't have any time. Can't you see I'm busy?"

"Yes. But why are you busy? Do you know?"

"What is there to know? It's not important."

"It's not important to know why you're doing what you're doing?"

"It only gets in the way."

"Of what?"

"Of doing what I need to do." Fear entered her eyes.

"Please," Sarah said. "I just want to understand more about you."

"I don't want to be understood. There's nothing to understand." The woman started walking off. "Go away. I'm in a hurry."

A day or two later, Sarah saw a man walking down the street in the block ahead of her, language flying off him in repetitive obsession almost impossible to look at. "Fuck me," "I want to get laid," even worse phrases like, "Sit on my aching purple cock" leapt off him in every direction. He stared at every woman who passed, looking at their breasts and butts. Sometimes he said hello or whistled. He was rating them too, she could see from the words. At the same time, his body was tense with the agony of his obsession. At various moments, "Help Help Help" twisted above his head. Sarah had seen language like this coming off men before, of course, if rarely this strongly. This time it was different. She hurried to catch up with him.

"I know you don't want to be this way," she said. "I know what's causing it."

"Hey Mama. You still got the stuff."

"Excuse me?"

The man grinned. "A little past your prime you know but hey, I bet you can still shake it."

"No," Sarah said. "I'm trying to help you."

"You can help me all night long," he said.

"Shut up," Sarah said. "I can tell you're in pain, and I can tell it's not your fault."

"That's right, Mama, I'm hurting, and it's not my fault. It's yours, coming along here strutting your stuff. It's good, Mama, and I need it to stop my pain. Stop my hurt, Mama."

"I know there's another part of you in there somewhere, if you'll just try."

"I got one part here that's really good. Wanna see?"

It was hopeless. Several other encounters went nowhere also. They were puppets, dragged along by forces they couldn't understand. Their original minds were somewhere and didn't want to be trapped, but she couldn't strip through the layers of alien force. In fact there was no core underneath those layers; it wasn't like some genuine self was buried inside them. Instead, their original selves and the alien force were intertwined, almost like cancer cells mixed with healthy cells, with no clear distinction between what was sick and what was healthy. The most outgoing ones had their personalities exaggerated to the point of parody. Still, to anyone without her power, they probably seemed ordinary, if a bit quirky, people going about ordinary business. It was easy, Sarah could see, for people to become parodies of themselves and still not really affect others around them, or even be noticed. The ones who were taken over by a kind of inner emptiness stood out much less, as if waiting for the right moment to vanish beneath the crowded streets.

"I don't understand," she said anxiously one evening to the new David as they sat at her kitchen table. "I can't reach any of them."

"Maybe they're not ready to be reached," he said.

"What do you mean?"

He rubbed his hand through his hair as if trying to push something out of his head. "They're not ready to hear you. What they think of themselves and what you think of them is so far apart that there's no way to bridge the gap."

"But I'm able to talk to *you*." Sarah grabbed his wrist insistently. "You have that emptiness, sure. But when I explained the situation to you even the first time, you were able to understand. I'm not saying you didn't have questions, or that nothing confused you, but you understood the essential problem."

"I sought you out though, remember."

"That's true," Sarah said, considering it. "Why'd you do that?"

David shook his head. "I could tell you knew something I needed to know, and I followed you to find out what it was."

"What accounts for the difference? You're all suffering from the same problem."

He thought about it. "Is it clear we're suffering from the same problem? Similar problems, yes. Maybe we all suffer from it in our own unique way? You've said so yourself."

"Yes, that makes sense." Sarah tried to slow her spinning thoughts and breathe more easily. "I'm starting to lose sight of things. Sometimes all I can see is my own frustration."

"You're not there yet, I would guess," David said calmly. "You're especially frustrated right now, sure. Maybe you need to step back and rethink it."

"Okay." Sarah tried to ease the tension in her shoulders. "Of course I can't approach everyone in the same way, as if I could just walk up to them and they'd understand. Each case is unique, although there are some shared patterns."

"Such as?"

"Being easily influenced." She felt herself setting into an explanation, for herself as much as him. "We're all of us to some extent the sum of our influences. Then there's the twist we add in our response to those influences. You can call that character if you want, or personality. It's a series of choices made in response to influences. The choices themselves don't exist before they're actually made, except that a lot of responses are habitual. Some people always follow the same pattern, some are more variable and follow multiple patterns, some follow patterns then disrupt their own patterns— which becomes a pattern."

"I've been trying to disrupt mine," David said.

Sarah smiled. "Right. Like you, some people develop a more definite sense of how they respond to external conditions. But even those who have a more conscious sense of themselves can't be conscious every time. Sometimes they're overwhelmed, too, perhaps permanently, just like somebody who's been overwhelmed for years can suddenly become more conscious about their conditions. I'm not talking about two distinct types of people. I'm talking about different possibilities for different people at different times."

"So if people are differently influenced at different times," David said, "then maybe at different times they're more capable of hearing what you're trying to tell them?"

"When the alien energy comes in," Sarah said, "something about that person at that time takes in the energy, maybe wants or needs it. So yes, maybe at another time they'll want or need something else. All this only brings me back to the original issue. How do I get across to people what's happening to them?"

"It sounds like with some people, you can't, at least not until they're ready."

Sarah stretched her fingers and arms, trying to slide away the frustration of the answer. "Maybe not. On the other hand, what that also means is that with some people, I can." She looked at the new David. "There must be others like you out there," she said. "The question is how many and how to find them."

*

Subject: Oliver Lowell
Third Psychiatric Interview
Lorton Prison
April 4, 1999

Dr. Rudolph Stein and Dr. Henry Whitlow

Q: We'd like to talk about your past. Family, hometown, friends, things like that.

A: What's that got to do with anything?

Q: Clearly you're an important person in this situation you've been describing. We want to know why you were chosen.

A: I'm not important. Just doing my duty.

Q: Your modesty is admirable. You're important to *us* because you're helping us figure out what's going on. We need to know more about you.

A: If you put it that way, okay.

Q: What was it like growing up? What was your family like? Your town?

A: I don't want anybody talking badly about my parents. They don't have anything to do with this.

Q: We appreciate your loyalty. They must be special to you.

A: I can take them or leave them. But they're my parents, and I don't want anybody talking about them.

Q: They both worked hard, it seems.

A: That's right. That's what you do in my town, work. Unless you're one of the college Liberal Jews. Then you do what you please.

Q: The way you say "work" sounds as though you don't like work much.

A: What's to like? Slaving like an animal so you can eat enough and sleep enough and have clothes enough to go on slaving like an animal.

Q: You drove a truck for a while?

A: Yes. The same thing over and over until you go crazy. I hear the sound of truck wheels sometimes when I sleep. The ba-dump ba-dump ba-dump going along the road at night when the rest of the world is quiet and you're stuck, headed nowhere. When I'm dreaming, it goes on and on like it did when I was awake, so what's the fucking difference?

Q: You quit trucking eventually? Went on to do some electrical work?

A: Yes.

Q: Was that any better?

A: No.

Q: What didn't you like about it?

A: Messing around in people's walls. Trying to get them hooked into the same system that made them miserable in the first place. Messing with people's wires is like messing with their minds. The TV and other wires keep them hooked up.

Q: What do you mean, hooked up?

A: Hooked up to the government messages that keep decent Americans slaving in misery. The TV sends messages constantly. Sooner or later, you can't tell the difference between the world and the television. It seems like it's letting you see everything, but it's keeping you from seeing. If you let it send you messages long enough, sooner or later you *become* TV. You think what it thinks and act the way it tells you. I cut myself off. You know how? For about a month I watched nothing but static, those black and white dots sizzling on the screen. Hours at a time. It burned the TV right out of me. TV's nothing but sizzling dots, you know that? If you think it's making a picture, that's because you haven't realized it's only dots.

Q: It sounds like between trucking and electric work, you've never done any work you liked?

A: People like me aren't supposed to do work we like. We're supposed to do work that other people want us to do.

Q: When did this idea first occur to you?

A: It's not an idea. It's the truth.

Q: When did you first realize it was the case?

A: I think I've known all my life. It's one of the first things I noticed, that work is killing everybody. Not like a plague, not wiping everybody out at once, but slowly and surely draining the life out of people. Work is supposed to give people pride, but it takes away their pride. It's supposed to give them families, but it takes away their families. I could see that from the time I was a kid. The strange thing is, the fact that I could see it made people hate me. People think it's a nasty violation of their privacy if you understand what's destroying them.

Q: You feel that people hate you because you know too much about them?

A: Of course. It's why *you* hate me. I know exactly what you guys are about, pretending to ask sympathetic questions when you don't give a shit. I know who you work for and why you work for them.

Q: Why are you bothering to answer our questions then?

A: It's my duty to help you see things clearly, even if I'm sure you don't want to and won't.

Q: You seem to have some history of mental health treatment. Could you explain why?

A: It was the only way they could get me after I shut down the TV voices.

Q: What was?

A: To put other voices in my head, then turn them off, then start them again and turn them off and so on.

Q: The voices you heard were a result of your treatment?

A: Treatment? Why don't we just call it training?

Q: The voices were put in your head by whom?

A: The government, of course, and their secret little groups.

Q: You don't believe you were given medical treatment to help you with mental difficulties, namely schizophrenia?

A: Sure I was having difficulties. The people you worked for caused them.

Q: So if you were to characterize your life before you were contacted by the people of another world, what would you say?

A: My life had no meaning before I was contacted.

Q: How so?

A: I've been telling you. Where I grew up, there was nothing to believe in. The people who did believe in things couldn't face that there was nothing to believe in. That's the kind of world you people have given us. If somebody comes along who *can* look the truth in the face, you call him a liar, insane, a criminal. You're sitting here listening to me say this, listening to me tell you what you are, and it's still having no effect on you.

Q: You seem upset. Maybe we should continue this conversation later.

A: Since you're not asking me whether I want to continue, I won't answer that. You know the world is tearing itself apart as you sit here asking me nonsense, and you don't even care. You decided in advance I was crazy, and now you're looking for something to back up what you already believe. And you know what? Even if I was crazy, I'd still be a better person than either of you.

*

The waiter's muscular forearms went taut as he set the food on their table in his tightly-fitting white shirt. He was a young guy, fresh, even glittering in certain angles of the restaurant's dim silvery light.

"This restaurant's so romantic," Geena said.

"What?" Jerry was trying to shake the buzzing in his head.

"It's so romantic that you've brought me to this restaurant. The view of the city is lovely."

"I knew you'd like it." Jerry looked over at Geena, whose face was oddly blurry. She seemed a shapeless blob plopped down in a chair. "Anything for my girl."

Geena giggled. "You look handsome tonight," she said. "That's a fantastic suit."

Jerry said nothing. Of course it was a fantastic suit.

The waiter came back with the final course of their meal. He leaned down over the table gracefully, then straightened up and slipped away.

"Is there something about the waiter you don't like?" Geena said.

"No. Why?"

"You keep staring at him."

"No I don't."

"But you just…"

"No I didn't," Jerry said.

Geena squinted with confusion. "My mistake."

"Don't worry about it," Jerry shrugged. He raised his wine glass.

"To a wonderful girl and a wonderful future."

"To a wonderful man." They clinked glasses. "You know," Geena said, "sometimes it still amazes me we're going out."

"Why?"

"It just seemed for the longest time that you didn't like me much. When you asked me out, I was surprised. Don't get me wrong. I was happy about it. But I've always wanted to ask. Did you change your mind about me or what?"

"I always had my eye on you," Jerry said. "I know quality when I see it."

Geena smiled. "Then what took you so long to…"

"It wasn't that long," Jerry said. "I was just waiting for the right moment."

"You're sure?"

"You're not doubting me, are you?"

"No. Just curious, that's all."

"I understand," Jerry said. "What can I say? I'm an interesting guy."

They turned to their food and ate for a while in silence. The restaurant wasn't too crowded and the decor was top quality, refined and restrained. The wide windows of the restaurant, on all sides, looked out from the 45th floor. Jerry could almost see Geena fading into the distance of the city, disappearing layer by layer until she was nothing. Where was that waiter? It was strange, but seeing him calmed the buzzing in Jerry's head. It wasn't really a headache. It started along with the phone call that afternoon, the same strange beeps he had been getting for several weeks now, as if some secret code were being relayed to him. The waiter couldn't have anything to do with it. He must work out a lot though, to get forearms like that. Why wasn't he coming by again?

"The food's very good," Geena said.

"I've had better," Jerry said.

When they were nearly finished, the waiter showed up again and asked about dessert. Geena said no. Jerry, who a moment earlier had told Geena he didn't want dessert, suddenly changed his mind and ordered dessert for both of them. The waiter walked off.

"Is something wrong?" Geena said.

"No. Why?"

"You just have a funny expression on your face, like you're in pain or something."

"You suppose that waiter's gay?" Jerry said.

"Just a little." Geena smiled.

"I don't like gay people," Jerry said.

"That's an old-fashioned view, isn't it?"

"Is it?" Jerry said. "Oh well."

"Oh come on," Geena laughed. "What could possibly be wrong with being gay?"

"They don't contribute anything to the future," Jerry said. He pointed disapprovingly at the air. "They're not going to have families. They get to play around, doing who knows what, while they leave the serious business of taking care of society to others." A rush of pain shot through his head; why wouldn't the buzzing stop? "A man should take care of business. He needs to be responsible for women and children. He has to be focused and hard-working. But gay guys—if you can call them guys at all—sit around and do what they want. Work as waiters if they feel like it, just for their own spending money. It's not only not fair, it's an insult to men like me who have to take charge."

Geena was staring at him searchingly, as if she wished she knew what he was talking about.

"Do you think I'm wrong?" Jerry said.

Geena smiled. "I think you're brilliant," she said, "even when I don't understand you."

Jerry grinned, and raised his wine glass again.

After dinner, Jerry suggested they go out on the town, though he actually felt tired. When Geena said that maybe he should just take her home, he quickly agreed. They pulled up to Geena's apartment in a cab and got out.

"I'll leave you here," Jerry said.

"Why don't you come in?" Geena asked. She leaned close to him, put a forefinger on his chest. "You've been a real gentleman these last few weeks, but you don't need to be too much of one."

"I don't know if I should," Jerry hesitated, grimacing. "I've got a headache."

"Of course you should," Geena said. "I guarantee you won't regret it."

The image of the waiter's forearms still burned in Jerry's imagination. Who the hell did that queer think he was? "Okay. I can come in for a bit. I might need some aspirin though."

"Anything you need, you can have." Geena grabbed his arm and pulled him forward.

A few minutes later, she put Jerry on the couch, a drink in his hand as well as the aspirin. "I'll be back soon," she said.

To Jerry, even with his head buzzing, it seemed like a scene from a movie. He was being treated the way a man should be treated. A drink, a classy apartment in the city, a beautiful girl of taste and refinement. Marinda could go screw herself. Sure, he didn't feel aroused by Geena. He tried to picture touching her and imagined her as mushy, a piece of rotten fruit. That was just his fuzzy head talking, the annoyance of having his manhood insulted by the waiter. When Geena came back he'd do her up right, make her crazy with longing for him.

He'd had sex with girls, a number of times, although none recently. In college he'd even had a girlfriend for several months, although eventually he lost interest. The more a girl liked him, the more bored he became. Sure, sex was the important part, but what was the point in having sex too often with a girl who let you go right ahead? When things were too easy, it was no wonder that sex wasn't interesting.

Geena came back, sauntering towards him as if unable to stand straight. She was wearing a sheer, light green nightie. Jerry couldn't decide whether she looked more like an old lime or a baggy slice of kiwi. She was glowing, bright and round with youth and energy. He wished she'd turn it off so he could sit in the dark with the mushy fruit. They all wanted him, these women. He wished he was home in bed.

"Hey there," she said. "How's my man?"

"Bring it on, baby," he said, squinting at her brightness.

Then she was sitting next to him and her lips were brushing his cheek. They tickled like a fly landing on his face. He reached out his hand as if to swat them. Sitting there pressed against him, she smelled sickly sweet, fleshy. There was an inner softness about her that might melt in his hands, get gooey all over him. A messy mud puddle. He became aware that she was saying his name, the syllables deep in her throat.

And just like that, her tongue was deep in *his* throat. Was she trying to choke the life out of him? It was sloppy and wet, every bit as mushy as he imagined. He pulled back, tried to figure out what was happening. Why were women so sloppy, undefined, vague? A real man—a man like him—couldn't be like that. Women wanted to take that away, to drown men in mush.

"What's wrong?" Geena was breathing heavily. "This is so good, what's wrong? Are you sick? You look sick."

"Nothing's wrong," Jerry said. "Come here."

Then her tongue was in his throat again. He wanted to gag, forced his stomach to stay down. This was what a man wanted, wasn't it? To have something to let his hardness melt into? He didn't want to melt. He felt too melted already, too much like he and Geena together would become a sloppy, melted pool of nothing. He couldn't feel his own muscle, needed to. His or anyone's. Anyone's? He pulled Geena close to him, grabbed the nightie and ripped at the buttons.

"You're an animal," she gasped.

"The ultimate animal," he said.

She was wearing nothing now but small sheer panties. The flesh around her waist and arms was blotchy, and her breasts… no. He shut his eyes. Dinner churned in his stomach and his head buzzed wildly. He had seen naked women before. Had he ever looked at one this closely? Did women really look like that? Like what? He kept his eyes closed. If he looked and saw, really saw, he had no idea what would happen. He felt his head rolling back, his eyes lost in darkness.

Her body pressed against him, warm, smooth, soft. "Oh Jerry," she said. "I've thought about this for so long. I want you so badly. I'm so happy you want me."

He reached out his arms. He was going to pull her to him, wasn't he, like a man was supposed to? Yes, he was going to…

He pushed her back, hard, off the couch. She cracked into the coffee table and shouted in pain. When he heard her shout, he opened his eyes. She lay there a moment like a puddle, then tried to stand. Her foot slipped out from under her and she fell heavily onto one knee.

"Why'd you do that?" Jerry said.

"Do what?" Geena's eyes quivered with surprise, perhaps with hurt.

"That. Whatever you did."

"I don't know what I did," she said. "I'm sorry, whatever it was." She stayed on the floor, disheveled, half-naked.

"You're not sorry. You did it on purpose."

"I don't understand. What?"

"Do you think I can get it on with a girl who does something like that? It's disgusting."

Geena's eyes sprang into tears. "I don't understand," she said. "I'm sorry I'm sorry I'm sorry, whatever it was. Why are you looking at me like that?"

"You didn't have to do it," Jerry said. Behind his eyes, the buzzing felt like it would split open his head. "You could have left me alone."

"Left you alone? But we're… this is our perfect night, isn't it? This has been our perfect night."

"It was until you…"

"What? Until I what?"

"You're going to stand there, no, lie there, and pretend you don't know what you did?"

"What did I do?"

"If you're going to deny it, I can't continue this conversation at all."

"I don't deny it," Geena said. "I'm sure I did it and I'm sure it was wrong. You need to tell me from your point of view what it was, so I don't do it again."

"You won't do it again," he said. "I'm not going to give you the chance."

"Oh my God, what are you saying?" Panic burst out over her body and she stood, shaking. "What are you saying to me?" She grabbed at him.

Jerry pushed her hands away. He didn't know who she was, could barely remember her name. "It doesn't matter what I'm saying. As far as you're concerned, whatever I do couldn't possibly matter one way or the other." He was already headed towards the door.

"You're leaving?" she practically screamed. "My God, Jerry, don't go. I'm apologizing as much as I can. I'm saying I'm sorry, I'm so so sorry."

"I don't care what you are," Jerry said. "Stay away from me."

Crying no, she lunged at him, tried to grab him again. Her flesh bounced in a nauseating way. Her fingers—they were clammy—

raked his forearm, and he slapped at them. "Don't fucking touch me," he said. "If you touch me again, I won't be responsible for what I do."

She took a step back, her eyes wide with confusion and, now, fear.

"Don't call me," he said, "ever. As far as you're concerned, I don't exist. Understand that?"

If she answered him, he didn't hear. He was out the door into the hallway, taking deep breaths so not to throw up, head pounding as if it intended to split in half. "Who does she think she is?" he said to the walls. He staggered down the stairs and into the hot night, where nobody could get near him or touch him.

*

Tony Stevens's eyes throbbed, which they did a lot, but tonight they throbbed even more. Ever since he'd quit his job at the Montgomery County Regional Services Center, people thought they could give him as much shit as they wanted. It had been a mistake to move back with his mom, even temporarily and with his dad long gone. The weeks he had meant to be there had become months. He'd thought about retail jobs, but he was a college graduate and made for better things. He was tired of doing crappy work for stupid people. His mother didn't understand, thought he was loafing, a feeling which showed in her face when she was sober and which she let loose when she was drunk, which these days was more often than not. She would even bug him when he brought home an occasional woman from a bar or party, like she had a right to tell him who could be in the house.

Still, living with his mother was better than getting back with his wife, who started bitching whenever he showed his face around her apartment. He wanted to see his son sometimes, really did, but who could stand to listen to her? He might still have been with her if she didn't criticize everything he did, never wanting him to go out alone and always asking where he'd been. Sure, he'd gone around with other women, a little after-hours fun here and there, but nothing serious. But she had to get up in his face all the time. Besides, after she'd had the kid she'd been no fun anymore, went to work all day, leaving the kid in day care, which was just wrong, then coming home and always saying she was too tired to party. Once she had the office job, she didn't even make dinner for him anymore, then complained if he stayed out for happy hour when it was the only way he could get something to eat. She was still bleeding him dry, always asking for money for the kid when she knew he wasn't working much. He gave her some here and there because he didn't want her to sue for child support. It was starting to look like she might do that anyway, so he'd decided against giving her more. If she was determined to fuck with him, he'd be damned if he was going to help her do it.

To top everything off, things were screwed with Stacey, his girlfriend. Last week at Mulligan's he'd arrived to find her already partying, laughing loudly, deep in conversation with two guys, one with a stupid-looking scraggly goatee. She didn't even see him until he walked up behind her. She stepped away from the guys and played like nothing was going on. She even tried to get him to leave the bar with her, probably because she thought he might kick those guys' asses. He told her she might as well fucking stay and walked out. He saw her car in the parking lot and scraped his key along its side. She could do what she wanted, but if she messed around behind his back, she'd answer for it.

So everything was fucked. How could he get his life together if every time he made the effort, someone tried to stop him? He wasn't like a lot of the low-class scumbags who hung out at Mulligan's on a Tuesday. His father was an eye doctor, and even though the man had a new wife and family up in Pennsylvania, he'd still left Tony's mother a nice house and money to get by, although she usually refused to give Tony any. Tony had never been that great a student, sure, because he had too many friends who liked to party (and what was wrong with that?), but he still had a degree in business from the University of Maryland. He'd even worked for a big economics firm a while before they booted him out for showing up late a time or two.

He'd never seen Mulligan's this much of a madhouse on a Tuesday. Add in a steamy June night and the air conditioning not working well and things were pretty much going crazy. People were bombed. He had drunk enough to feel rowdy, although he could swear each drink only made his eyes hurt worse. The place reeked of armpits and spilled liquor. Stacey hadn't showed yet. He was looking around the bar, trying to figure out what kind of losers came out on a night like this: some office-worker types, some dudes in Hawaiian shirts who weren't at the beach, and a lot of guys who worked in nearby stores or otherwise hung around the neighborhood. A lot of girls too, partying just as hard. He'd talked to a couple already, and probably could have taken someone home if he had been in a better mood. That would be the real kicker, wouldn't it? To be so pissed off that he couldn't get laid.

His eyes had been throbbing since the afternoon. His phone kept ringing while he tried to sleep through his hangover. Only, every time he picked up the phone, nobody was there, just this odd beeping signal, over and over. He would have turned off the ringer except he was waiting for some calls that never came. As if he didn't have enough to worry about without the phone company messing up his line.

He reached under his shirt. The pistol was still strapped there. A Ruger Semi-Automatic. Powerful. He'd been making a little money through a friend of his who sold some guns on the side, nothing official. The guy needed help here and there; Tony did a little when he had a moment. He didn't make that much money, but he did pick up a few handguns and rifles for around the house. For once his mother didn't complain; they seemed to make her feel safer. At one point when the phone was ringing, he picked up the Ruger and came close to shooting the dial. Instead he grabbed the strap that fitted inside his shirt and fixed the pistol there, hidden. Having the Ruger against his flesh, he was ready for anything.

One or two people had passed out. Others were tossing back shots and shooters like the drinks were speeding down an assembly line. In a corner some people were singing loudly. A few couples seemed ready to get it on right in the bar. At least two girls who walked in alone not long ago had already found someone to swap tongue with. He didn't see Stacey anywhere. She better not be off with some guy or there was going to be hell to pay.

He found himself staring at some asshole wearing a red hunting coat and cap and who had a goatee. Where had he seen him before? It was… oh. He was one of the guys talking to Stacey last week. Who did that asshole think he was, talking to people's girlfriends and walking around with a stupid goatee like he was a star in some shitass slacker movie? Maybe he needed to know that he better not talk to people's girlfriends if he wasn't ready to answer for it. Tony felt the Ruger in the strap, tight against him.

Years later, Tony was still unable to convince himself whether, just then, he began to hallucinate. So maybe it didn't matter that at his trial, no one cared either way. The ceiling of the bar started breathing, like someone lifted the roof for a moment and set it back down. Then came the rush, a big wave of what? Invisible, rolling through the walls and down from the ceiling. It slammed through his body and filled it and sent him jerking around demented. An odd film blurred his eyes, like some sort of filter, and his thoughts ran away from him, into and through the film, as if it was channeling and blocking what he could think. His head buzzed like someone was about to bring a chainsaw down on top of it.

Through the haze, he could see what was going on in Mulligan's.

It made no sense. Some people were totally undressed, a few were fucking on the floor of the bar with frantic thrusts and shrieks. Some were walking around like zombies, movements awkward and forced, eyes empty or filled with surprised pain. Tony wondered a moment if he looked like that too, then couldn't wonder anymore. A shot went off somewhere, then another. A man crumpled over a chair. The ceiling kept breathing. It was alive, shuddering. Whatever had started the whole thing continued to pour into the room, wave after wave of it, slamming into people's bodies and carrying them away.

He moved forward. Some part of his mind managed to notice what was happening. Most of him was focused on the goal he had just been given. Once you had a goal, why think about anything else? That thought passed through his head and so he had to be thinking a little, only it wasn't really like thinking. He no longer had options.

The guy with the goatee was sucking on the breasts of a woman, naked from the waist up, both of them like bad actors playing a sex scene. Tony moved towards them. The woman's head was thrown back, her mouth opening and closing like she was trying to speak some line she had forgotten.

Tony undid a few buttons on his shirt and fumbled under it for the gun, found it. He grabbed the guy with the goatee and spun him around. The guy flashed Tony a dazed, empty expression, like the personality had been sucked from his face. Tony felt the gun kick. The guy in the goatee flew out of his hands in a liquid roar and collapsed. Tony's arms and hands were soaked. Everything seemed far away. He turned to the woman, who stared at him with mouth slightly open, lips thick and inviting. He reached out and grabbed hold of her waist, pulled her towards him, her flesh against him, tongue all over his face. In his hands the gun went off again, kicking back powerfully. The woman collapsed too. Gun shots sounded elsewhere, mixed with shouts and orgasmic groans. Many more people were naked. Tony moved towards the bar. The whole place was still breathing. He breathed with it, as if its breaths were his. He sat on a stool, blankly.

He had no idea how long it was until sirens were rushing closer and the bar was on fire. He stood and walked outside into the parking lot, where several small fires had been set. Other people were moving around in the lot. A small grassy hill bordered the lot and Tony went over to it. He set the gun down and lay back against the grass, empty and utterly satisfied.

SEVEN

That morning, Sarah and David were sitting in a coffee shop, reading the paper, each drinking coffee and eating a muffin. It seemed like the two of them had already fallen into a routine, no matter the state of the world. To the people sitting nearby, or grabbing their coffee and going, they probably looked like an ordinary couple having a surprisingly leisurely mid-week morning, just another New York professional and his accomplished, artsy wife, David in an untucked button-down and slacks, Sarah in flat shoes, slightly flared jeans and a plain black shirt. With all the walks they'd been taking, and a better diet, David looked thinner.

"What do you think?" Sarah said.

"I can't even begin," David said.

The New York Times headline NIGHTMARE IN THE SUBURBS preceded a story about the Maryland nightclub, Mulligan's, where people had given in to some odd group hysteria. Shootings and stabbings. The detail that most covered the news though was that the police, when they arrived, found a number of patrons in what could be described only as an orgy, a mass sexual dementia that swept everyone up.

"Eight people dead," Sarah said, "in some out-of-control bar fight? And a lot of people in a sexual frenzy? It has to be what we think."

"It's just speculation." David's shoulders hunched towards his neck. "We don't really know anything. Still."

"The way the energy comes through has an essentially sexual element. What if that part went crazy?"

"Could be. But sexual energy gets out of control all the time."

"Sure," Sarah said. A man walking close behind her with a cup of coffee peered down at the headline of her newspaper before going out the door. "But this out of control? Affairs, violent obsessions, yes, but a mass orgy while people are being shot and stabbed? That seems a little more than pent-up frustration."

"It does," David said.

"I don't know what to do." Sarah sighed. "I have no way of knowing where something is going to happen. I can't be everywhere. Even if I could, what would it matter? Maybe the energy was so powerful it would have caught me up too. Just because I see it coming doesn't mean I'm immune."

"I bet it helps though. What did you do about things like this before? When some kind of disaster happened?"

"Before? Nothing. I mean, I couldn't, could I?" She stared around the coffee shop as if asking everybody the question.

"So why should you be able to do something now? What's different?"

"Because I understand what's happening."

"So because you understand what's happening, you should be able to stop it?"

Sarah looked at him. "You're right," she said. "Understanding something may have nothing to do with being able to affect it. You also have to have power. And I don't, do I?"

"No." David pushed some advertising sections of the paper aside.

"It's frustrating. What's the good of knowing what's wrong if you can't do something to make it right?" David started to say something but she waved him off. "I'm just venting," she said. "Maybe there's somebody I can help, a person or two."

"You've helped me," he said.

"Have I?"

"Yes."

"That's good." Sarah smiled. "It's not enough though. Helping your friends while the world goes mad doesn't quite count as effective response."

"How much more can you do?"

"I can try to help as many people as possible."

"Sure," David said.

Sarah shook her head, laughing with outrage. "Is this what's going to happen? My searching the news every day to see what parts of the world have been seized by alien energy? If I'm not there, how am I going to tell? All I'm going to get is the news, and the news is only going to say what it thinks I should know. So how can I possibly recognize the difference between a disaster caused by alien energy and one that would have happened anyway?"

David stretched as if getting tension out of his back. "Any idea what you want to do now?"

*

"How's the daily grind?" Herbert asked Marinda that evening, when they'd been seated at the table in the bar long enough to feel comfortable. He slouched in his yellow print shirt, leaning at an angle that made him look like he might throw himself across the table.

"It's not exactly love at first sight," Marinda said. She was wearing work clothes, pants and a vaguely masculine jacket in an understated beige, tight at the waist; it made her feel like a robot. "What's funny is I don't hate it either. It's just something to do, you know, like anything else I might do. Like I'm in this oddly silent cocoon, even though there's office noise all around me. I don't do much in the cocoon: carry this or that from here to there, make copies. It's not a good calmness though. More a numbness."

"It's essential to be alienated from work," Herbert said.

"I don't feel alienated." Marinda smiled wryly. "I don't feel connected either. It's more like a neutral non-being. There are decent moments. I like dogs well enough. Here I've been all my life not thinking that much about dogs, liking them just fine I guess, but hardly thinking about them. Now I find out that dogs are something these people think about all the time. It's a dog cult. There's this whole world of incredible disasters and pleasures, but that just gets in the way of thinking about dogs and the business surrounding dogs. There's something beautiful about it, except it's also weird. Imagine being committed to something so relatively trivial. Not that I care that much about doing something important."

"Don't you think happiness is nothing more than committing to something trivial?" Herbert said. "Besides, maybe it's not dogs who are trivial. Maybe it's humans."

"Right now I think happiness would consist of getting another drink." Marinda looked around. "Suppose that waitress is feeling too alienated to come over here?"

"I'm sure she's feeling alienated," Herbert said. "I envy her. We get to sit here doing what we want and are unable to feel good about it. She gets to be a waitress and feel terrible. At least she knows what her enemy is."

"Does everything you say tonight have to be some nihilistic comment?" Exhaustion washed over Marinda. "You're getting trapped in your own shtick."

"Sorry. I was trying to say nothing. I'll have to say less."

"Oh, here she comes," Marinda said, waving in the waitress's direction.

A moment later they had another round in hand, gin and tonic for Marinda, white wine for Herbert. The bar was small and crowded, like hundreds of other bars in New York. It was June and there had already been a lot of hot days, but they weren't so far into the summer that the city had cleared out. People walked by on the street outside, headed wherever they were headed. There were so many people, Marinda thought. They all had their own individual lives that she would never know anything about. A group at the table next to her stood up and left, leaving a copy of the *Daily News* behind. She picked it up.

"Can you believe that happened?" She pointed to the headline.

"I can believe that anything happened," Herbert said. "Nothing's so outrageous that it's not going on somewhere."

With typically ironic melodrama, the *Daily News* screamed what every other newspaper in the U.S. screamed that day:

**FRENZY OF SEX AND VIOLENCE
IN SUBURBAN NIGHTCLUB
8 DEAD, 20 WOUNDED**

"They must have gone completely nuts," Marinda said. "What on earth could have caused it?"

"Something totally random, I'd imagine," Herbert said. "The wrong combination of events at exactly the wrong moment."

Marinda shook her head. "Some people were having sex even while the shooting was going on? Is that some kind of new turn on? Screwing in the face of random death?"

"Or dying in the face of random screwing?"

Marinda restrained an urge to laugh. People had died; it wasn't a game. "I've never heard anything like it. I didn't know it was possible to invent new types of sickness."

"It's always possible to invent new types of sickness," Herbert said. "I've been trying my best, but too many others are far ahead of me."

"It was in the suburbs too, and the people weren't college kids or anything." Marinda stared, incredulous, at the paper.

"The most out-of-control violence in America happens in the suburbs." Herbert shifted in his chair. "There's no one to stop you because no one's looking."

"Nobody was ever looking when I lived there," Marinda said. "In southern California, teenagers can do just about anything and no one notices. But this seems pretty significant."

"It does sound significant." Herbert's face scrunched up. "That's what makes it boring. Significant things are never interesting. I'm much more interested in things most people don't think are significant."

"Like dogs?"

"Dogs are much more interesting than violence."

"I feel a theory coming on."

"I'm not sure we need to dignify it." Herbert leaned back and smiled as if something had occurred to him. "The concentration on what's significant might just help us miss everything significant. Or insignificant, if you will. What's the difference?"

"I'm lost," Marinda laughed, "and not for the first time."

"Aren't you lucky? See," Herbert leaned forward again, put his hands down so hard on the table that it jumped up slightly, startling them both, "there's this idea that some events and things are significant, and others insignificant. Apparently we should pay attention to the significant ones and not be distracted by the rest. Never mind the problem that there are competing versions of what counts as significant; there's still this idea that we need to distinguish.

So we spend most of our time concentrating on things that we or some others have decided are significant and ignore everything else. But if we're spending all our energy looking at these significant things, how much of our lives do we actually notice?"

"My life certainly isn't of earth-shattering significance," Marinda said.

"So what that means is we're missing most things. We're giving all our attention to some disaster in the news, or some conflict with authority, or some personal relationship that's supposed to solve all our problems, even though we'll have left it behind in a few months. And the rest of what's going on escapes us."

"Like what?"

"Who knows?" Herbert flailed his arms as if trying to gather up the room. "All the things that go on automatically, or the things on the street we pass by in a hurry. I have a plant with a leak at the bottom of its pot. If I put too much water in it, the water drips through, leaving a little on the window sill but sometimes seeping past that too and dripping to the floor. I don't know that it's going to happen; I'll go on doing something else, then hear this drip drip drip and look over, and these little drops are falling onto the floor. Who could possibly care, right?"

"You beat me to it."

"One day I sat there and looked at it for a while. There's this stain on the window sill, and a stain on the wall where the water drips down, and a little wet spot on the floor. It was absorbing, pun intended of course. There was a pattern. Not a method, because it was an accident."

"You're awfully close to saying we need to take time to smell the roses," Marinda said.

"Not at all," Herbert shook his head. "The person who's taking the time to smell the roses is replacing one concept of significance with another. I'm not saying we should stop to watch the water stain.

There's no way to think of it as a significant, not to the plant, not to me. How much of our experience is like that? Nothing changes because of it, and after a moment you don't even remember it. So what? How many supposedly important things do you remember either? They pass too."

"Your whole argument seems entirely too focused." Marinda took a drink. "All this purpose is wearing me out."

"I used to think," Herbert said, "that I was going to devote my life to pursuing the trivial. I don't want to be famous, rich, well-liked, well-respected—all the significant, powerful things that drive everyone mad. I don't want to be unknown, poor, or hated either. Far too melodramatic. But trivial, that seemed something worth devoting myself to. Besides, how much can we understand about supposedly important things if we don't understand that important things always take place against the backdrop of what's unimportant? Then I thought, what's all this about devoting my life? As if the things that have caused most trouble aren't the things that people have devoted their lives to."

"So you couldn't devote yourself to the trivial because that would make the trivial important and start the cycle again?"

"Right."

Marinda took another drink, pulled her elbows tight against her sides as if protecting herself. "How did we get onto this? Weren't we talking about sex and violence in the suburbs?"

"That's where it started. I don't remember why."

"Because eight people were killed in a nightclub last night."

"I'm sorry to hear it," Herbert said.

*

Jerry tried to call Marinda several times over the night and into the next day. He thought maybe she was just letting the answering machine pick up, but he went over to her place and no one was there. He left a message on her cell, though it was pointless. Marinda checked her cell only every three or four days at most, and often let the battery run down. She'd heard stories of how easy it was to get hold of cell numbers. Every time she turned it on, she was afraid she'd find a message from Steve. Jerry didn't believe the horror stories but hadn't been able to convince her. Weirdly, half the time he picked up his home phone, that strange beeping signal was there. He'd find himself getting lost in it a few moments, his head throbbing in time with it before he put the phone down angrily.

What had happened was partly, maybe mainly, Marinda's fault. Now she wasn't available to talk about it. He would never have gone so far with Geena if Marinda hadn't said what she had. She'd had no right and he had to prove her wrong, quickly. Geena was the most convenient way. But it was clear that Geena was a mistake. Why did most women have to be so soft, round, fleshy, disgusting? How was a man supposed to be a man if women couldn't take care of their bodies?

It was early evening. Unshaven and sweaty, he went into a bar and ordered a drink, brought it over to a window seat. Why did he keep screwing everything up? His father was a man, took care of everything, made tons of money, had women galore and ultimately a beautiful wife. He had showed Jerry what to do. Women wanted Jerry, and he wanted them too, so why, lately, couldn't he get it done? Why did he keep thinking about men, wondering what it would be like to press up against their strength, to give himself away to it? He startled. What the hell was wrong with him? His headache from yesterday had calmed, although he sensed that it could break out again any moment.

Marinda kept turning him down; that had to be the problem. He'd known her since they were children in California. Their fathers were friends, strong, successful men, although Jerry had to admit that Marinda's father had recently become flaky. Jerry first played with Marinda when he was six and she four. At an afternoon party he chased her around the pool and through the yard, then feigned indifference until she chased him. He didn't remember it, but both sets of parents talked about it. It was like he and Marinda were destined to be together. She was pretty too, although he had to admit that he'd never felt sexually aroused by her. But that was probably because he knew her so well.

He ordered another drink. Everything was falling apart. He felt a rush of hatred for Marinda, absolute loathing. She didn't do anything with her life and thought she was perfectly justified in screwing up his.

He felt drunk, though not enough. He sensed someone—some guy—out on the street staring at him. The guy moved towards the door. He was big and walked abruptly, with either hostility or anger. He also seemed familiar, but looking out into the dark and the blinking lights it was hard for Jerry to tell. The guy yanked open the door of the bar and a moment later, in his jeans and Pearl Jam t-shirt, he stood in front of Jerry, body tense, an animal about to strike. "I didn't know you were in New York," he said.

"Steve." Jerry made no effort to shake his hand, not that Steve held one out.

"I thought you went back to California with Marinda," Steve said.

"No. We decided against it."

"We? What do you mean? You're not telling me Marinda's in New York?"

Jerry looked at him. With taut arms and clenching hands, Steve was a strong man, uptight, who seemed dangerous. Jerry hadn't thought about Steve much since the guy disappeared from Marinda's life. He knew Marinda had a restraining order against Steve and had tricked him into thinking she'd gone back to California. He knew

Marinda insisted that if Steve ever found Jerry, or called him, that under no circumstances should he tell Steve anything about her, especially not where she was.

"Yeah," Jerry said. "She's in New York." He wasn't going to back down; he took a step closer to Steve. "Why should she leave because of you?"

"Where is she?"

"What do you want, her address? She doesn't want to see you. If you try to contact her, she'll call the cops."

"She's in New York." Steve's voice was rough, threatening. "Tell me where."

'No."

"That's too bad," Steve said. "People who mess with me end up regretting it."

Jerry scoffed. "You sound like a bad movie. I have a powerful family and powerful friends. Don't even breathe on me funny."

Steve smiled. "Never mind. I know she's here. It shouldn't be too hard to get details."

"She can have you arrested. You know that."

"Still pissed off she liked me more, huh?" Jerry startled; how could Steve have known? "You and her crazy family think you can cage her up. She knows better. Her thinking might be twisted right now, but I'll get through to her."

"Get through to her for what? To tell her you're out of your mind?"

"I can see what you are," Steve said. "A rich parasite exploiting the ignorance of others. People like you have no right to live."

Adrenaline surged through Jerry's body. "I'm glad you have a chance to tell me now, because it's the only chance you'll get."

"Don't think I can't see what you've done to her," Steve went on. "Told her lies and made her weak and dependent. You've stomped all over her. There's going to be no more of that. Once we're back together, she's going to see it all."

"Back together?" Surprise pushed briefly through Jerry's disdainful frown. "Are you fucking nuts? She hates you more than any person she's ever known."

"Believe what you want to believe," Steve said. "I'd tell you to watch out, only you'll never see it coming."

Jerry bristled. "Don't threaten me. I'll fuck you up so totally you'll wish you'd never heard my name."

Steve's stare was flat and removed. "I appreciate the information, Jerry. You know, if I hadn't run into you, I might never have found Marinda."

Jerry started to say something but swallowed it. The pit of his stomach lurched.

"I'll be sure to let her know to thank you." Steve turned away and went out the door of the bar.

Jerry's hands were shaking. He had to do something, but what? Another drink? Would that help give him time to decide? He walked over to the bar.

*

Cynthia looked at her watch again. Forty-five minutes late. She hoped something serious hadn't happened to Steve. She also hoped something not serious *had* happened. Steve was always ridiculously punctual. It wouldn't have been an issue, except for the whole last week she'd had the sense that things weren't going well. It shocked her that she wanted him so much so fast. The moment she knew it was the moment she realized something about him was uncertain.

There was nothing overt, but with men there often wasn't. Even when they were telling her what they were thinking, she always suspected there was something else they weren't saying. She'd never been able to figure whether it was something they knew or something they weren't even telling themselves. That was the thing that made men so impossible. They didn't want to think about what they were feeling so they didn't want to talk about it and probably didn't know what it was. Then, sometimes after months of awkwardness, came the blow up. Everything the man had been feeling but hadn't been thinking about overtook him in a panic, and he wasn't going to talk about the panic either, just act on it. Sleep with somebody else, or stop answering phone calls or quit his job and move across the country without saying why. Men spent all their time pretending everything was okay until they couldn't pretend anymore, then wham.

Her mind kept circling around the same questions. There had been hints with Steve, yes, but nothing more. Maybe she was misreading them. Why always jump to the worst conclusion? She didn't do that in other areas of her life. On the other hand, it wasn't like she had no reason. Still, with Steve there wasn't much to go on. Although sometimes he seemed too distracted, they'd slept together quite a few times and it had been more or less good and seemed to be getting better. But there was something distant about Steve that stayed distant, focused on the act more than her while it was happening, then drawing himself up afterwards into a tight shell, as if for him the world outside his own calculations didn't count. She used "calculations" rather than "thoughts" on purpose. She could sometimes see his eyes moving back and forth as if he was trying to add up the world to some conclusion.

Of course, when they weren't having sex it wasn't like Steve was a model of openness and giving. He never entirely lost his uptightness and was relentlessly wary. Although she tried to help him take things easier, it hadn't worked. Sometimes he would stare at her as if he didn't know who she was.

But with men, didn't she have to get used to a certain lack of recognition? Busy denying they had personalities, they were hardly ever interested in the personalities of women either. So maybe it wasn't Steve, but a condition of being a guy. Besides, many of the other conditions that seemed to go along with being a guy, Steve avoided. He always went where he planned to go, arrived when he said he would, and did anything he promised. He dressed well and his apartment was clean. He didn't check out every woman who passed him on the street; he was what her friends would have called "unflirtable," the kind of guy who couldn't be drawn in by a laugh or a toss of the head or even something blatant like a hand hit lightly against his chest or fingers squeezing his arm. Cynthia didn't feel worried he was going to take up with another woman, although he still talked too much about his ex-girlfriend Marinda, that weird California cult-freak chick. Still, she could even put that down to the genuine and restrained nature of his emotions. He had cared about her. He wanted a serious adult relationship. Sooner or later he wanted marriage, family, and a stable life. Wasn't that worth a little distant rigidness that would maybe go away over time?

But it came as a terrifying jolt when she realized, a day or two ago, that after dating Steve for nearly a month, she had never seen him laugh. Not even an understated one, or a witty, superior snicker, much less any good-natured howling. Didn't there have to be something wrong with a guy who didn't laugh? Then again, she'd had another boyfriend who'd laughed uproariously all the time, even during the final month they'd been together, when he'd been uproariously screwing some woman from his office. Steve didn't laugh, but it also seemed clear he didn't screw around.

Now he was over an hour late. When her intercom finally barked and his voice came over it asking to be buzzed into the building, she said "Sure" with a coldness that surprised her. It was just once, she reminded herself. Being angry would only give away that she was more worried than she should be.

She let him into the apartment. "You okay?" she asked. "I hope nothing's wrong. You were supposed to be here an hour ago."

"Everything's going to work out," Steve said. He was smiling in a way she'd never seen, like he was thinking about something thrilling, although it seemed like a smile from another planet. He was wearing a t-shirt and jeans, neat enough, but the sort of thing he wore at home, not when he took her out. "I always knew it would." His attitude wasn't even close to apologetic. He was almost swaggering, although he was also on edge, almost shaking.

"That's good," Cynthia said. "But I don't know what you're talking about."

"It's a relief," Steve said. "I told myself it would be confirmation, and here it is." He brushed past her, striding quickly towards the center of the room.

"I'm glad you're relieved," she said. "But I still don't understand."

"Marinda's in New York. She's been here all along. I don't know exactly where yet, but that guy Jerry is such an idiot, it shouldn't present any problem."

Cynthia felt momentarily dizzy. "Marinda?" she said. Steve stood there, still triumphant. "The weirdo religious chick who made your life hell for two years?"

"Right."

"She's visiting New York?"

"She never left. She just wanted me to believe she had. She lives here."

"She lives in New York? Marinda? The one you complain about endlessly?"

"Right."

She made an unresolved questioning motion with her hands. "So?"

Steve startled. "What?"

"I said, so? She's an ex-girlfriend you hate. What does it matter where she is?"

"She thought she was going to get away from me," Steve said.

"What are you talking about?" Cynthia knew her tone was

worried and hostile but she couldn't stop it.

"Who did she think she was, to think she could get away? She completely underestimates me. It's one of those things we'll have to discuss."

"What are you talking about?" Cynthia said again, more loudly than she'd intended. "She's your ex-girlfriend, so why does it matter? You're going out with me. What does she have to do with us?"

Steve stared at her finally, instead of focusing on some unknown elsewhere. "What are you asking me?" He clenched and unclenched his hands.

"What does your ex-girlfriend have to do with our relationship?"

"Relationship," Steve said. It wasn't a question. He was still staring at her, his face narrowed with scorn. "You think we're having a relationship?"

"What do you think we've been doing? Of course we're having a relationship. You've been sleeping over here, remember?"

"We're not having a 'relationship.'" Steve snorted as if he despised the word. "I don't recall the subject coming up."

Cynthia stepped back, stunned. "You don't recall the subject coming up? Maybe it didn't, not in so many words. What do you think has been going on with us? Just because we never talked about it directly as a relationship, that means nothing's going on?"

"I'm talking about a life and death matter here," Steve said. "Not some psychobabble about a relationship. You sound like you read women's magazines."

"Why are you talking to me like this?" Cynthia's cheeks were burning. "What do you mean, life and death matter?"

"I can finally make things right again," Steve said. "I've got the power."

His words seemed to be coming out of the mouth of someone she didn't know. A wave of fear shuddered through her. "The power? To do what?"

"I can take her away from them. They can't stop me this time. All that religious stuff, all the lies. I can sweep it away with the back of my hand. She doesn't have any choice."

"You're telling me you want to go back to your ex-girlfriend?" This time Cynthia's face flushed with anger. "That we're not having a relationship at all? You're standing here in my living room talking about going back to some other woman like I should have known you were going to all along? Why are you being an asshole?"

"Don't call me names," Steve said.

"What do you mean?" Cynthia said hotly. "You've been sleeping in my bed, having sex with me. You've been going around town with me saying you want to have a wife and a family and you can't even acknowledge that something's going on between us? Then you find out there's a woman in New York who won't talk to you, and all of a sudden you're having a permanent relationship with her?" She heard what she was saying and her rage stopped. "Oh my God. There's a woman trying to hide from you. And I know why, don't I? Oh my God."

"It's going to be different now," Steve said as if he hadn't heard her.

Cynthia backed away. "Why don't we talk about it another time? Why don't you think about things and call me later?"

"Can you imagine it?" Steve said. He was looking towards the window. "She's been here all this time and I didn't know. Why wasn't I paying more attention? I was distracted, wasn't I?" He looked at Cynthia. "Why did you distract me?"

"I didn't," Cynthia said. "I don't want you to think I did, and I don't want you to waste any more time. There's no reason for you to be here when you could be off doing what you need." She moved further away, towards the door, as if to usher him out.

"I can't fucking believe it." With the flat of his hand, Steve hit the couch beside him, hard. "Did you think I was going to hang around here forever, talking about nothing then going to some stupid job?"

"I made a mistake," Cynthia said. "Why don't you head on your way and not waste any more time?"

"You know what happened to Joseph," Steve said, "because of what he tried to do to me. Do you have no sense?"

"Joseph?" Cynthia shook her head, trying to process what he was saying, figure out how to get him to leave. "What does Joseph have to do with this?"

"You know what happened because he fucked with me. Then you fucked with me too." He took a step over to a shelf behind the couch, raked his hand across it and sent the things on it to the floor. Cynthia screamed.

"What, you're afraid?" Steve said. "You better be. If you think I'm going to let you off easy, you're even stupider than I thought."

Cynthia moved towards the phone. "If you don't go now, I'll call the police."

"You think I'm that obvious?" Steve said. "You think I'm going to stand here in your living room and hit you? It's going to be when you don't expect. You're going to be walking around or in your bed or at your desk and all of a sudden it's going to happen." He hit the couch again. "I can't believe how much time I've wasted."

He came around the couch towards her. She shouted at him not to and picked up the phone. He walked right past her, towards the door. "You thought it would work," he said. "You stupid mindless middle-class airhead bitch. You won't see me here again. But something else will be coming to remind you how you wasted my time."

He opened the door and slammed it behind him. Cynthia stood there, looking at the door and breathing heavily. Then fear hit her again and she ran and locked the door before going back to the couch and sitting, stunned and quiet, eyes blinking feverishly and watching the door to make sure it didn't move.

*

The sun stabbed through the window. Jerry groaned awake, trying to escape the light. He hadn't closed the blinds before passing out in his clothes. Cursing, he got up and shut the blinds and threw himself back on the bed. He had that wide awake head-throbbing energy. Sleep was impossible.

"What did I do last night?" He struggled to pierce the foggy hangover and remember more than smoke and the alcohol aftertaste that made his mouth bitter and dry. The sense that something was wrong ached through his temples—something more wrong than simply hangover remorse.

"Oh shit," he said, remembering. "I told Steve that Marinda was in New York. I've got to let her know. Shit." Last night, when he was drunk, he knew he had to tell her but couldn't bring himself to. He'd started to call several times but hadn't.

He went to the phone and dialed her number, heard the answering machine. He hung up without leaving a message. What could he tell her? He couldn't leave a message saying he'd been the one who let Steve know, but how could he leave a message saying, "Steve knows you're in New York," without explaining how he knew? His message could ask her to call him back, but why bother? He'd just call her again or track her down. Where would she be, this early on a Thursday?

The phone rang and he picked it up, hoping it was her. It was only that odd beeping again and he slammed the phone down.

It would drive him crazy to sit around here hung over, waiting for her to come home. God, his head pounded, and his stomach wasn't exactly settled. He went to the bathroom, chewed some antacid and drank a glass of water.

The water helped only a little. He wasn't going to make it through, not like this. Maybe a Bloody Mary?

He had a little vodka and Bourbon in the house, nothing he

was going to drink now. He didn't feel good enough to shower, even though his skin had an unpleasantly alcoholic sweatiness. He threw on pants and a shirt and shoes, picked up his cell phone and went out.

On the street, he left a message on Marinda's cell, asking her to call him. He knew she wouldn't get the message and that made it easier than leaving one on her home phone. A little later he arrived at the restaurant he wanted. Soon, Bloody Mary in hand, he waited for an omelet, home fries and toast. His head still throbbed. He kept thinking about Marinda and finally called her at home again. Still only the answering machine. She was always home in the morning, so where was she? He didn't leave a message.

The food came and he ate it greedily. Maybe he didn't have to tell Marinda he'd been stupid. He hadn't told Steve anything specific about where Marinda lived. Her cell phone worries aside, it was New York City—what were the odds that Steve would find her among seven million people? There was always the slim chance Steve would run into her on the street, but there had always been that chance before. Jerry's slip didn't really change those odds significantly, although Steve would be more watchful. Maybe there was no problem and he could just go about his business. He felt a wave of relief and finished his breakfast.

The relief lasted only into his second Bloody Mary. He couldn't just not tell her that a man she'd been hiding from knew what city she lived in and was probably looking for her. People ran into each other by accident in New York all the time. He and Steve had run into each other. He called Marinda again. Answering machine. He hung up, disgusted. He was trying to help her but she wasn't making it easy. Maybe she'd spent the night at some guy's place, maybe even that weirdo Herbert? If she had, there was no way to find her. But maybe she was just home, not answering the phone. He didn't want to risk leaving a message.

A little drunkenness was again seeping into his head. It seemed on top of and outside the throbbing, as if the throbbing was going on in some separate place that couldn't be touched. Did he need to tell Marinda? He couldn't decide. He'd made a terrible mistake, hadn't he? Maybe he hadn't. He had an obligation to tell Marinda, didn't he? But if she wasn't really in danger, why did he have an obligation? Even if he'd done something wrong, if it was going to have no results, why confess? He didn't want to admit he'd been foolish if there was no reason.

A little later, the second drink was gone. What next? Go home? He didn't feel able to sleep, even having eaten. He called Marinda again and still got no answer.

Maybe he needed to go to her place and see if she was there. He had done it yesterday and it hadn't worked, but he didn't have anything else to do and doing nothing seemed intolerable. So he'd go to Marinda's. And tell her what? He'd decide when he saw her. Out on the street he grabbed a cab.

While the cab moved through the traffic-heavy streets, he tried to figure out what he would tell her. The whole story, or just some part? Maybe say that Steve told him he already knew Marinda was in New York, because somebody else told Steve? Did Jerry really have to say he'd done it? She'd ask a lot of questions though. If she pulled it out of him after he'd not told her, wouldn't that be worse? But maybe she wouldn't find out. Maybe he'd just say, "I don't know," a lot, deny that he knew how Steve knew. Yes, maybe that was best.

On the other hand, if he didn't tell her how Steve found out, she'd probably start calling everybody she knew, trying to dig up if anybody had given her away. If for some reason it became necessary for Jerry to tell her later, the fact that he hadn't done it the first time would make things worse. Besides, since there was obviously a chance that Steve *would* find her, if he did he'd certainly tell Marinda that Jerry was responsible.

But I'm *not* responsible, Jerry told himself as the cab weaved through traffic. He hadn't done anything really so why get worked up? He had been surprised by seeing Steve, and the words had slipped out in shock. No, it hadn't been a slip, had it, drunk or not? He knew what Steve was asking and was angry at Marinda and he told Steve on purpose, entirely. There was no way he could tell Marinda that part, ever.

He still wasn't sure he needed to tell her anything. Maybe he was making a big deal out of nothing, because the big deal was his having betrayed her when he hadn't, not really. If I'd given him her address or phone number, then I would have betrayed her, he thought. I just made one slip—well, not a slip if I did it on purpose—but just one mistake and maybe it's minor. Steve probably won't run into her. New York is *huge*.

The cab finally reached Marinda's street. When it pulled up, Jerry decided that coming to her place hadn't been a good idea. If she was home, he'd have to tell her face to face whatever he told her. At least over the phone, if she started screaming at him, he could hang up. Now, he'd just have to take it. Take what? He hesitated in the cab, almost told the driver to keep going. At the last minute he didn't, paid the fare and stepped out.

On the street in front of Marinda's building, he hesitated again. He needed a plan when he walked in. If he tried to invent one at the last minute, he would likely slip up again (well, not really *again*, because the first time hadn't been a slip, had it? Or maybe it had?). He didn't want to tell her something that he didn't need to tell her because he couldn't think clearly.

But what was he going to do, stand here on the sidewalk with a hangover? The new alcohol was beginning to fade, but the hangover wasn't. Marinda could certainly pour him a drink. He didn't need to tell her everything the moment he walked in. He could sit back, relax, gauge her mood and see if that had some effect on his decision. Nothing was unavoidable. He didn't have to stand here like he was waiting for an executioner.

He went up the front steps and punched in her code on the apartment intercom system. He expected her voice any moment. A sick dread rumbled in his stomach. Maybe it wasn't dread, just his stomach feeling bad and his mind trying to turn that into dread? Her answering machine picked up. He pushed the hang up button. Maybe she was in the shower. He punched in her number again, but as he did, he felt certain she wasn't home.

He stood there a few minutes until his certainty was confirmed. It had been stupid to come all the way here. If she hadn't been answering the phone, she probably wasn't home. Why had he thought that coming here and calling from downstairs would make her magically appear? Maybe it was better to come here than to think up some other way to waste time until he could track her down? It was like her not to be around when something important was happening.

His chest tightened with annoyance. Here he was, going all over town with a hangover because he knew something she needed to know, and where was she? Whenever he went out of his way for her, he could count on her not to do the same. He was sick and worried and not even sure he needed to be worried and who knew where she was, screwing some guy she'd picked up or at the beach at somebody's guest house, having a good time while he wasted a morning trying to find her. Goddamn you, Marinda, he thought. Why do I keep fucking up my life for you?

It wasn't like she loved him. She had turned down his marriage proposal flat. This whole problem with Steve had happened because she had called him, Jerry, gay to his face. If he hadn't been angry about that, when he'd spoken to Steve he wouldn't have told Steve where Marinda was. Why had he blamed himself all morning for something that wasn't his fault?

In any case there was no use standing here. Where should

he go? Home? Maybe she'd be back soon, and he should just find something to do in the neighborhood. It was only a few blocks down to an area of bars and restaurants. He needed a drink badly. His hands had a prickly hangover shakiness. If the throbbing in his head wasn't as painful as before, it was lodged deeper in his brain, like some repeated signal telling him what to do.

So he walked away to get a drink. A few minutes later he found himself in a restaurant. It was still barely noon and the bars were still closed, though a few liquor stores would now be open. He ordered a drink and said he'd look at food in a minute. He had a seat by a window and peered up and down the block, at the newsstands, closed bars, a strip joint, two porn shops, a shoe store, a hardware store and other miscellaneous businesses. What a neighborhood to have a hangover in.

Why had Marinda called him gay? If she hadn't, none of this would be happening. He wouldn't have made the mistake of trying to sleep with Geena when he wasn't attracted to her. He could almost hear Marinda laughing, saying see, I told you, you're gay. If only he'd had sex with Geena. But he hadn't been able to, and there was Marinda in his head, saying marry you? Are you kidding?

So if she hadn't said that, nothing would have happened with Geena and he wouldn't be feeling low and thinking everything was wrong. And if he hadn't been feeling like that, he wouldn't have been out drinking by himself. And if he hadn't been drinking by himself, he wouldn't have run into Steve, and he wouldn't have told Steve. And if he hadn't done that, he wouldn't have had to get so drunk. And if he hadn't gotten drunk, he wouldn't be hungover this morning, wouldn't be in this restaurant ordering a drink and feeling confused.

He looked over at one of the porn shops. Girls girls girls, huh? It was just that Geena wasn't his type. He'd had sex with plenty of girls. Not recently, true, but nobody knew that but him. Why was it anybody's business? He was picky, sure. A man of his taste and position was supposed to be.

Maybe going into the porn shop was the boost he needed. Get some pictures of naked chicks in action, good-looking ones. What could it hurt, and maybe it would help. Besides, he had nothing to do. He couldn't talk to Marinda until he could find her.

He called her again, although this time with no sense that she'd be there. He had no idea what to tell her, but it didn't worry him right then because he didn't expect her to answer. She didn't.

He paid for his drink and crossed the street towards the porn shop. He pushed the small steel door and went in. It was bigger inside than it looked from the outside. A number of men were wandering around. The rug smelled of mildew and some kind of sweet unidentifiable cleaning fluid. Magazines were tossed in multiple bins, videos in racks covered the walls, there were a couple of peep-show booths in back. Some of the magazines were seriously hardcore, the women being gang-banged or fist-fucked. A few bins had gay magazines too. He frowned at them. It was like Marinda was following him and not there both. While he looked around, picking up this or that magazine, his eye kept wandering over to the gay bins. Why did they have to be there?

He picked up some girly mags, hardcore sex ones, held them aggressively. Then he had a thought. Maybe he should go ahead and buy a gay one, look at it for a moment at home and prove how much the whole idea revolted him. It would be a test. He would look at a few gay pictures and be disgusted and turn to the girly mags and have confidence again. He didn't like the idea that the cashier would be ringing up a queer magazine for him, but the cashier was ringing up other purchases with blasé oblivion. Hell, what did a cashier who worked here care what anybody bought in a store full of fist-fucking pictures?

Still, he didn't look at the cashier when the magazines were rung up. The cashier told him the cost in a flat voice, put the magazines in a bag, then Jerry was on the street again, feeling gross, a little humiliated, but more like a man too. He was going to look at some pictures of girls and see what there was to see. He would take the test and go back to looking at girls.

Jerry hailed another cab. Maybe Marinda was out of town. He could call her from his place and that would be soon enough. If she wasn't in town, then there was no chance that Steve would run into her, not right away.

Jerry's head didn't feel good, but the throbbing was less intense, muted, as if the drinks or the walk or whatever appeased the messages the hangover was sending him. He would need another drink eventually, but he could get some liquor at the store near his apartment and have the drink at home. Maybe in another hour or two he would even be able to sleep.

He still had no idea what to say to Marinda, but now the problem didn't seem pressing. He'd try her again later. She wasn't around and there was no telling when she would be. There was no reason to stay worried about something he couldn't solve right now and that maybe didn't even need solving. Even if Steve did track her down, he wouldn't do it in the next day or two, even probably the next week or month.

The cab left Jerry in his neighborhood. After a trip to the liquor store to get the reinforcements he needed, he was back in his apartment, having a scotch. He dialed Marinda's number half-heartedly, knowing he probably wouldn't get hold of her. He didn't. He sighed, relieved. He could put it off awhile. What greater pleasure was there in life than putting off a problem?

Sitting on his bed, drink on the nightstand beside him, he pulled out the magazines. He had quite a mix. Large-breasted women, a couple beautiful blonds, some Asian pieces, all of them getting fucked. Exactly what he needed. There was that other magazine too. He left it in the bag. Thinking about it, he felt sick again. What could there be to look at other than some guys engaged in grossness? Strong guys, macho-looking guys, subjecting themselves to who knows what kind of indignity? Having some other guy touch them all over, screw them in the ass or mouth? Did anyone really behave like that? They were men, but they weren't acting like men, so were they men? Be a man. What did that mean?

He looked at the girly mags. The girls were bent over, twisted into all sorts of ridiculous postures, showing the filthy holes in their bodies. Yes, this would make him feel like a man…but the images left his mind detached, floating. The girls looked pathetic and artificial, exposed like scientific specimens. That was the thing about porn magazines. They were never as interesting as he wished they were.

The phone rang, and he startled. Shit, he thought, it's Marinda. Maybe he would let the answering machine pick it up. It rang once, twice, three times while he sat there. Then he pounced on it.

No one was there, only those repeated odd beeps that came over his phone so often lately. He was used to the beeping by now, at times would even act like he was trying to decode it. The beeps throbbed in time with the muffled remains of his hangover. Phone and hangover, back and forth, connected and disconnected in some twisting rhythm that, as he listened, seemed filled with a mystery he was close to deciphering. There was mystery in so many things, Jerry thought, hearing the continuing beeps. Things seemed obvious at first, then faded away into darkness, a silence where there should have been words but weren't. Maybe he had everything he needed, but what did he really know? There was a surface to things that seemed so lively, accessible, his. When he reached out to grab those things, they dissolved in his fingers.

He still had the phone in his hand. Why? He thought about Marinda briefly. She seemed far away, unreal. Even if there was a problem, it wasn't urgent. Oh right, he realized, she's been working, that's where she must be. Geena told me. He thought briefly about trying to find her, then hung up the phone and went back to bed.

The girls were still pathetic, more like dissected frogs than human beings. There was always the other magazine though. He felt pleasantly drunk now, the hangover throb still there but far away, lost in a haze. He pulled the other magazine out of the bag.

The men had well-defined bodies, muscled and tight. They shoved themselves into each other with reckless fury made motionless by the camera. He moved to put the magazine back in the bag, stopped and held it in front of him, staring. Through the haze of alcohol distance, he noticed his whole body had tensed and that tears of shame were reddening his eyes. Then the alcohol distance was gone. I won't look at these, he thought, arousal bursting all over his body, face burning. He started again to put the magazine away, didn't. He stared at the pictures through stinging eyes, his mind casting around for protection. He thought of Marinda. Who was she? What did she have to do with him? I won't look, he thought, staring, crying, body contorting with desire. "No," he said, once, loudly, then fell silent. The world vanished, except for him and the motionless thrusting of the men.

EIGHT

At work, Marinda could never tell if she was awake or soaring through a permanent dream. It was regular temping: xeroxing, ordering paper, answering phones, checking this list against that one, occasional in-depth computer projects that didn't involve in-depth thinking. Her mind would often float free, thinking about someone she knew or imagining herself painting. Temping was painting's emotional opposite. Painting was intense and fitful, temping bland and frequently seamless. She was working, but she wasn't using any complex abilities and also not using herself up emotionally. She kept debating which was better, the safety of achieving nothing with no more than a hazy, empty ache, or the momentary thrill of creativity and connection followed by a devastating crash. The second was obviously more valuable. But could she handle it? Here at *The Contemporary Dog*, at least she always knew what would happen.

Marinda worked mainly for Dan Roberts. He was about forty-five, with two kids, a wife he mentioned much less often than the kids, and an understated, self-deprecating humor. His hair was going a stately grey and he was stocky, with powerful shoulders. He had an air of stability that she should have found boring but didn't. He had become her symbol for the job because he was like it. There were never any surprises, but on the other hand, there were never any surprises. Most men she knew, even her father, either swung from mood to mood or steamed like a pressure cooker until they blew. The world wasn't divided into men like Dan and men like Jerry or Steve, not quite, but if it had been, the Dan types had more than a few advantages.

Marinda had been doing somewhat more interesting work during the last week. For an upcoming series of articles, she had been asked to review the bank of breeds and their histories and fill in missing information. She had been researching some breeds she'd never heard of. Dogs had a complex history. She couldn't say that the information was mind-boggling, but there was something soothing, almost comically enjoyable, in reciting facts about Thai Ridgebacks or Otterhounds. She had never been an expert at anything, and she felt intrigued by what it might be like to know something in such detail that others came to her about it. If the detail was minor in the larger scheme of things, did that matter? It was pleasant to quote the obscure.

Two women in the office had been particularly friendly. Debbie and Stephanie—professionals on the job, party girls off. Debbie, plump and blond, a little like Geena, had unlike Geena a vicious dry wit and never took anything seriously. She dismissed sarcastically all sorts of things without any desire to examine them further. Stephanie was wilder. A pretty, large and athletic woman, her laughter boomed across the office, and her piles of brown hair were as unruly as she was. She made everybody feel like they were involved with her in some hilarious secret. Instant-Intimacy Girl, Marinda thought the first time they met.

It was late morning on a Wednesday when Dan came up to Marinda and said, "Come talk to me about 2:30? I want to throw something your way."

"Sure," Marinda said. "Is there a problem?"

"Not at all. Something you'll find interesting, I hope. Let's talk then."

Marinda nodded, and Dan went about his business. His tone piqued her curiosity. Of course, nothing could happen in this office that would be all that outrageous. Still, it was slightly out of the ordinary. Even slightly out of the ordinary was better than more of the same ordinary, even if the ordinary did have its attractions.

Lately, Marinda often ate lunch on a small shaded bench in a garden she had discovered near the office. There were never more than a few other people in the garden, and she could read or let her mind drift. It was hot out, dead summer even if it was still June, and an hour of heat after the metallic chill of the office's central air was a relief. She thought about what she might do that weekend; she had stopped going out much during the weeks and didn't miss the nightly craziness. Herbert was around of course, and she wondered what Debbie and Stephanie would be doing. Being single was wearing on her. Maybe Debbie or Stephanie knew somebody she might like. Marinda had never needed a boyfriend at all times. She preferred being by herself to being with the wrong guy. But being with the right guy, if such a guy existed, would be nice.

She hadn't been back at her desk long when Dan said, "Got a minute?" and she looked up to see it was 2:30. She joined him in his office, pleasant though hardly huge, with leather furnishings and a big window behind his desk. She startled a little to see Debbie sitting there too.

"Another meeting," Debbie said with cheerful irony.

Marinda sat down and smiled curiously.

Dan took a seat too. "It turns out one of our researchers—you know Sandra Jordan, yes?—is leaving."

"Sandra is? She seems to like it here."

"Great offer somewhere else that's really well suited to her. What would you think about taking her job, permanent full-time? You've been with us a month now and everything you're doing is excellent. It would save us the trouble of a search, give us a great employee, and give you something more permanent. A good deal all around, seems to me."

Marinda looked over Debbie, who was grinning. "You're offering me a permanent job?" It had never occurred to her that she'd be here more than a couple months. "Really?"

"Really," Dan said. "You've been handling the breeds project fabulously. There's no reason that can't continue. You'd be making yourself more informed about dogs, essentially, and all sorts of related things, depending on what we need, and passing along what you know. The position is called Research Associate."

"I'm flattered," Marinda said. "I'll need the details of course."

"Debbie here can talk to you about contract: salary, benefits, and so on. You don't have to decide right now, although we'd like to know in the next day or two. I want to stress, though, that I think you'd be great for it. You've done fine work. Everybody here likes you."

"I appreciate that," Marinda said. "I like you all too." Was she saying this awake, or still in the seamless dream? "I'm definitely going to think about it."

"Great," Dan said. "Let Debbie fill you in."

After Debbie did that, Marinda went back to her desk. She was flattered. Even though she had done well at jobs in the past, she always thought of herself as so weird that people who worked in offices would see through her. Here, they liked her. Did she like them? Could she imagine accepting a permanent—well, for a year or two anyway—job researching dogs and doing whatever else came up? As opposed to what else she might do? Work at another job in another office where she might like people less? Stay home and stare at a canvas, not painting, every so often beg her father for money?

Stephanie swooped by her desk. "Hey girlfriend, want a drink after work? I'm a plant, you know. I'm supposed to talk you into staying. Just thought you should hear the truth before I do talk you into staying. Don't tell me you have other plans. I know better."

"I don't have other plans," Marinda said.

"Great. We're on our way, Sisterhood."

Yes, on our way, Marinda thought after Stephanie left. Towards something she had believed for years she was trying to avoid—a regular job, regular hours, the whole mind-numbing routine. But how bad was it? Was it anymore mind-numbing than being in a bar at 2 a.m., night after night, talking empty ironic nonsense in the name of some freedom that didn't even feel good? What had that been about? Rebelling against something, her father maybe? Or doing exactly what he wanted and thinking it was rebellion? Some rebellion. I'll have another gin and tonic and change the world. It all meant something else, of course, when she thought about painting, the intensity of it, the power. But also the despair. She painted because she wanted to feel despair, then didn't paint because that was an even better way to feel it. Despair over what, Marinda, she asked herself. That your father's a confused and selfish man who tries to control your life? That you believe you're special but don't have the will to prove it? What's so special about believing you're special? Everybody believes that.

What would she do if she took a job a like this permanently? Get up every morning on time, do her work in a daze, go for a drink after? Go to parties or take trips on the weekends? Date some guys, sooner or later marry one, have kids and buy a house and grow old, and never know either overwhelming terror or overwhelming joy? But who said she wouldn't know those things, or that she'd know them if she took some other path? If painting couldn't give her a sense of accomplishment, maybe some other work could.

Besides, even if she took the "permanent" job, it didn't have to be permanent. She could go back to painting if she needed or paint in free moments if she felt like it. Or was the choice more final than that? Once she took on a new way of being—and it *was* that—maybe it wouldn't be possible to go back. To what? For now, the only thing that taking the job would cost her was a possibility that seemed no possibility at all.

So she would have a drink with Stephanie and hear her out. Research Associate about dogs. Who would have thought? She shook her head, laughed, and turned back to her work.

*

"I'm starting to remember." David appeared against the door frame, splashes of sun across his face.

Sarah was doing freelance editorial work at the kitchen table. Although it was hardly absorbing, it was detailed. Her mind took a moment to break free. "You…?"

"I'm remembering," he said. "Some things pretty clearly, others in flashes."

This time, she understood. "Are you serious? You remember David Carroll and…"

"No," he said. "Not much about David. About where I came from. I'm not David, more than superficially. That is, I'm as much David as David wanted to be. Most of him was gone already."

"Who are you then?"

"I'm not entirely sure. I just know I'm seeing things."

Nervously and curiously, Sarah stared at him. "Starting when? How did it happen?" She motioned for him to sit at the table with her. "Tell me all of it."

"Some time yesterday." He sat down. "Then last night as I was sleeping. I guess I stopped resisting. I think I've been blocking everything, not wanting to know. I didn't want to accept what happened to me. But over the last few weeks I've begun to accept it, and now I'm beginning to remember. As if the procedure is being counteracted."

"The procedure?"

He put a hand against the table unsteadily. "I think something was done to my brain."

She reached out to steady him. "You can go slowly. There's no rush."

He exhaled heavily. His face looked pale, not ill so much as like he was recovering from illness. "It's not all that clear to me. Something was wrong, and I chose to ignore it, and then I underwent a procedure. It wasn't the only solution, or even a solution at all, not really. It just made sense to those in charge."

"The procedure?"

"Do you know what happens if you can't dream?"

"Literally? If you were stopped from dreaming, you'd die quickly."

"Yes," he said. "One way or another."

"I don't understand."

He took a deep breath, struggling to get the words out. "I have images of streets, of people in them. Of rancid air and undrinkable water. A sense of threat permeating my skin. Then the government got involved. They described it as a health initiative. A total, non-stop barrage of public information made sure that's what it seemed. Still, many of us knew the procedure was more than that. It was an open secret."

Sarah felt her shoulders go rigid. She was about to hear something appalling, she knew. "What was it?"

"I think," David said, "it was designed to control the flow of dream information." One hand squeezed his face anxiously. "To repress bad dreams. 'Dream alterations' is the phrase that keeps running through my head, I'm not sure from where. Really, though, you could probably say it was designed to repress dissent. And I knew it, although in some way I didn't, quite. I didn't want to."

Sarah shuddered. "What did you do?"

David shut his eyes, then opened them. "I submitted to the procedure."

"What? I thought you said you knew what it was."

"Yes. There were many people like me, at least I have the feeling there were, strung between two worlds in a way more and more untenable. I knew it was wrong, but I did it. I must have been afraid of what would happen if I didn't."

"And other people?" Sarah said. "If you did, they did."

"They must have, yes. Maybe even gladly. Everybody wants to feel better, right? Be part of a happier, healthier society? That's how it was sold. There was a huge rush to be first. I think there were penalties for not doing it, but I don't know how often they had to be enforced."

"You walked into a hospital under your own power and let somebody alter your brain?"

"They weren't quite hospitals, in the way you mean. The public health centers. Yes, that's what I did."

"I'm sorry," Sarah said.

"So am I," David said. "I don't know if I'll ever be not sorry again."

"So what happened? You felt better?"

His face scrunched as if it hurt. "For a day or two, I felt quite light. Then everything fell apart. It was like my brain was trapped inside something and was beating against it, desperate to get out."

"No one had anticipated that was going to happen?"

"I can't say." David shrugged. "And I can't remember things after that nearly as well. I still functioned in a basic way, I guess, got food, stayed out of the rain. Maybe I even still went to work, at least for a while. But the world had lost its meaning."

"Why? Sarah said. "The procedure had that effect?"

David considered a moment. "I've been thinking about that all morning, and I'm only guessing. If you shut off part of a person's mind, the rest of that person's mind begins to change too. That's even true—maybe especially true—if what you're trying to shut off is that part of people's minds that's anti-social, cruel, even murderous. By trying to eliminate what's wrong, you only make everything wrong. You can't eliminate the dark side of the human mind without distorting the rest."

"And obviously you weren't the only one affected," Sarah said. "The changes must have been huge."

"I don't know much about that either." David's shoulders sagged; he looked exhausted. "Did people give way to their negative urges? Did they give way to supposedly positive urges that became negative? I don't know why I did what I did. The part of me that had gone away was the part able to create meaning." He shook his head. "I know this is all vague. Don't you see? Whatever they'd intended, what they had done was eliminate crucial parts of my imagination. After a while I stopped doing even the things I did habitually: making coffee, setting the alarm, checking what time it was. Even the parts of us that have learned to function without knowing why stop functioning, eventually, if we're not able to think about why we do things, even if when we do think about it, we don't come up with answers. We don't need to imagine because our imagination gives us answers to our questions. We need to imagine because imagination is basic to who we are. A world that can't dream is a world that goes mad."

Sarah was trying to take it all in. "But that's not the whole story," she said, "or you wouldn't be here."

"No. But I can't say I'm here because I'm some hero." He folded his arms on the table and his head sunk down towards them.

"There's no need to condemn yourself." Sarah put a hand on his arm. "The details will do."

"A few people resisted," David said. "I think that's why I'm here. The government must have been trying to track them down, of course. My best guess is they were saved by the vastness of the disaster, and because they had avoided the procedure. Even proponents of the procedure must have gone mad in some way or other. The underground managed to survive probably because its members could still think. They found me somehow, and decided they could help me."

"Why you?"

He looked at a patch of shadow on the kitchen wall, eyes moving as he thought it through. "Somehow I was still capable of understanding. I don't know why. They figured out that maybe more could be done for me if I was sent away. My mind, I mean, my imagination. They knew how to do it, although I guess they didn't really know what would happen. So they gave me a choice, and there was enough of me left to make a decision. I could stay in a world where I would have moments of clarity among hours of mindless pain, or I could be sent away, with the chance of arriving somewhere I might be able to live more fully. I remember the discussion as well as anything else I remember, I think because they pumped me full of a drug that shocked me temporarily out of my daze."

Sarah was staring at him, amazed. "They knew how to send your consciousness out of your world?"

"That's what they said."

"How?"

"A technology system called the Crab. It was based on a theory, about the interrelated nature of psychic energy, how minds are inevitably caught up in other minds, how what we experience is a relation of what others experience. They told me that the technology didn't work often and didn't work well, but sometimes it worked."

"They didn't have any ethical problems with launching out and taking over whoever's mind happened to get in the way?" Sarah scoffed.

"If the theory is right," David said, "the energy couldn't land anywhere that someone didn't want it to."

"So the underground's use of the Crab is causing what we're seeing here, people's minds being seized?"

"Only partly." David breathed deeply again, centering himself, as he'd been doing throughout his story. "The government was aware of the Crab, they told me. It was busy trying to project its own energy sources out of the world in the same way, with the goal of confronting the energy created by the Crab. Its leaders must have been afraid that the changed dream energy might come back into their world so strongly it could destroy them. If the Crab works right, it results in someone like me, a new consciousness emerging in the mind of someone who wanted to change their old consciousness. But what kind of energy is the government projecting if its goal is to stop my new state from occurring? Something that locks people forever into the problems of their own consciousness, making them unable or unwilling to transform themselves, to imagine any condition outside their own. That's what I'm guessing."

"But it's not that simple," Sarah said. "Maybe your situation is, but not any of the others I've found. The energy's all mixed up. There aren't two clear sides. Don't you see?"

"I do see that," David said.

"Whatever is going on," Sarah said, "none of it's coming out the way anybody intended."

"I guess not," David said. "Nothing worked right there either."

"And if you take a world where almost nothing's working right, and project it onto a world where almost nothing's working right…"

"You get a world where almost nothing's working right." He rubbed his eyes.

Sarah looked stunned. "But is it a different world, or the same one?"

"It's a different one, of course. Maybe what you mean is, how different?"

"I guess that's right," Sarah said. "That's an outrageous story. Are you sure it's true?"

"Sort of." He shrugged. "Some parts are pretty clear. Some of it is guesswork."

"Okay," she said. "This is going to take a while for me to process. Still, assuming it's true, some if it at least, you've told me things that help me make sense of what I've been seeing."

"How so?"

"What you said about being willing to remember, being willing to change. We are, all of us, changing all the time. The big question is how we feel about those changes. We can fight them, try to shut them down. Then we get stuck, unable to be either what we were or what we're becoming. Or we can try to acknowledge and accept them, move forward differently. That's the crucial thing: being able to accept who we are. If we can do that, a lot of things are possible. If we can't, we're just building a wall around ourselves."

"I understand." David's eyes moved from side to side, as if he was thinking carefully. "I'm not sure what I'm supposed to do about myself though. I'm not from here, but there's no way to go back even if I wanted."

"And the original David Carroll? His mind is just gone? Or lying around back in your brain somewhere?"

"I think David's relieved he'll never have to make a decision again."

"You expect me to believe that's a good thing? He probably wasn't a nice or helpful man, but still."

"Maybe it's just the change David was looking for?" His expression seemed to draw up into itself. "I'm not sure. But for some reason and in some way, I'm alive. I have to do something about it."

"I hope I can help," Sarah said. "I'm not sure what I can do, except keep talking with you about it, trying to help you see who you're becoming, who you might be."

"That might help a lot," David said.

*

Pleasantly buzzed, Marinda walked into her apartment building. Debbie and Stephanie had taken her out after work for food and a couple drinks. Stephanie could turn the minor events of her day into hilarious stories. Matters of boyfriends and families became, in her intimate and excited telling, grand epics, full of confusion and error. Debbie had a habit of punctuating or inflecting things Stephanie said, a rhythmic, ironic counterpoint in which human behavior became a groping slapstick, funny to watch and even funnier to comment on afterwards. Neither had much to say about the world beyond their own experience, but what they knew, they knew well. Marinda enjoyed their company. Not every night, thank you—she imagined they could easily make her claustrophobic—but the evening was a friendly, relaxing break from the uncertainty of her life. It wouldn't be bad to work with people like that. In fact she needed no more convincing.

She opened her front door, turning the lock and pushing the wood lightly and happily with her palm. Once inside, she tried to close the door. A pressure she didn't understand pushed back. "What?" she said. The door pushed against her harder, caused her to stagger. A man stood there, silhouetted, and closed the door behind him. Then she could see who it was. She gasped—practically choked.

"You can't be here," she said. "I'll have you arrested."

"That's okay," Steve said. He was dressed in a stylish blazer of the kind he had sometimes worn when they had gone on dates. "I just want to talk. You can have me arrested afterwards if you feel like it."

"How'd you get in?"

"Doorman. Said I was your boyfriend and you told me to meet you here, but you weren't back yet and could I wait in the lobby. He was very helpful. Didn't seem to notice when I took the elevator up."

"But it's his job to…"

"I have a habit of getting what I want," Steve said, "especially lately. I need to tell you about it."

"I have nothing to say to you, Steve, and you have nothing to say to me." Marinda tried to make herself sound forceful and angry. "Leave now, or I'm going to make sure everybody on the floor hears me."

"I wish you wouldn't talk to me that way." Steve's mouth grew small and narrow. He pulled something from his pocket and rubbed it against the side of his face. A gun. Marinda went silent, watching him. "I don't want things to get out of control," he said. "I need to tell you what I've been up to and you need to listen. You're going to be impressed."

"All right." Marinda tried to keep her breath even. "You'll leave afterwards? And put the gun away? How can I possibly listen if I'm doing nothing but staring at that gun?"

Steve waved the hand without the gun. "Turn on the lamp and sit down."

Marinda did as she was told, taking a seat on the couch.

"I still don't blame you." He stood in front of her, his body rocking. "You were under a lot of pressure, and I wasn't as understanding as I could have been. I was under pressure too. But Marinda, could you have taken any worse advice? Your family's religious nonsense, crap from that guy Jerry. You know it's nonsense, don't you?"

"Yes," she said.

Steve smiled, reminding Marinda how much it had always pleased him to be agreed with. "It made me angry. I have to admit, I'm not always good at controlling my anger. I wouldn't say this to just anyone, you know. Most people think I'm perfectly in control.

Some even think I'm rigid." He smiled again, as if he had successfully complimented himself.

"Why are you telling me? What do I have to do with it?"

"It's been hard for me since you left." Steve's face grew more serious. "I have a feeling it's been hard for you too. You'll have to tell me about it. You didn't understand, and I didn't know how to make you understand. Now I do. After you left, though, god, it all came apart inside me. When I realized your family forced you to get that restraining order, I was frantic. I still don't understand why they were out to get me so much. It's even harder to understand why you went along with it."

Marinda struggled to absorb what he was saying. It was hard to concentrate on him and not the gun. "How did you find me?"

"Jerry told me you were in New York. He was very helpful."

"Jerry told you where I lived?" She pushed down further into the couch as if trying to vanish.

"Not quite. I have a lot of extra time at work, and one thing I've always been interested in is surveillance techniques. I've read a lot of articles, and it was great to have a chance to use the advice. I figured I wouldn't have to watch him long. And I was right; he came over here first thing, the morning after I ran into him. He was pretty upset you weren't home. Since then, I've been waiting for the right moment." He caught himself. "But that's off the subject. You made me doubt myself, Marinda. No one's ever done that but you. I don't like it."

"I'm sorry, Steve, but what can I do about it?" Marinda, stunned, was trying to speak as rationally as possible. "We weren't working out, that's all. Can't you just leave it there?"

Steve bristled. "You don't understand yet." His pushed the hand not holding the gun outward, as if shoving the room away. "I'm trying to explain. I wish you wouldn't interrupt. The whole feminist thing, I think the worst thing about it is women try to talk when it's not their turn." He rubbed his face with his free hand. "I know you still feel like

I do, Marinda. Remember when we used to talk about how things were meaningless, how the world was screwed up? It was our bond, it's why we were—are—soulmates. We'd sit out on the roof of your old apartment building and look at the city and think how messed up people were, how trapped in their little pointless lives. Remember?"

"Yes," she said, "but I…"

"And we were right," Steve said. "We hadn't experienced much yet, so we couldn't really know, but we were right. We could see how much had been stolen. A world where the only thing that matters to anybody is money and their own selfish pleasure. Their little affairs, little jobs, little houses, little families. No one cares about bigger things. No one cared about your art, no one cared about all the things I wanted to do. We were right about all that, Marinda. I think what went wrong—I've had a lot of time to think—is that we didn't know how much pressure the outside world was going to put on us. We thought love was enough. We were right about that too, but we didn't know how hard it would be to keep loving. Remember the first time I got really angry? You were telling me you wanted to believe in God even though you couldn't, and I was trying to tell you your Dad wanted you to believe because he didn't want us to be together. You couldn't see that, and I couldn't see why you couldn't see it. It was an accident, shoving you like that and tipping over your shelf. But I was angry. Will you please forgive me for that?"

"I forgive you," Marinda said. "But Steve. I couldn't, and can't, be with someone who has no control of themselves. It's not a matter of what either of us believed."

"I know," Steve said. "That's why it's so good, all these things that have happened recently. Now I've found you, it proves everything I've been thinking is true. You won't believe it when I tell you."

"Won't believe what?"

"I can make things happen by willing them to happen. If I have a dream, I can make it come true."

"I'm glad you're feeling so confident," Marinda said.

"I mean literally."

"I don't understand."

Steve's chest welled with pride. "I had a dream one weekend that some guy at work who I hate got his ankle broken. When I came to work on Monday, it had happened."

"That's a weird coincidence."

"No," he said. "I made it happen by dreaming it."

"I don't get it," Marinda said. "What's the joke?"

Steve smiled knowingly. "No joke. When I dream things, they happen. I wasn't sure for a while. But I dreamed that I found you, and now I have."

Marinda squirmed on the couch, then stopped. She had been with Steve for two years. His temper was out of control and he could be verbally and physically violent, and she had gotten a restraining order. But never, never, had it occurred to her that he was insane. Weird and unbearable, yes, but insane? She'd never known anybody personally who was insane. Had she? There was a man in her apartment with a gun, a man who believed his dreams literally became real. She had spent two years with him and even had thought she loved him.

"Why are you here?" Marinda said. "What do you think can happen?"

"We don't have to waste our potential anymore," Steve said. "We don't have to let this world destroy us."

Had he always been crazy, Marinda thought, sitting quite still, or at some point had he crossed a line? Did people cross a line? One day they were confused and abusive and the next they were crazy? "What do you mean?"

"We fell apart because the world seemed too much for us. You wanted to be a painter, Marinda, and you *were* a painter, a wonderful one."

"You always got angry when I tried to paint," Marinda said. "You thought I wasn't paying you enough attention."

"I know." His voice was falsely contrite. "That was the frustration talking. I admired the way you would throw yourself into your painting and come out with these pictures that said so much about being lonely or ignored or misunderstood. You had vision. You could see the world. I had dreams too, Marinda, even if I couldn't always figure out what they were. Did I want to be a writer? To make lots of money so I could get back at the people who had money already? There's so much potential in each of us, Marinda, and there's so much more when we're together. Tell me you remember."

"I do," Marinda said, and meant it. "But we were young, Steve. I don't think we believed what we said. We were just talking. We weren't thinking about what we meant."

"No," Steve barked. She startled. For a moment she had been telling him what she really thought. That had always been a mistake even when he didn't have a gun. "We *did* mean it. Okay, yes, we didn't know what we were up against, we were too young for that, but we had the right idea. We just let the pressure get to us. That doesn't have to happen again. Not now."

"Why?" Marinda said. "What's changed?"

"Me," Steve said. "I know who I am now, what I'm capable of. I didn't before. I was afraid but couldn't admit it. I had all these dreams but all I could think was that people were going to crush me. I didn't have any faith in myself, didn't have the stamina to struggle against the things the world was forcing me to be. Dreams aren't enough. You have to have faith that tells you that if you want something badly, you can make it true, even if the whole world says you can't."

Marinda shut her eyes, frowned. Was it possible that insanity could sound sensible? She had to get him out of the apartment, she knew that much.

"But I need you," Steve went on, "or it's going to fall apart again.

Together we're capable of anything, Marinda. You can be everything you ever wanted, brilliant, famous, admired. And I can be what I've wanted too. People will understand the importance of what I have to say. I can't do it without you. What do you think? It doesn't have to be yes or no right this second. I know I can prove to you I'm right. All I'm asking is that you try it, see if you like us being together again."

Marinda held tightly onto her chair. She had no idea how to get rid of him. "Okay," she finally said. "I'm not sure I'm completely convinced yet. But I'll try it, just like you say."

"That's great." Steve grinned. "You're the smartest girl I've ever known, Marinda. I knew I could make you see it. I just wish this all could have happened sooner."

"What do we do now?"

"I'm not sure. I'm so happy. I don't know what it's like to feel this happy."

"Me either," Marinda said. "We can't just sit here."

"What?"

"There's so much to plan, to discuss. We need to celebrate."

"That's great," Steve said. "I don't know where to start though."

"We don't want to hang around here. This apartment is too much about the past, Steve, about all the things that went wrong. I've been hiding from you here."

"I hate this apartment," Steve said.

"I hate it now too," Marinda said. "Let's get out of here." Outside, maybe she could get away from him? She had no idea how.

"And go where?"

"I don't know, out on the town." She smiled flirtatiously. "It's not even midnight. We're even already dressed for it. Let's go dancing, or look at the water. Let's stay out all night long. If you're right—and I think maybe you are—then we can do what we want. To hell with morning and jobs and lives doing what other people tell us to do."

"You're amazing," Steve said. "It's like you can see the things I see."

"I think I can," Marinda said. "I think I can see everything you see."

Steve came over to her and kissed her on the cheek, hard, then pulled her into a standing position against him, into an intense hug. "Marinda, it's so amazing to hold you again, to kiss you. I can't believe it."

"I can't either," Marinda said. She pushed up on her toes and kissed him on the cheek. "Do we have everything we need?"

"What do you mean?"

"To celebrate."

"I guess so, yes."

"This is so fabulous."

"Isn't it?" Steve said. "I love you so much."

"I love you too," Marinda said. "Ready?"

"For anything," Steve said.

Marinda grabbed him by the hand, slipped her fingers tightly into his and smiled. "Come on."

She opened the front door, and a moment later they were out in the hallway. "Oh wait," she said automatically, barely thinking, like she had done countless times with Steve and everybody else. "I left my money on the table."

Steve let go of her hand and then, still automatically, she was inside her apartment. Shocked, she realized that the door stood between them. She snapped back to the door, slammed it and locked it in one quick motion.

"What are you doing?" Steve shouted.

Marinda dropped onto the ground, away from the door. She scrambled over to the phone.

"Cut it out, Marinda," Steve said.

She dialed 911; the operator came on just as Steve began pounding on the door. "Let me in," he shouted. "Goddammit."

"My ex-boyfriend's in my apartment building, and he's got a

gun," Marinda said into the phone, holding one hand against her ear so she could hear above the pounding and shouting.

"Let me in," Steve said. "Don't ruin everything."

Marinda was talking into the phone, giving her address and answering the operator's questions. Steve shouted in the hallway, loud enough to wake everybody on the floor if his pounding on the door hadn't done that already. "Don't do this to me," he was screaming, "don't destroy everything."

Marinda tried to give the operator the details. Steve was still shouting. She turned from the phone and shouted herself. "The police are on their way, you hear me?"

There was silence in the hallway. Then came a loud crack that for a second Marinda thought was a gunshot. It wasn't; probably Steve had cracked the gun hard against the door. "Let me in, Marinda. Don't do this. I thought we understood each other."

"They're on their way," she shouted again, phone still in her hand as she ducked behind the couch, onto the floor, waiting for the gun to be fired or the door to cave in, for the end of everything to come crashing down.

Silence. She paused, breathing heavily, and pushed herself tightly against the wooden base of the couch, trying to hide. The silence continued, and continued, and then it continued. She didn't move. He could still be there. But he wasn't, it seemed, although she didn't move away from the couch until the police knocked on the door at some time that seemed endlessly later.

NINE

"Maybe I don't want to dream anymore." Marinda leaned forward on the table, her lightly striped summer dress hanging loosely around her. "Maybe dreams are just an excuse to impose your fantasies on other people."

"What are other people except an excuse to impose your fantasies on?" Herbert said. In shorts, a tee-shirt, and sandals, he looked calmly impervious.

It was another bar, another Friday night. No reason to be there, no reason to do much else. People moved around, showing themselves off to each other. The air-conditioner was churning, giving a tinge of damp coolness to the otherwise stuffy room.

"There's got to be an in-between," Marinda said. "It's possible to recognize that other people aren't like you, don't think or feel like you. When I consider how much time I've spent fantasizing about things that were never going to happen, how much time hoping the world would conform to what I want it to be, it makes me sick."

"You're becoming a hard-headed, no-nonsense realist," Herbert said. "That's not imposing a fantasy?"

"I'm sure it is." Marinda sighed. "I'm not becoming no-nonsense, though. I'm all nonsense."

"Fun to punish yourself, is it?"

"The most fun." She looked around the bar at people engaged in furious conversation, or looking bored or uncomfortable, or striking their most mannered cocktail-ready postures. "I still can't fathom it. He actually believed I was coming with him. He thought that all on his own, he had the power to change the world."

"Being crazy can make it difficult to be effective," Herbert said. "Any news about the trial?"

"It won't happen for months," Marinda said. "I wish the whole thing would go away. I suppose I could not show up, right? Take a last minute trip to Paris?"

"It's a nice fantasy," Herbert said. "What about Jerry?"

"My mom tells me he's still 'resting at the Center.' I'm sure he's having a very expensive recovery. I don't know if I can ever to talk to him again. He nearly got me killed and didn't even have the courage to warn me. Under the circumstances, a nervous breakdown is the least he can do." A waitress hurried past, almost bumping their table. "Maybe the whole thing taught him something? People do learn about themselves. Don't they? Tell me they do."

"They do. But what they learn, that's the question. Are you leaving New York?"

"I was thinking about it," Marinda said, "but I don't see why. Where else would I go? Will running away change the problems I brought with me? I have to live somewhere. Maybe the question is not where I'm going but what I'll do with the place I'm in."

"Sounds like a good question," Herbert said. "With luck you won't answer it too easily."

"I thought I was going to stick it out at *The Contemporary Dog*," Marinda said, "but now I'm not sure. I guess I'm doing okay at it, and it brings in money. So what? I could get another job if I need to. I suppose I might as well do it for a while, until something else comes along."

"Your future's not going to the dogs?"

"You never get tired of that joke, do you?"

"I'm proud of the limits of my imagination."

Marinda smiled wanly. "At least you know it *has* limits. When I think about the people I know and the way they live their lives, I think we all must have missed something, not given it a chance or seen it coming. All I've known is privileged people, Herbert. All I've seen them do is screw themselves up or screw up other people, or both. So it's one of two things: privilege really is privilege, and everybody I've known has just been unable to handle it. Or else privilege isn't really privilege; it's bad values running out of control, and those who believe in it are either deluded or lying. Which is better? That they believed in the right things but didn't have the character to see them through, or believed in the wrong ones? To think it's me and blame myself, or think it was other people and blame them?"

"Do you mean, which is better, self-pity because of what others have done to you, or self-pity because of what you've done to yourself?"

Marinda looked at Herbert. His flat, unreadable expression was perversely reassuring. "Okay," she said. "You're right. But it's been hard, so you can take it easy on me. My father's turned into a wacko, I spent two years dating a guy who was insane and who stalked me to my apartment and who I'm going to help put in jail, and a boy I grew up with was the one who helped my insane ex-boyfriend find me, then had a nervous breakdown. Is that enough for one summer? I wish there was something to blame it on. How about polluted air or too much radioactivity in the water? Or I know: signal beams from another planet."

"That's another nice fantasy, no doubt. I thought the point was to avoid that."

"But how?" Marinda said. "How do you work with things as they are and still be okay, when the way things are is so absurd it almost seems like they're a fantasy in the first place? How do you not give in to fantasies when the way things are is not much more than a tissue of fantasy?"

"Maybe there's no solution to that." Herbert shrugged. "Or to a lot of things. That's the big American fantasy, isn't it? That every problem has a solution?"

"But some problems do have solutions," Marinda said. "All I'm asking is, what kind of attitude do I need, what do I have to do, so I don't live my life in a fog of fantasy and regret?"

"Maybe you'll find out," Herbert said, "and maybe you won't. Maybe even if there is a solution, you can't force it. Maybe the only thing to do is see what happens and do the best you can." He leaned back in his chair and took a long sip of his gin and tonic.

"Maybe," Marinda said. "And here I thought I was going to be a sheltered little rich girl."

"You *are* a sheltered little rich girl, dear."

"I am." Marinda touched the back of Herbert's hand. "Isn't it crazy?"

*

When Steve finished talking to his lawyer, the guard took him back through the noisy, putrid jail to his holding cell. The guard's face wore the same grim mask of impersonal indifference that seemed a practiced style with everyone Steve encountered here, although there were occasional moments when people spoke to him like he was a person. Some parts of the indifference were comforting. People told him what to do and gave him no choice, but beyond meaningless insults that really had nothing to do with him, no one shoved his opinion in Steve's face or forced him to think anything he didn't want to. It was one more indication of how pathetic everything was that only once he'd physically lost his freedom, no one tried to take it away from him psychologically anymore. They just assumed it was gone, pushed him around. There was no battle because he'd already lost.

The lawyer was confident that Steve's lack of prior record would serve him well in the trial, although the presence of the restraining order worked against him. The bail hearing was tomorrow. He might not even have to serve jail time. If he did, it would be minimal, a year or two at most—he hadn't shot the gun—before he would be paroled. A year or two was a long time, but at first Steve didn't care what happened to him, now that Marinda had betrayed him again. But in the last day or two he had begun to think it did matter, a lot.

He lay back on the grimy mattress and looked through the metal bars at the wall opposite, as he had done repeatedly in the days since his arrest. His cell smelled of rot and disinfectant. How could he have been so wrong? Believing Marinda loved him, believing the world would fall into line the way he wanted? It was arrogance, he could see now, the first flushed recognition of his power carrying him into recklessness. He had thought through how to find her, but not what would happen once he had. She had been too far away from him for too long. It didn't excuse her betrayal, but it made it unsurprising.

Next time, of course, he wouldn't forget, and he wouldn't be so restrained in the use of his power. As much as he had mishandled things, she had almost been persuaded. She had been coming over to his side until her bad habits reasserted themselves.

Here in the jail though, it was hard to tell how powerful he was. He knew who he wanted to hurt and why, but couldn't get his dreams in line. The dreams lectured him about his foolishness. Maybe he would get the ability back when he finally knew how long would be locked up.

In most cases, what he would do to people later seemed clear.

However, he went back and forth on the issue of how to punish Marinda. Obviously her betrayal couldn't simply be ignored. On the other hand, he recognized that he was in some part responsible for her reaction. Besides, he still loved her. She didn't deserve it, but love wasn't always deserved. It also involved keeping your faith in people when they let you down. Marinda would have to be punished a little, yes, but only so she would understand how important it was to love him right. Sometimes when he thought about how much kindness he was going to show Marinda when she didn't deserve it, he felt good about himself again, despite other people. They wanted to destroy his power and his faith in himself. They couldn't, not as long as he remembered that he intended one day to be good to Marinda.

Thinking about that future, he relaxed, and it seemed possible to sleep. He smiled, closed his eyes, and drifted into dreams.

*

It had been a violent spring, and a violent summer, and it would be a violent fall. The disasters on the television, those of a world too vast for anyone to feel everything, continued to flash across screens, large and small, in rooms and windows and on the street, while people went into stores or dropped off packages or drank their morning coffee, shaking themselves into wakefulness. It was hard for Sarah to keep it straight, to stop the deaths from blending, from becoming nothing more than stories the media used to keep ratings high, more unreal than real to the people who watched them cross screen after screen. They were real of course to the people who experienced them, who lost friends or neighbors, husbands or wives, parents or siblings or children. The media tried to give you the illusion that everyone was inescapably part of these events, but even if you felt sympathy, Sarah realized, you were still a voyeur, staring at people you didn't know who stood there, devastated, being watched by you.

In April, two boys walked into their school in Colorado, opening fire on students and teachers, killing more than a dozen, targeting African Americans and professed Christians until finally turning their guns on themselves. A student at the school said, "It was like being in a horror movie." In May, a man was arrested for killing three teenagers in a Washington, D.C. coffee shop and perhaps several others elsewhere over a five-year period of robberies and murders. The summer brought more incidents. A hotel handyman in the Rocky Mountains admitted to killing a number of female tourists and a female forest ranger, claiming he had tried to control himself but couldn't. An air conditioner repairman in Seattle killed several people at the company that had fired him. In Illinois, a college student who dropped out to become a member of a white supremacist group began shooting black men and women on the street before dying in a gun battle with police. A man in Georgia killed his wife and two children and, several days later, walked into two day-trading stock companies and started shooting, killing nine people and wounding more, finally killing himself in his car at a gas station. In California, a thirty-seven-year old man walked into a Jewish community center and shot three young children, one sixteen-year-old girl and a seventy-year-old day care worker.

"Sure you're ready to go?" Sarah asked David. "It's not a pleasant world, and I've gotten used to having you around. It's not every day you get to be friends with someone from another planet."

They were standing on the street in front of her building, next to the used Jeep David had bought, his credit still good for the moment. The street was noisy this summer morning, as it always was weekdays. Even in the July heat, people went to work, delivery trucks moved through the streets and dropped off goods, tourists blundered along. Language was everywhere. They could both see it on poles, buildings, and cars, and Sarah could see it on people who passed them on the sidewalk.

"I've gotten used to being around you too," David said. In shorts, a light shirt and thick sneakers, a flannel shirt in hand, he looked like he was going hiking. He wasn't really David of course, but he had to have a name, and that was the one on the cards he carried. "It's nearly the only thing I've gotten used to. But yes, it's time. If I'm going to live in this world, I better start doing something about it. I'll be back here any time you call though. You know that."

"Thanks," Sarah said. There were three others now, two women and a man, ones she found and was able to reach. They understood enough and were starting to understand more. "I swear sometimes it's like I'm a teacher or therapist."

"I know it's not exactly a revolution," David said, "but it's something."

"Maybe." Sarah smiled and pulled anxiously at one of the belt rungs on her jeans. "How many others are there, you think? A thousand? Ten thousand? Fifty or a hundred thousand? Maybe a million? What about other cities and states and countries that I'm not going to get anywhere near? What's going to happen to all of them? Besides," she said, "even if I do find a few more, who invited me to explain anything to anybody?"

"I invited you," David said. "I guess anybody else who wants your help will let you know. That could be a lot of people."

"I could start my own chain of alien energy recovery centers. Put them in suburban tech corridors all over the U.S. Maybe add a sports annex and teach raquetball."

"The guru opportunities are endless," David said. "Try to avoid them."

Sarah's smile was chagrined. She thought about all the people who had been affected by the alien energy, or who might be later. How would they change? Would they become a mutually agreeable synthesis of the persons they had been? Would the alien consciousness supplant the other, sweep it into oblivion in order to seize a vacant and accessible body? Would the repressed parts of their personalities come out, or would they become more repressed? Would they become worse people, better? Would they be lost, wild, despairing, furious, blank? Would they leave their jobs or the people they loved, or just slip back into their old lives in new ways, maybe not even in new ways? Was it possible to be seized by alien consciousness and not alter your routine?

"Do you think some of them will recognize what's happened, or know what to do about it?" she asked. "They'll have to learn somehow. Will some be able to teach themselves?"

"I don't know," David said. "I've been trying to teach myself, but I needed—and still need—your help very badly."

"I don't suppose it's the kind of life you were hoping for." Sarah shook her head. "I can't imagine you saying to yourself that you wanted to go to another world so you could have an angry ex-wife, get sued for alimony and child support, resign your university position and run up your credit card debt."

David nodded shyly. "It's a little more than I might have asked for. On the other hand, a credit card problem is better than having no world left to live in." He took a step forward to avoid a man, hurrying and oblivious, who brushed closely behind him.

"If those are your options."

"They are." He smiled ironically. "How perfect could I have expected some other world to be? Besides, a lot worse things can happen than appearing in another world as a member of the middle class, however thin my savings might get in the next few months. It's just a matter of fitting myself to expectations, then doing something with them."

"Don't fit yourself too well," Sarah said. "Look what it got you last time."

David looked at the ground. "I'll try," he said.

"You're really going to be a journalist again?"

"It's what I know how to do. I can't teach history."

"Around here you could. Although I suppose your point of view might be considered nontraditional."

David laughed. "I could certainly make a case for the value of multiple perspectives." He stepped forward, grabbed her hand. "I'll see you next week. And I'll call as soon as I'm set up in the apartment. You're meeting with everyone this afternoon?"

"Yes. And there's good news; there may be one more. At least they said they were going to try to bring her in."

"That's amazing," David said. "You didn't even have to find this one. Who would have realized that some of us might have the ability to recognize others? I'm not able to. Every time I think I understand the limits of this condition, I find a new variation that makes me rethink it."

"I don't mind rethinking it," Sarah said. "Keeps me on the lookout. Still, I've been wondering. If ten thousand, a hundred thousand, or even a million people became aliens, would life be that different?"

"What do you mean?"

"We live in a world," Sarah said, "you and me both, in which anything that's possible sooner or later takes place. There's nothing so outrageous, unbelievable, or nightmarish that it hasn't happened and won't happen again. So how much can anything change even if everybody is seized by alien energy? How much different can anything be in a world where every conceivable thing has already happened to someone?"

Concerned, David looked at her. "I hope it won't be too much for you."

"Me too," Sarah said. "People who watch the skies have a high rate of burnout." She laughed. "I'll remember to wear sunglasses."

David opened the door of the Jeep. "Oh brave new world and all that," he said. He jumped behind the wheel.

Sarah turned her head questioningly. "Was the original David good with quotes?"

"Not very. He knew a few."

"Some brave new world," Sarah said. "Looks a lot like the old one."

"Depends who's doing the looking, doesn't it?"

"I don't know," she said. "Sometimes I think it depends on what you do with your looking. But that could be misleading too." She looked away from him, down the street, and shaded her eyes with her hand. "I'm afraid of what's going to happen."

"Yes," David said. "More than before?"

"I don't know. There's no point in measuring."

"Well," he said. He turned on the engine.

"Yes," she said.

"I feel a little short on words."

"There are so many words," Sarah said, "and we're so wrapped up in them. Then we try to bring them close, and suddenly we realize they're not like us at all."

David scratched the back of his head and put his hands on the wheel. Sarah stayed on the sidewalk as he pulled out into the street, into all the words. Then he was out in them, on his way, and she was out in them and on her way, and it was just another morning. Who knew what it would hold for anyone?

*

Working for *The Contemporary Dog*, Marinda picked up the habit of going into art galleries on her lunch hour. It started one day when she was tired of sitting and reading in the garden near her office. Like many others, she ate quickly at her desk while she worked and used her lunch hour for other things, running errands, reading, meeting someone for a conversation. Several years earlier, when she had first been in New York and was painting, she had gone to galleries a lot, but then stopped. She was glad to be going again.

It was amazing how much bad art there was in New York, terrible knockoffs of established approaches, transparently one-dimensional new gimmicks. At times it told her she was right not to be painting anymore. At others it made her want to scream that she could do better. Certainly it made clear that there were many artists who should have done what she had—stop. Still, even when art was bad, it was no more or less insignificant than any other kind of work on which everything seemed to run, waitressing or bartending, stock trading or being an executive vice president. If people had to do something, why not make bad art? It was harmless. Or mainly harmless—wasn't there some harm in emptiness of any kind, a way it had of dragging other things into emptiness along with it?

She rarely went to the galleries according to any plan. She just wanted to see whatever was around. One afternoon she found a tiny street of the kind common enough in New York, if one looked, a street she might never have seen if she hadn't been wandering. She liked secret streets, the New York inside New York, a spot of occasional reticence in a city obsessed with display. This particular street curved around a tight corner and seemed to be residences only, until she turned the corner and saw several shops and a small gallery. The street was hidden enough that she wondered how any business on it could survive. Of course many of New York's tiny backstreet shops were hobbies for people with money and who for reasons like tax write-offs didn't mind losing some of it here or there.

The gallery was in an attractive building with an ornate iron stairway that felt like it had been waiting, for her, many years. She expected to find the door locked and to have to ring. It was open, and she walked in.

There were a number of small paintings on the walls, most of no interest to her. When she went into a back room where only three paintings were hung, she stopped.

Although she tried a few times, she was never able to explain to anyone the effect that the paintings in that room had on her. They weren't ridiculous, though they ought to have been. Their amateur raggedness was startling and energetic, as if the paintings were flying off their canvases and out of the frames. They weren't subtle; if anything they were some kind of twisted folk art, American naive gone psycho. They pictured domestic scenes: a family dinner, a backyard during a family barbecue, an intimate portrait of figures sitting on a couch. In each painting, no more than one or two of the figures were human. The rest were aliens, depicted with the usual clichés: big eyes, round heads, thin necks, all slightly blurred, not quite ruined by poor technique.

In the first painting, a young woman and three aliens sat at a table set with plates and dishes of food, an ordinary American dinner of fried chicken, potatoes, and corn. An alien stood at the head of the table; another alien was serving. The young woman stared directly at the food on her plate, not looking at the others, her face with an anguished expression she was trying to hide, uncomfortable and afraid as she sat there. Were they really aliens, grayish blue and blurred, or did the young woman only think of them that way?

The backyard barbecue scene was populated by aliens also, one wearing a red and white apron as it leaned over a grill. Other aliens moved through the backyard, standing here or chatting there. Among them was the same young woman again. Her expression was so crudely drawn as to seem dull, even blank. Or was that the artist's intention? It was hard to tell what the artist had the skill to do and what had happened because of accident and ineptitude. There was another human figure at the barbecue, a young man in slacks and button shirt, a guy who probably had a job somewhere like a hardware store or a car dealership. He stood near a fence, looking over it, away from the party and towards the houses and sky beyond the backyard, as if he wanted to be far away. The young woman didn't mirror in the slightest his urge to escape, didn't register desire or pain. She was just there.

In the last painting, the young woman sat on a sofa. Next to her sat another grayish blue alien, almost superimposed on the sofa like a picture from a magazine pasted onto the painting. Behind the young woman and the sofa stood another alien. One hand and its long blurry fingers were draped over the woman's shoulder in a parody of emotional support. Were the fingers touching her lightly or holding her down? It was an unimpressive, flower-print sofa, the image of a typical American living room, the back wall hung with what were probably family pictures. The woman stared straight at the viewer as if in a formal family portrait. Her expression was uncertain. Was she challenging the viewer to say something was other than it should be? Was she asking for help or didn't she care? Could it really be painterly failure that made it so difficult to tell? Or was the uncertainty meant to suggest that she didn't know how she felt, sitting on a couch with an alien beside her and another behind her?

Marinda couldn't understand the tension she felt while looking at the paintings, her relaxed lunch hour spinning into strangeness. Maybe the pictures were just bad pop parodies without good technique to pull it off? But how would that account for her hot prickling skin and difficulty breathing? Marinda looked for the gallery clerk. There was no one behind the small desk and chair. The room was quiet. Maybe the clerk had gone to the bathroom, or down to the corner for something to eat, leaving the front door unlocked? Marinda looked back at the paintings, and they looked at her. According to the paintings, aliens were here, everywhere, behind her, next to her, around the corner, having families, going to work, setting the table for dinner.

"I hate it," Marinda said, "I hate it," but she didn't know what she hated. The paintings, what they suggested, herself, the gallery, all art, New York City, the world? "I hate it," she said again. There was no link between her and what she hated, or not what she hated but had the need to *say* she hated, for no clear reason.

She couldn't get at the feeling when she tried to talk about it. She would describe the paintings as ludicrous, or as funny, even as terrifying, but how to explain it was not the paintings, but the way that she was *in* the paintings, or not in them? How could she be in them? How to explain the feeling of being at the heart of something gone wrong while meanwhile no such thing was there?

"I'll take you to see them," she said to Herbert several times. She didn't mean it and she didn't go back, just like she wasn't going back to her own painting either, not now anyway, not any time soon. It wasn't long until she wasn't even remembering the feeling she'd experienced, but inventing it again, when she needed it, making it up so she could bring it to her once more, trying in her mind to get at it, to know again what it was like to stand beside that cheaply misdrawn horror and desolation, an alien hand draped over her shoulder.

*

It was cold and dark in Mytros.

He had never gotten used to working the night shifts, although he didn't know why. If it was painful, it was an ordinary pain and not worth thinking about. He couldn't think clearly when he tried to think anyway, so why try?

They had trained him to use the equipment. He wasn't good at it, was always losing focus even though he had memorized the directions, could recite them. Often the problem came in translating the words from the manual to the equipment itself, which seemed to hold back from being understood and was all grey areas and mistakes. The equipment registered what wasn't there and didn't register what was. Sometimes he was called an expert. He acted as if he believed it, but the equipment was beyond whatever expertise he had. If he operated it successfully at times, it was only in the midst of errors and omissions on his part and frequent breakdowns in the machinery.

They were doing the evening sweeps. He sat in the control room, which was walled off, with its own separate side entrance, between the cab and the long body of the truck, where the sweep teams slept. He tried to concentrate on the monitors. There were no windows; windows would only distract him. Only the drivers had to know where they were. Even for them, knowing didn't matter much inside the Safe Zone, since they were following the predetermined sweep plan. As long as they recognized which turns to take according to the grid, and could see street lights and signs, night in the city could take care of itself until the monitors lit up and there was something to do. Sweeps out in Chaos were far more dangerous. The three months a year he spent there were the worst parts of the job. Sure, anything could happen even in the Safe Zone, but it was much less likely.

Then the monitors did light up, finally, as they always did once or twice a night, sometimes more. He was always startled when he received an Indication, felt the welling up of a fear so old he couldn't have identified its source even if he thought to try. This time the Indication came from an impressive source, although probably not impressive enough.

"Improper Dream Activity." He spoke into the intercom to the cabin of the truck, as he had many times. "Measure 6.3."

"A pretty large surge," came back over the intercom. "Not individual, right?"

"Doubtful, obviously. More likely a party."

"Any sign it's a Crab?"

"No," he said. "Can't be certain though, so use caution."

"Pinpoint."

"Gonna have to turn around. It came and went fast."

"Shit," the intercom said. "I hate turning around. I want to be home by morning."

"I don't make the rules," he said testily. "I'm alerting the sweep team now. I think this one's big enough you'll want to notify base."

"All right, all right. I'm doing it, okay?"

"Okay." On the intercom, he switched over to the sweep team. All four were probably asleep in the body of the truck. He envied the sweep teams sometimes, no requirement to pay attention except in moments of action.

"We're turning back on an IDA 6.3," he said. "Be ready to sweep if we strike a location."

"Sure man, whatever," a groggy voice came back.

"Hope you enjoyed your nap," he said. "Nice job you guys got."

"Better have woke me for a reason," the voice said.

They turned around. The monitors stayed motionless. That happened often. More frequently than not, a powerful surge led to nothing. Improper Dream Activity was hard to locate. It moved and was wildly variable. He was supposed to keep track of the team's strike rate, the percentage of properly identified IDA relative to number of Indications, and his team was doing pretty well, almost 20% this season. The rates were never accurate of course. If you liked your team and wanted to keep it together, failing to record a vanished Indication now and then was just the way one worked, no more serious a transgression than stealing pens from the office. One had to be careful, though, not to let too many vanished Indications slide. Should a team's rate get near 30%, leadership became suspicious.

"We're turned around," the driver's voice came over the intercom, "but I don't hear you barking."

"Nothing yet," he said. Then he got a flash. "Oh, here it is." He felt the truck slow. "Recording only 3.1 now. Probably kids playing around."

"If there's a Crab, they must have moved it. Address?"

"Got a lock," he said. "125 Ludlow." He switched on the red light to indicate immediate sweep options.

"We're ready to go in," came back from the sweep team.

"125 Ludlow," he said again.

"We're on it."

He heard the back of the truck open, the sound of the sweep team leaping into the streets. Then came silence and waiting, his turn to rest while the team was in action, although once a month or so he would pick up an Indication even while stationary, because IDAs often moved.

Sure, it was probably kids having a party, but you never knew. Maybe there had been a Crab. The original Indication was almost high enough. Crabs were as much legends as anything. No base ever recovered more than one or two a year. Even those were usually defective. Everybody wanted a Crab, since to recover one meant an immediate increase in status, both officially and among the guys. Someone who had recovered a functional Crab gained a reputation hard to take away.

Not that anyone in the sweeps knew much about Crabs, beyond the details of their mechanical composition and the fact that they were used to let IDA escape. It was the major tool of the underground. Discussing the significance of Crabs was forbidden. There were people, he had heard, who secretly talked about them. He wanted nothing to do with that. It was dangerously close to committing an IDA oneself. Members of the Force did sometimes break down and commit IDAs; there was always a risk. He prided himself on never having gotten close to that particular career buster.

Then came the noise of the sweep team loudly returning to the street. His intercom screeched on. "Nobody there," the team leader said. "If there was something, it's gone."

"Any residuals?" he asked.

"I got a few brief RDA flashes, nothing consistent or intense. There was one almost 2.0." RDA—Residual Dream Activity from a now vanished source—could sometimes be high. A hot spot of RDA, 7.0 or higher on the RDA scale, often indicated the presence of recent Crab activity, since an active Crab was volatile and could spew IDA in many directions.

"I guess that's it then," he said. "Damn. Something was there, for a moment. Whatever it was, it was intense."

"That's great," the sweep team leader said, already bored again, probably ready to go to sleep the moment the truck was on its way. "What do you expect us to do, chase traces all over the city?"

"We can move on," he said. The sweep team clambered noisily into the truck and he switched over to the cabin. "Ready to go," he said. "No luck."

"Imagine that," said the driver. "Turning around for no luck."

"I'm just doing my job, okay? Maybe you should stop complaining and do yours."

"Complaining? Hell, I ain't complaining. It's better than cruising Chaos."

"Right," he said. "You want to keep having this conversation, or get home by morning?"

"On our way, Chief."

The truck started up. Soon it was moving on its regular, numbing pace through its pre-defined course on the Mytros city grid. There was a lot of IDA out there, hiding in basements or on rooftops, moving secretly, drifting consciously or unconsciously, sometimes happening by accident. Eventually, that night or the next, they would encounter some and with luck find the source, a few sixteen-year-olds putting out cigarettes on each other's arms, a woman slashing at imaginary enemies with a knife, a man stockpiling sex toys. And somewhere out there was more mysterious, deadly IDA as well, the product of an active, organized underground whose members he had only several times seen, desperate and lonely men or women who barely looked human. Yes, it was all out there. But it was hard to think about it tonight, and harder to worry about it, cruising the silent blocks of the Safe Zone, waiting to go home, to eat and sleep, then getting up to do it again, driving this block and that, following the course, his mind wandering nowhere because there was nowhere for it to wander.

Mark Wallace is the author of more than fifteen books and chapbooks of fiction, poetry and essays. *Temporary Worker Rides A Subway* won the 2002 Gertrude Stein Poetry Award. His critical articles and reviews have appeared in numerous publications, and he has co-edited two essay collections on contemporary poetics. Most recently he has published a novel, *The Quarry and the Lot*, and a book-length poem, *Notes From the Center on Public Policy*. Raised in the Washington, D.C. area, he currently lives in San Diego, California.